THE TEMPLE OF FORGOTTEN SECRETS

AFTER THE RIFT, BOOK 4

C.J. ARCHER

WWW.CJARCHER.COM

CHAPTER 1

*T*he man I'd known as King Leon was buried on a rise at the edge of the royal estate. The site offered a view of the palace, and the grave was marked with a hastily carved headstone. Theodore suggested a mausoleum be built to honor him, but no one else had championed the idea. Balthazar went so far as to suggest the headstone shouldn't acknowledge Leon as king at all.

But that would be a sign to the world that Leon had gained the throne through trickery. While it was the truth, it wasn't the official stance of the ministers and noblemen. They didn't believe magic was involved, despite hearing his dying confession.

Those of us who knew about the memory loss that plagued the palace's inhabitants did.

I was still in shock, some four days later. It was one thing to use the sorcerer's magic to become king, but it was another to lie about it to those affected. It wasn't just the palace staff who'd suffered from Leon's actions; residents of The Thumb had lost their livelihoods when the magical event known as The Rift cut off their peninsula from the mainland to make Glancia a richer nation. The people of Mull had also suffered as the Vytillian refugees from The Thumb swarmed into our village looking for work, shelter, food and basic necessities.

Months later, there still wasn't enough accommodation,

employment or basic necessities to support the newcomers pouring into the village, and the locals were angry at the rising costs. Unrest simmered, occasionally boiling over onto the streets, particularly in the village's underbelly, The Row.

The one good thing to come of Leon's death had been the hush that had blanketed Mull ever since the crier announced his demise. Troubles were set aside to discuss what his death meant to Glancia in general and Mull in particular.

The whisper of war was on everyone's lips. Without an heir, Glancia had no king. The two highest ranked nobles, the Dukes of Gladstow and Buxton, were rumored to be gathering support from among the other nobles to claim the throne for themselves. Both refused to allow the other to become ruler, and neither was prepared to hand the country over to a foreigner.

The only legitimate claimant to the throne was King Philip of Vytill, a distant cousin to King Alain, Leon's purported father and the previous ruler of Glancia. To be swallowed up by Vytill went against every nobleman's sense of honor and pride. They'd rather die than see him sit on the throne.

The Glancian townsfolk weren't too enthused by the notion either, but it didn't matter what we wanted. We would bend with the wind, no matter which way it blew. We would become Vytillian citizens if it was deemed the best course, or our men would become soldiers if the nation descended into a war over the succession.

I felt hopeless as I waited, along with everyone else in Mull, for the dukes or King Philip to make the first move. Gladstow and Buxton had remained at the palace, each of them occupying a different wing from which they schemed. Neither was prepared to give up the seat of power, even though the palace hadn't existed mere months ago and the official Glancian capital was still Tilting. The glorious building had become a symbol of Glancia's newfound status as a rival to Vytill, and symbols of wealth and power would become important in the coming weeks and months.

I saw little of Dane and the other servants in the four days since Leon's burial. Four days of frustration as I waited for him to come to the village or send me a message. Four whole days wondering what he would do now that the truth was out.

Too long wondering if he would leave and go in search of his past.

If he did decide to leave, what would become of me? My days stretched on into nothingness in Mull. With my apothecary work taken from me by Doctor Ashmole's wife, I had little to do. The few pregnancies in the village weren't enough to keep me busy, and there was only so much cooking and cleaning at Meg's house that I could stomach. Besides, I couldn't impose on her family forever.

On the fifth day after the burial, I decided to visit the palace. Meg came with me. She claimed she merely wanted to go for a walk, but I suspected she was as keen to see Sergeant Max as I was to see Dane.

The palace looked exactly the same. There was no sign that the king had recently died and the country was now facing uncertainty. The gilding still glinted in the sunshine, the northern and southern wings still dwarfed the twin pavilions, and two guards still stood at the front gate.

"The captain didn't tell us to expect you, Josie," the one named Ray said with an apologetic shrug. "Are you here to meet him?"

"Not specifically," I said. "I came to see how everyone is faring after…" I glanced at Meg. "After the king's death."

Ray shifted his stance. "I don't know how I feel. Numb, I suppose."

"I know how I feel," the other guard spat. "Angry. That prick lied to us for months. He *stole* our lives from us. And now he's gone and we can't get answers."

"It's frustrating," I said heavily.

"*You* don't know. You *can't* know."

Ray thumped the other guard's arm. "Don't get mad at her. It ain't her fault."

"Sorry, Josie," the guard muttered. He stepped aside. "Go on through."

"We shouldn't let her in without an appointment or the captain's instruction," Ray said.

"It's just Josie, you idiot."

I gave them both grim smiles and hurried through the gate before they changed their minds. As we crossed the large forecourt, I braced myself for Meg's questions.

They came as soon as we were out of earshot. "Were they talking about the king? What did the guard mean by stealing their lives?"

It was time to tell her. Both the large outer and small inner forecourts were relatively quiet. Sedan chairs traversed from the palace door to the gate and back again, ferrying noblewomen. Nobody walked past us. Most of the men would be inside discussing the succession, and the women were either with them or walking in the formal gardens on the other side of the palace.

I stopped Meg at the fountain. We were far enough from all buildings that no one could be lurking nearby and listening. It was easy to spot anyone who came close.

"I should have told you this days ago, but I wasn't sure it was my place to do so," I said. "It's time you knew."

"Let me guess your next sentence. You don't want me to tell anyone, not even my family."

"You're smart."

"I know you too well," she countered. "Go on then, Josie. Out with it. What's the big secret the guards have all been hiding?"

"It's not just the guards, it's everyone at the palace, including the king."

I told her everything I knew about the memory loss and magic, and I finished with the king's dying confession. Her jaw dropped a little more with each sentence. When I finished, she simply stared at me.

"Have you got nothing to say?" I prompted. "You must have questions, although I doubt I can answer them. We all still have questions, perhaps more than ever. The king died without giving any answers."

"I'm trying to fathom it all," she murmured.

I squeezed her arm. "It's a lot to take in."

"How do the poor servants feel, knowing the only person who could give them answers is dead?"

I gazed back at the two guards at the gate. "It's no wonder they're angry."

We walked off in the direction of the garrison at the tip of the northern wing, each of us lost in thought. Considering this was Meg's first time at the palace, I'd expected her to be more awed by its grandeur. My news must have overwhelmed her.

"Why do they remain?" she asked. "Why not go in search of their families?"

"They don't know where to begin their search. At least here, they're together. They're among friends in the same predicament." I indicated the palace. "This is the only home they know."

There were more guards in the garrison than usual. They lounged about, resting their booted feet on the table, napped in chairs, or picked at the bread and cheese. I was greeted amiably upon entry. Some nodded, and others smiled or greeted me by name, while Max ushered us inside.

"Come. Sit." He pulled out a chair for Meg but not for me.

She sat, tilting her head to the side in an attempt to obscure her birthmark. No one was fooled. Some of the men stared at the plum colored patch on her jaw and neck for a few brief moments before returning to their conversations and ale. Meg was the only one who seemed to care. At least she'd come today. Mere weeks ago, she would never have dared.

Max sat beside her, while Erik pulled up a chair. "Two pretty ladies in our garrison today." The Marginer beamed. "We are lucky."

"You have many pretty ladies in the service commons," I chided him.

"Aye, but they are not here now. You are." He took my hand and kissed the back then did the same with Meg.

Max rolled his eyes. "Go and find something to do, Erik."

"There is nothing to do. All is quiet at the palace."

"Then go and polish your sword."

One of the men snickered.

"And not talk to Josie and Meg?" Erik crossed his arms and shook his head. "You cannot have them both to yourself, Max. I will stay. Hammer would want me to." He winked at me.

I couldn't help laughing. Erik always had a way of cheering

me up with his open exuberance. Meg, however, eyed him carefully. I suspected she wasn't quite sure what to make of the big guard with his thick accent, tattooed forehead, and long blond hair. We'd always been told that folk from The Margin were a squabbling, disorganized horde of barbarians, who luckily had no interest in crossing Hawk River into Glancia. Erik was the first one we'd ever seen. If all Marginers were like him, it might not be so terrible to let them come.

"Did you come to see Hammer?" Max asked me.

"Not particularly," I lied. "I brought tea." I pulled out a jar of mildwood leaves that Meg and I had gathered from the slopes of Lookout Hill and dried in her mother's kitchen.

"Tea?" the guard named Tom scoffed. "What do we want tea for?" He picked up his cup. "We have ale."

The guard sitting next to him shifted suddenly, and Tom hissed under his breath at him. He set down his cup and turned to me with a hard smile.

"Although tea will be nice in the mornings," he said. "Thank you, Josie."

"I'll deliver it to the kitchen on my way out," I said. "Would you like me to look at your leg or did he not kick you that hard?"

"Er..."

"Forgive them, Josie," Max said quickly. "We're glad to see you, whether or not you bring tea."

"Also, they are fools," Erik added. "Especially Tom."

"Oi!" Tom cried. "*He* kicked *me*. Where's the sympathy?"

Max cleared his throat. "My apologies, Meg. They're not usually this irritating."

"They are," one of the other guards shot back. "They'll get worse after a few ales. If I were you, Miss Meg, I'd be long gone before then."

Meg smiled weakly. "Duly noted, thank you."

The guard smiled back at her.

Max scowled.

"There are more guards than usual in the garrison," I pointed out. "Why aren't you all on duty?"

"There's not much to do without the king," Max said. "We used to have a minimum of six men escorting him at all times, and others stationed outside his rooms or along the path if he went for a walk."

"The dukes don't want you to do that for them?"

"Doesn't matter if they do," Tom said. "We work for the monarchy, not the nobles."

I didn't think his reasoning very sound. After all, if they were seen to do nothing, they were in danger of being dismissed to save money. At this perilous time, the treasury shouldn't be spending more than necessary. Hopefully the ministers were too caught up with political machinations to notice idle servants.

"It is strange without the king," Erik said quietly.

Max arched a brow at me and nodded at Meg.

"She knows about the magic," I told him.

"I'm still coming to terms with it all," she said.

"So are we," he added. "Everyone feels restless since Leon admitted it. No one knows what to do next."

"Has anyone left?" I asked.

"Not yet, but I think some will."

"Where's the captain?"

"Meeting the sheriff in Mull to discuss security."

"I thought there was little for the guards to do in the village now. It seems quiet."

"We thought so too, but the mood is shifting again," Max said. "The shock of the king's death is wearing off, and the old troubles are resurfacing. There's talk among some of protesting about rising costs and the influx of Vytillians from The Thumb."

"Let me guess," Meg said wryly. "Is Ned Perkin the instigator?"

"That's what Hammer's gone to find out."

"Ned needs to be put in his place, once and for all. He and Ivor Morgrain. Do you know, he tried telling me he was no longer a friend of Ned's? I didn't believe him."

"Why not?" I asked.

"Because he made a particular point of asking me to tell you. He's simply trying to win you over, Josie. Thank goodness you're smart enough not to fall for him and his lies."

"Aye," Erik said with a decisive nod. "She is Hammer's woman."

"She is no one's anything." Meg swallowed her next words and sank into her chair, her face reddening. She'd retreated into her shell again after briefly emerging. I wished she wouldn't. She had worthy opinions that ought to be heard.

Erik grinned. "She *is* Hammer's woman. This man Ivor will learn it the hard way."

"Ignore him," Max said to Meg. "He's as subtle as a hammer picking flowers."

The door opened and Balthazar entered. He paused upon seeing Meg and me, then resumed his plodding pace toward a spare chair. Theodore entered behind him.

"Josie!" He threw his arms around me. "It's good to see you."

I introduced them to Meg, and just as I finished, Dane and Quentin arrived. Like Balthazar, Dane paused upon seeing me, and like Theodore, Quentin threw his arms around me.

"I hope these lugs haven't been boring you to death," Quentin said.

"You're the boring one," a guard muttered.

Theodore poured two cups of wine from the jug on the sideboard and handed one to Balthazar. "We've missed you, Josie. What brings you here today?"

"A lack of work," I said. At his frown, I added, "We're bored."

Balthazar waved his cup to take in the other guards. "And you hoped to find entertainment here?"

"Your company is always a delight, Balthazar."

He grunted but a small smile ghosted his lips as he sipped.

"Max was just telling us the village is growing restless again." I addressed myself to Dane, who'd yet to say a single word. I couldn't fathom what he thought of my presence in his garrison.

"The sheriff has his concerns," he said. "After meeting with him today, I now share them."

"Why?" Balthazar asked. "What did he say?"

"The two factions in The Row are fighting again. But that's not the biggest threat. Ned Perkin conducts meetings in The Anchor every night, and his followers are growing."

"Apparently his speeches are rousing," Quentin added. "Sheriff Neerim says Perkin is a born leader and the people listen to him."

Meg clicked her tongue but didn't say anything. I suspected she had strong opinions but was keeping them to herself out of shyness.

"What does Ned want?" I asked. "The issues are beyond simple resolutions. The population explosion can't be easily resolved, nor can prices simply be lowered. Not until supplies increase. The ships can't bring in more supplies until the harbor is dredged to allow for bigger ships, and homes can't be built without land and materials, or the money to purchase them."

Dane eased himself onto a chair with the softest of sighs. It was the only sign that the wounds caused by the animal trap still troubled him. "Perkin is focusing on the housing shortage," he said. "He's reminding everyone that The Row is taking up a significant parcel of land."

"By keeping the poorest of the poor off the street," I pointed out.

"We already know he doesn't want to rehouse the poor," Meg said. "He made that clear at the last village meeting. Ned is shortsighted. He can't see that the consequences of removing The Row will be devastating for the people living there."

"And lead to even more unrest," Balthazar added.

"There'll be unrest before that happens," Dane said. "Perkin is planning protests. The sheriff is worried and has sent for reinforcements."

My village was becoming less and less like the home I knew. Sometimes I longed for the days when the annual fair brought the most excitement. Other times, I remembered that I would never have met Dane if The Rift never happened.

"Let me know if I can be of assistance," Balthazar said to Dane. "Life is quiet here at the palace lately. Too quiet. There are no revels to plan, no grand dinners to organize, and more and more nobles are leaving every day."

"You should put your feet up and relax," Quentin told him.

Balthazar tapped his leg with his walking stick. "These feet can't go up. I have to do something. If not, I might as well be dead."

"At least you still have *some* work to keep you occupied," Theodore said with a sigh. "I am a valet without a master. In the last

9

few days, I have rearranged the clothes in the royal wardrobe five times and taken stock of all jewels and personal effects four times."

"Become a guard," said one of the guards. "You can't be any worse than Quentin."

Quentin rolled his eyes. "At least his company will be more interesting than yours."

Theodore chuckled. "I'd rather rearrange the wardrobe again. I've also been running errands for Balthazar. While we still have staff here at the palace, he has work to do, if significantly less."

"Once the dukes leave, the rest of the nobles will follow," Dane said. "When that happens, the palace really will feel empty."

Balthazar lifted his gaze to Dane's, and a worried look passed between them. "And the number of staff we currently have will become unnecessary," Balthazar said. "If the dukes want to decrease costs, that's where they'll start."

"Is it their decision to make?" I asked. "Or the finance minister's?"

"The finance minister died two days ago," Dane said. "He succumbed to his illness."

"And Dr. Clegg?" I asked, referring to the finance minister's private doctor. Dr. Clegg and I had clashed on numerous occasions, even though I had the king's support. It didn't concern Leon that I was a woman. He only saw me as a doctor. It had been his one good trait.

"He left," Dane said.

That meant Doctor Ashmole was the only qualified medic within miles.

"Lord Claypool is the new finance minister," Dane said. "But he is still coming to terms with the position."

"Miranda's father? I'm glad. He seems sensible. Which duke does he support?"

"A good question," Balthazar said. "Publicly, he's not saying. His lack of allegiance was why he was appointed finance minister so swiftly. Neither duke opposed him. Besides, they've been busy these last few days. Very busy. They were appointed co-regents, giving them complete authority over decisions affecting the realm. But they must agree. Financial savings will be an area they agree on."

"One of few," Max added. "I heard they argued throughout most of that meeting. And to think, they were allies when Leon was alive."

"Their aims aligned then. They don't anymore."

"They claim they won't fight each other for the crown," Quentin piped up. "They promised they wouldn't ruin the country with a war of succession."

Ray snorted. "If you believe them, you're a fool."

"Which one has the strongest support?" I asked.

"Hard to say," Dane said. "Few noblemen have publicly acknowledged their allegiance. We suspect many will do so once they leave the palace and return to the relative safety of their own estates. Until then, only the dukes know."

"Perhaps not even they," Balthazar said. "Some lords will play both sides until they can see what the outcome will be."

"You know quite a lot about the nature of powerful men and politics," I said. "Perhaps you were an advisor before you lost your memory."

"I would have been recognized by one of the noblemen," he pointed out. "And I like to think I'm more of an observer of human nature than of power and politics."

"Are they not the same thing?" Theodore quipped.

Balthazar lifted his cup in salute. "So it would seem."

"Do you think the dukes will depart soon?" I asked.

Dane nodded.

"And what of Lord Barborough? Has he returned to Vytill?"

"Not yet," Dane said. "He has been ordered to leave, but he remains here, like a stain that can't be removed. The moment he's caught spying, however, he'll be escorted out of the country. So far, he has stayed out of the way and not been seen speaking to any of the nobles."

Theodore pointed his wine cup at Balthazar. "Bal has a theory about that. He thinks Barborough is still here because he wants to find the gem."

"Of course he wants the gem," Balthazar said.

"Why?" I asked. "It's useless to anyone but Leon. Only the one who found it can use the sorcerer's three wishes."

"Barborough might have lied about that."

It was a sobering thought. Lord Barborough, the Vytill spy and magical expert, had seemed like he was telling the truth, but how could we know for sure?

"All the more reason to keep it hidden," Dane said. "And for no one but me to know where it is. Barborough can't be trusted. He might have been the one to break into Josie's house and tie up the Ashmoles so he could search the place unhindered. I won't risk anyone's safety."

Not a single guard grumbled. They trusted Dane.

"You no longer think it was Brant?" I asked.

He hesitated. "It could have been him."

He got up and limped to the door. If I hadn't been looking for the limp, I might not have noticed it at all, it was that slight.

"Captain, may we speak in private?" I asked.

He paused then gave a single nod. "I was on my way to meet with the dukes to discuss security. You can walk part of the way with me."

He held the door open and I brushed past him. The touch was fleeting, impersonal. I ached for more. We'd shared too many tender moments for me to accept this standoffishness. Perhaps when I got him away from his men, he might be more like himself again.

"Meg?" I asked. "Will you be all right here?"

She offered me a shy smile and a nod.

"We'll take care of her," Quentin said. "Won't we, Max?"

Max got up to refill Meg's cup only to have Quentin take his seat. The youth beamed at Meg.

"Did you know I'm learning to become a doctor?" he asked.

"No, no, no," Erik protested. "That is not good talk for a pretty lady." He turned to her. "Tell me about you. I want to know everything."

"Oh." Meg blushed again and glanced over their heads at Max.

He smiled weakly and refilled her cup.

I walked with Dane along the corridor, one of many in the

maze of passages that connected the service rooms to the more opulent ones inhabited by the nobles. This corridor was empty, the only sound that of our footsteps on the flagstones. I knew from experience that the closer we drew to the palace's better rooms, the busier these hallways would become with footmen and maids going about their work.

I put a hand to Dane's arm to stop him. "Can we talk here? In private."

"Of course," he said matter-of-factly. "Is this about Brant?"

"No, but I do have questions now that you've brought him up. Have you seen him since he ran off after the king's death?"

"He's here at the palace."

"As a prisoner?"

"No. If I put him in the cells, he'll be too easy to find. I suspect if he's found by the dukes or advisors, he'll be executed for murdering the king. I prefer not to have that on my conscience."

"Is it wise to have him roaming free?"

He crossed his arms over his chest. "You're questioning my decision."

"No! No, I'm not. You know him best, and if you think he isn't a danger then I trust you."

His gaze narrowed. "You *are* questioning my decision."

"I wouldn't dare. You're the captain of the guards, and I don't even belong here."

His eyes turned smoky. Or it could have been the poor light cast by the wall torches playing tricks. "Some would say you belong here as much as anyone."

"Are you one of them?"

He lowered his arms and walked off. "You can come here whenever you like. You're most welcome."

"I'm not finished yet."

He stopped up ahead. "There's more?"

I indicated his foot. "How is it?"

"Fine."

"Then why are you limping?"

"I'm not."

I tilted my head to the side. "I've seen men limping before, and I've seen men attempt to disguise their limp. You fall into the latter category. Remove your boot and roll up your pants leg. I need to inspect the wound."

He settled his feet a little apart. "I have somewhere to be."

"It'll only take a moment."

"It's too dark in here. You can't see properly."

I removed one of the wall torches. "Any more excuses?"

"It'll hurt," he said with a pout in his voice.

I laughed. "Not as much as it will if it gets infected. Do as I ask or you might be worse off if it's not healing properly."

He sighed and undid his bootlaces. "You're a dragon."

"A dragon who's going to make you feel better." I bent to inspect the wounds left by the teeth marks of the trap. Most were healing well but the deepest was red and swollen at the edges. "You need to put anneece on this before it gets worse."

"Do you have any?" he asked as he rolled his pants leg down again.

"You have to buy it from Mistress Ashmole. Rub an amount of the salve onto the wound to thoroughly cover it then wrap a bandage around the area. That will keep the anneece from rubbing off on your clothes or the bed sheets. Do that day and night until the redness disappears."

"I'll buy some when I'm next in the village."

"Today, Dane. The sooner you treat it, the quicker it'll heal. Leave it too long and the infection will fester. If you can't make it to the village, I'll buy a jar myself and bring it back this afternoon."

"Very well. Balthazar will give you some coins. And Josie?"

"Yes?" I said, too eagerly.

This time I was sure his gaze softened as it settled on me. "Be careful."

I wanted him to say more, something intimate and tender, just a few words to lift my heart until I saw him again. But he did not.

"The danger is largely over now," I said. "Barborough doesn't need me to gather information for him."

"The Deerhorns might still be a threat."

"They'll be too occupied with matters affecting the realm."

"I hope you're right." He inched toward me only to stop. His focus sharpened, captivating in its intensity. "I worry about you in the village. It's too far away from here. From me. I can't keep you safe."

I took his hand. The soft leather of his glove warmed my fingers. "I'll be careful. I'm with friends."

He didn't look convinced but said nothing as he turned away.

I didn't see the figure but I heard his racing footsteps a moment before his arm circled my throat from behind. I didn't need to see him to know it was Brant. His odor was more fetid than usual but it was distinctive.

Dane whipped around, drawing his sword in the same motion. His eyes were cold now, flat, his features set. "Let her go or I will run you through without hesitation."

Brant's arm tightened, a noose around my neck.

I scrabbled at it, gasping in air and succeeding only in choking. Brant's low chuckle and hot breath made the hairs on the back of my neck stand up.

"Let her go!" Dane shouted.

"Not until you give me the gem."

CHAPTER 2

"You kill her, and I'll kill you," Dane said. "It's a simple equation, Brant. Let her go and I'll spare your life."

"Give me the gem," Brant snarled.

My throat burned, but the more I struggled, the more his arm squeezed.

Dane's fingers flexed around the sword handle and he took a small step forward.

"Stay back!" Brant shouted. "Don't come any closer. I have a knife to her back, and I *will* use it."

I tried to signal to Dane with my eyes that Brant lied. He didn't have a knife. Nothing dug into my back. His hand fisted in my clothes, pulling my shirt and jerkin tight, but that was all. I would have felt the sharp sting of a blade if he held one.

Dane didn't seem to understand my signals, however. His face was unreadable as ever, his focus entirely on Brant, waiting for the moment to charge and overpower him.

I could help him choose that moment. Brant might not be armed, but I was.

I tucked my hand into the slim pocket of my skirt and wrapped my fingers around the surgeon's scalpel. Ever since Lady Deerhorn kidnapped me, I'd carried it for protection.

"Get me the fucking gem!"

Brant's shout made me jump which obscured the movement

of my arm as I arced it backward and stuck him high up in the thigh.

He cried out and his grip loosened. I stomped on his foot, punched his wounded leg, and slipped out from the circle of his arm. He swore in frustration and pain, but could do nothing except surrender at the point of Dane's sword.

"You fucking bitch! You cut me!"

Blood smeared the small hole in his pants at his upper thigh. "Next time I'll aim higher," I said.

That shut him up with an audible gulp.

Dane put pressure on his sword, driving the tip into Brant's chest. "You were already on thin ice," Dane said. "No one will care if I kill you now."

"You should care," Brant spat. "If you kill me, you'll never get your memories back." His lips stretched. "That got your attention, didn't it?"

"What are you talking about?"

"I have the king's remaining wishes. I can wish for our memories back, but I need the gem."

"What do you mean you have the wishes?"

"There are two and I can use them. The sorcerer will grant me what I want if I have the magic device. I know it as surely as I know I'm standing here now, arguing with you when you could be getting the gem."

"I don't believe you."

Brant shrugged. "Why would I lie? Fetch the gem, let me make the wish and we'll find out, won't we?"

Dane shook his head. "If it were true, Barborough would have said so."

"What if he didn't know the wishes could transfer? Or what if he did and decided to lie about it? I know you want your memory back, Hammer. Trust me." Brant put out his hand, slowly, so as not to rile Dane. "Give me the gem and let me wish for our memories to return."

Dane shifted his stance. "It's not up to me. Go back to the garrison. We'll discuss it."

Brant swore and shook his head. "You're the captain! The leader! Make the decision."

"I'm the captain of the guards, not of the rest of the staff. It's not my decision to make when it affects us all. Go to the garrison and keep your hands where I can see them."

Brant rolled his eyes but did as asked. I went to follow him, but Dane held me back. He touched my throat, stroking his thumb along the tender flesh.

"You did well," he murmured. "I like that knife." He gently pried open my fist to reveal the scalpel. I hadn't realized I'd been clutching it so tightly. "You don't need it now."

Even so, I did not pocket it, and he did not sheath his sword until we reached the garrison.

A low rumble of voices greeted us as well as glares directed at Brant. He snatched up a cup and filled it with ale from the jug at the sideboard.

"Listen up!" he said, raising the cup. "I've got something to say. Something you'll all want to hear."

Almost all of them turned to Dane with questioning looks.

"Listen to him," was all Dane said.

Brant moved around the room, walking behind the seated men and Meg. Their gazes followed him, wary, watchful, as if they expected him to flick the backs of their heads as he passed, or worse. Brant preened from the attention.

"Get on with it," one of the guards muttered.

"Patience." Brant pulled out a spare chair and sat on the back, his feet resting on the seat, elbows on his knees. "I inherited the king's remaining wishes when I killed him."

Silence. Again, several men looked to Dane.

"Why are you looking at him?" Brant snapped. He jerked his thumb at his chest. "I have the two unused wishes. They transferred to me after the fake king died."

"How?" someone scoffed.

"Why?" asked Quentin.

"I don't know," Brant admitted. "Maybe they jumped into me because I was closest to him when he died, or maybe I got them because I'm the one who killed him. But I do know I have them."

"The sorcerer tell you that?" asked Ray.

"It didn't tell me with words, just…just a feeling, I suppose."

Erik snorted. "You want us to believe you?"

Brant turned an icy glare onto him. "I don't care what *you* believe, Marginer."

"But you care what I believe," Dane said. "I'm the one with the gem, and if I don't believe your story, I won't give it to you."

Brant straightened. "I'm telling the truth."

"Then why did you wait so long to come forward? Leon died five days ago. You've had ample opportunity to talk to me."

Brant lifted a shoulder in a shrug.

"Because he wanted to keep the wishes for himself," Balthazar said.

Brant studied the men who'd been his colleagues, his friends. At least he had the decency not to lie to their faces and deny the accusation, but he showed no contrition either.

"It *was* you who searched my old house and tied up the Ashmoles," I said. "Not Barborough. You were looking for the gem."

Meg gasped.

"Why not just ask Hammer for it?" Max asked.

"Because I knew he wouldn't give it to me," Brant snapped. "He doesn't want you all to get your memories back."

Again, everyone looked to Dane.

"You think that of me?" Dane asked. "That I would deny everyone the chance to have their memories returned?"

"Aye, if you don't trust me. You think I'll use one of the wishes to gain my fortune."

"Or punish your enemies," Balthazar added. "Hammer might trust you enough to give you the gem, but I don't. And unless we all agree, you're not getting it."

"It's not up to you, old man. Hammer has it, not you."

"This affects us all. We all get an equal say and unless we come to an agreement, the gem stays hidden until we can be sure we can trust you."

Brant pushed off from the chair, kicking it over as he lunged toward Balthazar. It took both Dane and Max to hold him back. Brant struggled against them until Dane wrenched his shoulder back. Brant hissed in pain.

"I lost my memory too!" he cried. "Why wouldn't I want to use a wish to get everyone's memories back?"

"There are too many unanswered questions," Balthazar went on, "not to mention too many doubts about your character. How do we even know you're telling the truth? You had ample time to tell us but you didn't, not for five days."

"I hoped to use the third wish for myself and I thought you'd stop me. There, happy now?" He shook off Dane and Max and marched back to the fallen chair. He picked it up but didn't sit down. "But I won't try that now, and *that's* the truth."

"Forgive us if we don't accept your word," Balthazar said.

Brant sat heavily on the chair and dragged his hand through his hair. He didn't meet anyone's gaze.

"And another point," Balthazar went on. "How do we know you're not working for someone else who wants the gem? I suspect the Deerhorns and Barborough would like to possess it."

"Why would they when they don't have the wishes?" Brant asked.

"We only have your word that you have them, and I've already stated how worthless that is. I imagine both the Deerhorns and Barborough would want the gem in case they can somehow obtain the wishes. I wouldn't put it past the Deerhorns to think they could bargain with the sorcerer, and I wouldn't put it past Barborough to pretend not to know what happens to the wishes after death. He might know how to get them. He might already have them."

"*I* have the wishes!"

"You might have struck a deal with the Deerhorns or Barborough, saying you'll get the gem for them if they use one wish to get our memories back."

Brant rounded on Dane. "Why are you letting him say all these lies?"

"I told you before, I am not the leader of all the staff, just the guards," Dane said. "We have equal say in what happens to the gem, and Balthazar is allowed to voice his opinion."

"But he's wrong!" Brant ground out through a clenched jaw. "I have the wishes, and I need the gemstone to use them. Don't you want your memories back?"

"You know I do," Dane said.

"Then give me the fucking gem!"

"No," Balthazar said again. "Not until we know we can trust you. We've already seen how much damage can be done with just one wish. Imagine what can be done with two." He put up a gnarled and knotty finger as Brant protested again. "We have a responsibility to be careful with those wishes. You might have them, but those of us who are aware of the sorcerer's power have a duty to see that they're used wisely. I will *not* sit by and allow you, or anyone else, to become another Leon."

"That's easy for you to say," Brant spat. "You're old. You've lived the best part of your life. All you've got to look forward to is a grave. The rest of us want to live our lives and we can't do that until we know our pasts."

"You think I want to go to my grave never knowing what I've done in this life?" Balthazar shook his head. "I am not advocating letting the wishes go to waste. We will use one to retrieve our memories. But I want to make sure you are not the one wielding all the power for your own selfish reasons. I am yet to determine how to do that." He nodded at Dane. "It requires discussion. I suggest we take some time to think about it and not act in haste."

Brant kicked the table leg and crossed his arms. "This is pointless."

"I agree with Bal," Theodore said. "Captain?"

"So do I," Dane said. "We need time to plan for all possible outcomes."

"*None* of you believe me?" Brant asked.

"I believe you," Yen said. "But I don't trust you not to use one of the two remaining wishes for yourself. I agree to delay while we consider it. We've waited this long to get our memories back, what's a few days more?"

"Aye," Erik chimed in.

The rest of the men nodded, although not all looked entirely convinced. Some would be impatient to get their memories back, no matter the cost.

"Bal, pay Josie for a jar of salve she's going to purchase then organize a meeting with the heads of staff," Dane said. For someone who didn't like to be called their leader, he certainly gave orders as if he were. "I'm late for a meeting with the dukes. Brant, stay here until I get back."

Brant muttered under his breath and crossed his arms high up his chest.

Balthazar rose and handed me some coins then walked off with Theodore. Dane held the internal door open for them. Before following them through it, he looked back at me.

"You're returning to the village now?" He posed it as a question, but I suspected he was making a suggestion. A strong one.

"After we speak with Remy," I said. "I'd like to see how he's faring."

Max collected his sword and belt from the hook. "I'll escort you."

"We don't need an escort," I said without thinking.

He paused. "I need to see someone in the kitchen anyway."

Erik chuckled. "Bring me back some chicken."

Remy was in the makeshift class that had been set up in the corner of the service commons courtyard. He and two other students listened to maid-turned-teacher, Olive, as she spoke to them about the history of Glancia. She stopped so Remy could speak to us.

"Olive's been teaching us about stuff that happened a long time ago," he said with bright-eyed enthusiasm.

I'd offered the boy from The Row and his mother a room in my house when the situation in the slum became dangerous. When the governor's office had sold my house to pay the fine I'd incurred from illegal doctoring, the Ashmoles had leased it and thrown us out. The Divers couldn't take Dora and Remy into their home as well as me, so Dane had found Dora a place in the palace kitchen. She was the only servant with a memory and her son was the only child on the estate.

"Olive taught me about famous kings and battles, and inventions. Did you know, Josie, Mull is hundreds of years old?"

"That's very interesting." I glanced over his head at Olive. She wouldn't have known the history of the nation either. Or, rather, she wouldn't have remembered it.

She held up a thick book. "The palace library is extensive."

We left them to their studies and intended to head home, but got only as far as the large forecourt. I spotted Kitty, the Duchess of Gladstow, and Lady Miranda Claypool approaching from the palace and hailed them.

"I'm so glad to see you both before we leave," I said, taking Miranda's offered hand.

"Were you going to leave without even speaking to us?" Kitty pouted, but it was a pretty pout and held no rancor.

"I'm coming back this afternoon and would have sought you out then."

She turned to Meg. "Is this true?"

Meg bobbed a hasty curtsy. "Yes, Your Grace."

"You don't need to use our titles," Miranda chided. "You're a friend of Josie's, and that means you're our friend too. It's Meg, isn't it?"

Meg nodded. "Yes, er, ma'am."

"I'm Miranda and that's Kitty. You'll get used to calling us by our names, although getting used to *us* takes a little while. Particularly Kitty. She's far too proper and uptight."

"I am not!" Kitty snipped. "I'm no different to Meg or Josie, except that I wear finer clothes. Put me in a village dress and no one will know the difference."

Miranda burst out laughing, and I giggled into my hand, not yet confident enough to laugh in the duchess's face. Meg simply stared at me, horrified.

Kitty's lips twitched until she gave in and smiled. "I suppose I am a little different. It's not my fault. I was born like this." She indicated her rose-colored gown with the matching military style jacket, white ruffled collar, and polished leather boots. "It's breeding."

Miranda rolled her eyes. "That's an argument for another day."

Kitty looked as if she would protest, but Miranda got in first. "We're heading out for a ride. Will you walk with us to the stables?" She glanced back at the palace then leaned closer to me. "We have some questions to ask you."

"We certainly do," Kitty said as we walked. "Do you remember listening in to my husband's conversation with Buxton, that sergeant and the Deerhorn brat?"

It was my turn to glance back to the palace, but no one

followed us or lurked within hearing distance. "You haven't mentioned it to anyone, have you?"

She vigorously shook her head. "It doesn't matter now that the king is dead."

We were close to the gate so I signaled for them both to remain quiet. I smiled at the guards who opened the gates for us, and waited until we were out of earshot to speak again. "The question of the king's legitimacy to sit on the throne is no longer important," I said. "But it's wise not to discuss it."

"But what about..." Kitty put a hand over her mouth and whispered, "Magic? Did the sergeant prove it to my husband?"

Meg and I exchanged glances.

Miranda gasped. "Hailia and Merdu."

"Don't say a word to anyone about magic," I told them.

"No one will believe us anyway," Kitty said. "Nobody has mentioned it."

"As far as we are aware," Miranda finished.

"Oh, I am well aware of many things," Kitty said. "I've been spying on my husband and listening in to his conversations."

"Kitty! That's dangerous."

"But quite informative. Do you know what I learned?" Her strides lengthened, and considering she was quite tall, the rest of us had to quicken our pace to a trot to keep up. "I learned that he's been meeting with Violette Morgrave."

I stopped. The three of them stopped too and rounded on me.

"Josie?" Miranda prompted. "What is it?"

"Lady Morgrave is a Deerhorn," I said.

"And quite as manipulative and nasty as her mother. So?"

"I'm sure the Deerhorns believe the tales of magic. They also wanted her to marry the king so that she could become queen. If she is meeting with your husband in secret, Kitty..." I swallowed the rest of my words. It was too cruel to voice my opinion to her.

"It's all right, Josie," the duchess said levelly. "I have suspected for two days that she is seducing my husband." Kitty might not be too bright, but a woman had an instinct about such things.

"Why?" Meg blurted out. She didn't blush or try to hide her birthmark, nor look as though she wanted to slink away from the sudden attention focused on her. She simply looked shocked. "He's already married, and to a beautiful young woman too. Why would he look at another?"

Kitty lowered her gaze. "Because she could give him children and I am barren."

Meg bit her lip. "Oh. I'm so sorry, I didn't mean to pry. I shouldn't have spoken out of turn."

Kitty took her hand and offered a weak smile. "You have nothing to apologize for. The truth is, my husband has grown restless for an heir and I am unable to give him one."

"It could be just a matter of time," I assured her. "It may still happen."

"I know that, and you do too, but Gladstow doesn't care. He refuses to even come to my bed, lately. He says he's too busy. But he's not too busy to meet with *her*, is he?"

Miranda hugged Kitty's arm. "The Deerhorns are a pack of wolves. They smell blood and attack without mercy."

"Wolves are nobler creatures than the Deerhorns," Kitty said.

We walked on in silence, and all I could think about were the implications of Lady Morgrave attaching herself to the Duke of Gladstow. Did the Deerhorns consider him the best candidate to win out of the two dukes and they hoped Violette Morgrave would once again be the mistress of the most powerful man in Glancia?

Whatever the reason, I knew for certain that she didn't intend to be his mistress for long. She intended to marry him and become queen if he secured the throne. If he thought Kitty was barren, he might agree. But that meant getting rid of his wife.

I lifted my gaze to see if Kitty knew it. She stared dead ahead, lost in her own thoughts. Miranda, however, looked as worried as I felt.

"Perhaps you shouldn't ride far today," I told them. "And not into the forest."

"But I long for a lovely sedate ride," Kitty said.

"We'll stay on Grand Avenue," Miranda assured me.

"I also think you should tell everything you just told me to the captain," I said.

"Why?" Kitty asked. "Is palace security affected by their

affair?"

"It might be." Miranda and I exchanged glances. "The thing is, Kitty, your life might be in danger from the Deerhorns," I said.

Kitty gasped. "That's a diabolical thing to say! Honestly, you've become too involved in palace intrigue and can no longer see the good in people."

"I know how the Deerhorns are," I said, lowering my voice. "Lady Violette Morgrave's family murdered her husband so that she could marry the king. Is it such a stretch to think they would remove you too so that she could marry your husband?"

She blinked watery eyes and bit her lip.

Miranda wrapped her arm around Kitty's waist. "We'll stay together from now on. Send someone to fetch me if you wish to go out. Or even better, you can move into my room."

Kitty drew away. "I do appreciate the offer, dear Miranda, but your room is hardly big enough for the two of us. Besides, if I am to win back my husband, I need to be available to him, particularly in the evenings."

"Why do you even want to win him back? He's a prick for what he's doing to you."

"Miranda, language. Just because you're with Meg and Josie doesn't mean you can use village slang."

"He is a prick, Kitty, and you should wake up to the fact that he might never come back to you. You are still the Duchess of Gladstow, however, and will be until the day you die. Let's just make sure you outlive your husband, shall we?"

Kitty touched a hand to her stomach and her pretty cheeks paled. "What shall I do?"

"Be careful," I said, "and inform the captain."

* * *

MISTRESS ASHMOLE BLOCKED my entry to the house with more conviction than any of the guards at the palace gate. Her pinched lips and flared nostrils were more forbidding than their weapons. I wouldn't be getting across the threshold unless I was in desperate need of her husband's services. Perhaps not even then.

That was all right with me. I didn't want to enter the house I'd called home for my entire life until mere days ago. I didn't want to see the changes she'd made to the rooms my mother had furnished as a newlywed or the surgery my father had died in. I did wonder if the larder was as well stocked with medicines as I'd kept it, but not enough to invite myself in.

It was one of those medicines I needed now for Dane's injury.

"Why do you need it?" she said when I asked to purchase a jar of anneece salve.

I blinked back at her. "What do you mean? I need it because I need it."

"It's for infectious wounds."

"I know."

Her gaze raked up and down my length. "You don't appear to have anything wrong with you."

"It's not for me. I'm buying it for a friend."

"Then I can't sell it to you." She went to close the door but I thrust my foot into the gap.

"I can pay," I said, stupidly.

She sniffed. "I can't sell it to you if it's not for you. That's the rule."

"Whose rule?"

"Mine."

"How do residents who are infirm get their medicine?" I pressed. "Horatio Grigg lost both legs to infection and cannot walk. His daughter-in-law would pick up an ointment whenever he needed more. Do you not sell it to her? Does *he* have to come here in person? That would be difficult for him."

"It's perfectly all right for family members to buy on behalf of their loved one. *You* don't have family, Miss Cully, and you already admitted it was for a friend."

I drew in a deep breath but it didn't help. I was very close to losing my temper. "My friend doesn't have family in the village. How do you propose he come and get what he needs if he is infirm?"

"*Is* he infirm?"

"He's injured."

"That's not what I asked." She pulled hard on the door,

banging it against my foot. "Please leave or I will send for the sheriff."

"He has better things to do," I said.

"Agreed."

I stepped back, but she opened the door wider instead of shutting it. Yvette Baker slipped through the gap, one of her five children in tow. She dipped her head as she passed me, not meeting my gaze.

"Sorry, Josie," she muttered. "I'm real sorry, but Pip has a rash."

"It's all right, Yvette." To Pip, I said, "Doctor Ashmole will clear that rash up for you."

The boy scratched his wrist where a red welt spread from beneath his shirt cuff. "His hands are cold and he smells funny."

His mother dragged him away so hard he had to run to keep up.

I returned to the Divers' house, muttering as many swear words under my breath as I could before reaching the threshold. Mistress Diver would not like me using sailors' language in front of her children. It didn't help ease my temper, however, and I dashed off a message to Dane in anger. Meg's two younger sisters agreed to take it to the palace.

I visited one of my patients in the early afternoon. She lived at the edge of the village, and the quickest route was to pass by the dock. But the dock area was a busy place these days, not only with sailors, porters, builders, and carts of all sizes coming and going, but also with men looking for work. I had a good chance of running into Ivor Morgrain there. The less I saw of him, the better. He seemed to think I'd make him a good wife. The notion was both amusing and horrifying.

Delle was close to her time, but she was healthy. The baby's heartbeat sounded strong through the ear trumpet I placed to her belly, and Delle seemed prepared for his or her arrival. I assured her the discomfort was normal and instructed her to send for me as soon as her contractions started.

The sun was setting and afternoon shadows shrouded the village by the time I left Delle. I traveled back to Meg's house the same way, avoiding the docks. Most of the workers would soon be finishing for the day and either heading home or to one of the inns, but not yet. For now, Mull almost resembled the quiet, sleepy village I'd known my whole life. The market and shops were closed, and women were at home preparing the evening meal. Some children played in the streets, but their numbers thinned as I moved out of the residential district toward the village green.

I took a shortcut down one of the narrow alleys behind the shops, but regretted it as soon as I entered. The reek of piss and horse dung hadn't been so strong the last time I'd ventured this way. Avoiding the dung and the filthy puddles pooling in the wheel ruts meant leaping and sidestepping as deftly as a dancer, and took all of my concentration.

The whinnying horse lifted both my attention and gaze from the cobblestones. Up ahead, a man stood on a cart. He pushed a barrel with his foot to another man waiting to receive it at the end of the cart. The second man hoisted the barrel onto his shoulder and carried it into one of the many storerooms lining that side of the alley. The first man pulled back a canvas on the cart, revealing four more barrels. He tipped one onto its side and rested his foot on it, waiting for his friend to return. He spotted me and quickly lowered his hat over his forehead and turned away, but not before I saw his face.

Ned Perkin.

I hurried along the alley, pulling my coat tighter at my chest as a gust of wind teased my hair and skirts. I shivered, despite summer's warmth lingering into the early autumn days.

The shadows weren't so deep in the broader streets. I nodded at Peggy as she locked the door to the Buy and Swap Shop and waved at Rory the boot maker as he also closed up for the day. At the corner, someone swore and another man took offence at his language. The swearer walked off, but the other stepped in his path and shoved the swearer in the chest. I wasn't sure who threw the first punch.

It was as if someone had lit a torch and waved it to attract moths. Men emerged from the shadows and flocked to the fight, shouting, pushing, and throwing punches. So much for a quiet walk home.

I quickly veered off and hurried away. The incident had heightened my senses, and I began to notice everyone and everything. A man slouched in a recessed doorway and another four lurked nearby, lines of anger scoring their foreheads. I caught snippets of their earnest conversation. I didn't need to hear all of it to know they were complaining about rising rents and the lack of affordable food for long-time locals.

Further ahead, in the middle of the street, two men I recognized as Mullians shouted at two strangers while a whore tried to get their attention. Prostitutes were rarely out this early or this far into the village. The sheriff usually left them alone as long as they weren't visible outside The Row.

I kept my gaze low, my medical pack close, and my wits about me.

My heart felt heavy. Mull had become a wild frontier where the law couldn't contain the burgeoning crime. Dane was right. The lull that had descended over the village after the shock of the king's death was wearing off. There would be more fighting, more crime, and perhaps even riots. It wouldn't be contained to The Row, like it used to be. It was already spilling into the streets that had always been safe for me to walk down. How much worse would it get before something was done?

Knowing the governor and the Deerhorns, it would get much, much worse before they took action to alleviate the rising pressure.

I turned another corner and immediately spun around and walked in the opposite direction. Riding on horseback up ahead were Lady Deerhorn and the governor. I prayed to the goddess that she hadn't seen me.

The goddess wasn't listening.

Hooves pounded on the cobbles behind me, so fast that I knew they wouldn't stop in time. I dashed to the left, slamming into the brick wall with bruising force. The horse galloped past so close that droplets of its sweat sprayed me.

Lady Deerhorn's purple riding cape billowed behind her like a tail, only to settle over the horse's rump as she stopped up ahead. She wheeled the horse around and rode back to me.

"Next time, get out of my way, Miss Cully," she snapped.

I didn't bother to respond. We both knew she'd seen me and had deliberately ridden close to scare me.

"You rode right at her!" It would seem I had a defender in the shadows, someone who wasn't as scared of Lady Deerhorn as me, or perhaps someone who didn't know she had no heart.

Two of the governor's men rode past, heading in the direction of the voice. I hoped the fellow had got away before he was punished.

"Don't worry, my lady," said the governor, steering his horse alongside Lady Deerhorn's. "My men will find them. You shouldn't have to put up with this kind of behavior in your own village." He glared at two men dressed in worn boots and ragged clothes as they passed by. Their hungry eyes stared right back. "Mull is going to the dogs."

Lady Deerhorn ignored him. She only had eyes for me, and what cruel eyes they were, too. Even in the dull afternoon light, the shadows avoided those icy orbs, making them look even paler, colder. "It's dangerous for a girl to be out in the village this late in the day on her own," she said. "You should be at home." The horse shifted suddenly and she pulled hard on the reins. The horse jerked his head in protest. "You wouldn't want to be raped or kidnapped, would you, Miss Cully?"

I refused to show fear, but my body betrayed me as a shiver rippled down my spine.

The corner of her mouth ticked in delight. "The king can't save you now."

I inched away, keeping my gaze on her. She moved her horse to block my path.

"Thank Lady Deerhorn for her concern," the governor barked. "Merdu knows, you don't deserve it after the things you said at the village meeting."

I'd spoken out against the Deerhorns' plans to raze The Row and replace the homes of Mull's poorest with expensive housing the slum's residents couldn't afford. They'd shelved their plans after the people protested, but they would blame me for being the voice of the villagers, no matter how reluctant I'd been to speak.

"Leave us," she ordered the governor.

He frowned but dutifully wheeled his horse away to see if his men had found the man who'd called out.

I swallowed and held my pack to my chest, preparing to run. Lady Deerhorn had kidnapped me in broad daylight once before, but that had been in my own, quiet street. She wouldn't do it here with witnesses around. I hoped.

"You look like a frightened rabbit," she said. "Don't worry. I won't hurt you. Unless you don't give me what I want, that is."

I remained silent. I refused to play her games.

"Sometimes I can't decide if you're mute because you're clever or because you're stupid. No matter. I'll tell you what I want, since I know you're curious." She leaned down a little and lowered her voice. "I want the magic gem."

My breath hitched. "I don't have it, nor do I know where it is."

"The captain of the guards knows, and you're fucking him."

"We're just friends."

She raised her hand to slap me, but I dodged out of the way and she lowered it again. "Don't treat me like a fool," she hissed. "I want the gem. The real one, not the fake you gave to the king."

"Why? If you believe the stories, which you do or you wouldn't want it, then the wishes can only be used by the one who found the gem. That was the king, and he's dead. The gem's magic won't work for you." I wouldn't tell her that Brant claimed he had the remaining wishes in his possession now. If I did, he might not live much longer. Those wishes were too valuable for Lady Deerhorn to merely let him keep them, and it seemed the only way to get them was upon the death of the wish holder. Unless they'd already come to an arrangement between them.

"Just find out where the gem is, Miss Cully," she said, almost sweetly. "Or I'll see that you won't be rescued by your captain next time I kidnap you. He'll be too busy trying to save his own skin to think about saving yours."

"He won't tell me," I said.

"You have two days." She kicked her heels into the horse and rode off.

I ran in the opposite direction and didn't stop until I reached the Divers' house, where Dane was waiting for me.

CHAPTER 3

I had to sit through polite conversation between Dane and the Divers before he finally took his leave. I walked him out, feeling Mistress Diver's watchful gaze on my back until I shut the front door behind me.

"Did you get the anneece?" I asked him.

"It's in my saddle bag. Josie, what's wrong?" He took my hands in his. "You've hardly said a word since arriving home, and you seem anxious."

"This isn't my home," I said without thinking.

"I came as soon as I could get away. I didn't think there was any urgency. You seemed angry when you wrote the letter, not worried."

"How do you know I was angry?"

"You underlined the word 'refuses' twice and called Mistress Ashmole a sour-faced wasp." He rubbed his thumbs along mine. His hands were bare, his riding gloves tucked into the saddle strap. "Tell me what has happened since then."

"I met Lady Deerhorn."

His thumbs stilled. "What did she do?"

"It wasn't so much what she did as what she said. She wants the gem. She's given me two days to get it."

"Or?"

"She didn't go into specifics. I explained she can't use it without the wishes but that didn't deter her."

He let my hands go and turned to his horse. "I'll deal with her."

"How?" When he didn't answer me, I caught his arm. "Dane, look at me."

He turned his head to the side, presenting me with his profile. It was something, at least.

"What can you possibly say to her that will stop her wanting the gem?" I pressed.

"I'll think of something."

It wasn't an answer but I suspected it was all I'd get from him. Whether he already had a plan to deal with Lady Deerhorn, or wasn't yet sure how to, I couldn't tell.

Something she'd said to me seemed particularly relevant now. "Be careful." I took his hand and rubbed my thumb along his, as he'd done with mine. "You don't have the king to protect you anymore."

"I don't need his protection." He drew on his gloves and took the reins but didn't mount. He touched my jaw and his features softened. "I don't want you to be afraid of her anymore."

"I'm not."

We both knew it was a lie.

He mounted, favoring his injured foot. "Stay indoors. If you have to go out, don't go alone."

It was pointless to argue with him when he was right; I shouldn't go out alone. The problem was, Meg might not want to come with me if Delle gave birth in the middle of the night.

* * *

DELLE DID NOT GIVE birth in the middle of the night, and Meg was perfectly happy to accompany me in the morning. Mistress Diver was reluctant for Meg to attend a birthing, telling her that girls shouldn't be exposed to one of life's raw moments at such a tender age. I told her it hadn't affected me. She let Meg go but expressed her displeasure by pounding her fists into the dough she was kneading with more force than necessary.

Delle gave birth to a girl with a healthy voice in the afternoon. With the baby's grandmother and aunt on hand, and the father hovering nearby, I felt confident to leave the new mother to enjoy her daughter. They all promised to fetch me if something seemed amiss, no matter how small, but the birth hadn't been a difficult one, and I expected no complications to arise.

Meg and I left with my payment filling my skirt pocket. When it poked its head out and chirped, I thought it best to carry the little chick instead, lest it fall out.

"What are we going to do with you?" I asked the ball of yellow fluff.

"It can stay in our room," Meg said, patting the chick's head. "We'll find a box for it."

"And when it grows too big for the box?"

Meg took the chick from me and snuggled her cheek against the soft down. "I don't know, but we'll have to keep it away from my mother." She looked the chick in the eye. "She'll be quite happy to cook you and serve you up at dinner. But I won't let her, I promise."

"She'll leave it alone if it lays an egg every day," I said.

Meg checked the underside of the chick. "How do we know if it's a boy or girl?"

I looked between the legs and shrugged. "My medical knowledge doesn't extend to chickens."

I wished Delle's husband had paid me in ells instead of a chick, but they were struggling to make ends meet, like everyone else, and I couldn't ask them.

We'd been too intent on the chick and not taking notice of our surroundings until suddenly the streets got busy. The dock workers had finished for the day. They streamed toward us in groups, some chatty, some sullen, all looking tired. Some nodded or smiled in greeting, but many were strangers to me.

"Merdu and Hailia," Meg muttered. "It's Ivor. Don't look!"

Too late. I looked and Ivor saw. He trotted up to us, a tentative smile on his lips and a hopeful gleam in his eye. "It's good to see you, Josie. You look real pretty today."

"Thanks." I waited for him to greet Meg, but he simply continued to smile at me. "Meg's here too," I pointed out.

He finally looked at her and nodded a greeting. "Why are you holding a baby chicken?"

"It's Josie's," Meg said. "Delle had her baby,"

Apparently that didn't interest Ivor enough for him ask further questions. "Josie, can we talk alone?" He didn't wait for my answer, but steered me away from Meg.

I jerked my arm free. "We have nothing to say to one another."

"Just listen."

"I have listened to you," I said. "Unless you have something new to say to me, I'm not going to listen to you repeat yourself."

He clicked his tongue and heaved out a breath. If I needed any more proof that I would make an unsuitable wife for Ivor, his frustrated sigh was enough. I was about to point it out when he spoke first.

"I just wanted you to know I'm not friends with Ned Perkin no more. I ain't seen him for days, and I don't want to. I'd rather have honest work." He grabbed my hand tightly, crushing my fingers. "My job at the docks is secure. I can support us both now."

I pulled my hand free. "Stop doing this, Ivor. I don't care whether your job is secure, or how much money you make. I'm not going to marry you."

He crossed his arms and scuffed his toe against the edge of a raised cobblestone. He looked more vulnerable and contrite than I'd ever seen him. I almost felt sorry for him. "You used to like me, Josie, but everything changed between us when I became friends with Ned Perkin. I don't see him no more, though. I promise, I want nothing to do with him." He reached for my hand again, but I stepped away. He swallowed heavily. "You got to believe me, Josie. Me and Ned are no longer friends. He's going to bring trouble down on his head, and I don't want that. I want to be a good man. For you."

Part of me wanted to walk off without another word. If he thought the only reason we weren't together was because he associated with Ned Perkin, he was a fool. But he was right in one respect. We'd known each other a long time. We may not have been close, but we had grown up together. The way he'd treated me recently, however, dampened any sympathy I felt for him now.

"Whether you are friends with Ned or not is irrelevant to me," I said, moving out of the way of other pedestrians. "I have no feelings for you, Ivor, nor will I ever. I've told you before, I would rather never marry than marry someone I don't care about."

He dashed the back of his hand across his mouth. When it came away, his lips were white from pursing.

"What kind of trouble is Ned making?" I asked to fill the silence. "Is he up to something?"

He lifted a shoulder. I turned away and strode off.

"The captain won't marry you!" he called out. "He's hiding something. All the palace servants are."

Passersby stared at him then turned to me. Some shook their heads or rolled their eyes, while others muttered agreement. Meg took my arm in hers and we headed off together.

Ivor followed. "You can't trust people who keep secrets." He sounded close. Too close.

Before I could turn to confront him, he'd grabbed my shoulder and wrenched me around to face him. His breaths came hard and fast, and he bared his teeth. He wasn't a big man, but he looked fierce in that moment. He was also unpredictable. I regretted ever feeling sorry for him. He didn't deserve sympathy.

"Let her go!" Meg snapped at the same time I pushed his hand off.

"Why won't you listen!" he cried. "There's something wrong with the servants. They ain't…" He let the sentence dangle, merely shrugging his shoulders to explain himself.

"Aren't what?" I asked. "Aren't real? That's ridiculous, Ivor. You shouldn't listen to rumors."

"They ain't like us," he finally finished.

I shook my head, both in disagreement and disappointment. "That's your reason for not trusting the servants? That they're not from Mull?"

He shrugged again.

Meg transferred the chick to one hand and poked Ivor in the

shoulder with her finger. "That's so typical of you. You and many others in this backwater. I didn't know I lived in the same village as so many hate-filled people."

"We ain't filled with hate," he shot back. "We're just scared. Scared of losing our homes, our jobs, our wives."

"Those of you with homes won't lose them," Meg told him. "Nor will anyone who already has a job, unless you take too many breaks or do poor work. And if a man's wife strays, then it's his own fault for not keeping her happy. Come on, Josie. Don't waste another moment talking to him." She spun around and marched off, ignoring the stares. Some of those who'd heard her looked impressed, others bemused. I'd never been prouder of her.

I lengthened my strides to catch up to her. "That was a rousing speech," I said.

"I have strong opinions on the matter," she said. "In fact, my opinions grow stronger by the day. The more I get to know the guards, the more I like them. The Vytillians are mostly good people too, despite a few bad ones. Marnie and her husband are kind, decent folk. It's not their fault The Rift destroyed their livelihoods. I'm sure they wish they were back there now instead of subjected to hate from Mullians."

We walked for a while in silence until I felt the tension in her ease as her pace slowed. "So you like the guards more as you get to know them better," I teased. "Any one in particular?"

"Don't, Josie. I'm not in the mood."

I stayed silent for the remainder of the walk.

* * *

WE WERE WOKEN by shouts and someone banging on the door. "Josie! Josie, help!" It must be either Delle's husband or the husband of my other patient. *Hailia, please don't let it be too bad.*

By the time I reached the door, Meg's father had already answered it. The man standing there clutching his arm and coughing was not a family member of any of my patients, but I knew him well.

"Wallace, come in, come in," Mr. Diver said. "What's wrong? Is that smoke I smell?"

I smelled it too. Then I saw the glow above the rooftops. "Merdu," I said. "Fire!"

"The Row," Wallace gasped out between his coughs. "It's burning."

"All of it?" Meg asked.

Wallace nodded gravely. "Me and some who live near it tried to help, but it was too hot. And the smoke…"

"Lyle!" Mr. Diver shouted as he ran back inside. "Lyle, get up! Get dressed!"

Outside, several other men up and down the street were dashing out of their homes, pulling on coats and gloves, blankets or pails slung over their shoulders. If The Row were on fire, they'd need more than that.

And then I saw the stream of people making their way to the Ashmoles' house across the way. Women and children, mostly, and a few men barely able to stand. They coughed and spluttered, and cradled injured arms. They cried, some even wailing as they hurried forward, carrying a limp loved one. The air was clogged with smoke and the sounds of pain, misery, and utter desperation.

There were so many, and all heading in the same direction. To my old house.

"Josie, can you look at my arm?" Wallace asked.

"She can't help you," Meg said. "You know she can't. I'm sorry to turn you away, but you have to go to Doctor Ashmole."

"He already has too many patients," Wallace rasped.

"I know but—"

"Please, Josie. No one will notice if I come in. Patch me up so I can go back and help fight the fire. If it spreads, all of Mull will be in danger."

The figure of Mistress Ashmole appeared in the doorway opposite, candlestick in hand. She let in the first person in the queue and refused entry to the next in line. The woman cradling a baby slumped against the wall as a coughing fit overtook her.

Mistress Ashmole glanced toward us and lifted her candle higher.

Meg bundled Wallace outside and he trudged away, cough-ing, and joined the queue outside the Ashmoles' house. One of the patients in the middle of the queue, a man clutching the side of his face, stepped out of line and approached her.

"Wait your turn!" Mistress Ashmole snapped. She disap-peared inside and slammed the door shut. I heard the bolt slide across.

"Why won't she assess them and prioritize the order according to the severity of their injuries?" Meg asked.

"She doesn't know how," her mother said. "She's over-whelmed."

I headed back to my room and quickly dressed.

"No, Josie," Meg said, blocking the doorway. "You're not going over there. Doctor Ashmole will just have to see them one at a time. Perhaps he will look at the queue and pick out who to see first."

He might, but it wouldn't matter. He was only one man, one doctor. Even if I did help prioritize the patients for him, he could only work so quickly. Most of the injuries would be burns and there was little to do except slather on the sap from the pomfrey tree. But Mistress Ashmole wouldn't have enough of it, and the patients would be coming all night.

"There is something we can do," I told them. "Doctor Ashmole will need more sap and bandages. Much more."

Meg's eyes lit up. "We'll ask the other women in the street to help us collect as much as we can carry." She snatched up her cloak and flung it around her shoulders, not bothering to put on a gown over her shift first. "We'll take it to Mistress Ashmole."

Mistress Diver met my gaze. "And bring some back here?"

I nodded.

"Mother!" Meg cried. "You can't ask Josie to do that."

"It's my choice," I told her. "I won't stand by when I can do something."

"It's too dangerous. It won't be a fine this time. You'll be imprisoned. Or worse."

"Bring the patients in the back way through the courtyard," I said. "We'll swear them to secrecy."

Meg made a scoffing sound.

Her mother picked up Meg's boots and handed them to her. "They'll agree if it's going to save them and their loved ones."

I hoped I could save some of them. Burns were difficult to treat, and breathing in smoke could be just as deadly, if not more so. Some people would die from their injuries. I prayed it wouldn't be many.

CHAPTER 4

I prepared the kitchen as best as I could while Meg and her mother gathered pomfrey sap in the forest. I tore linen into strips, cringing as I did so. It wasn't my linen. But Mistress Diver would have done it if she were there, and I knew she would have it no other way.

Torren Bramm, a fisherman, came to the front door, coughing so hard that he could hardly speak. His eyes watered and both of his hands were wrapped in cloths.

"You can't come in," I told him. "Not this way. Go around the back. Don't let the Ashmoles see you."

He nodded, understanding my meaning, and left, his body bent as another cough wracked him. Torren was a good man, and I knew his daughters well. He wouldn't cause trouble for me.

I realized as I returned to the kitchen that only the men would come to me for help. Few people from inside The Row knew I had medical knowledge, so they would not come. Long-time locals from outside The Row who tried to put out the fire would be men. It was they who would approach me when they saw the long queue of injured at Doctor Ashmole's house.

Before I reached the kitchen, someone else banged on the front door. It was another man I knew, a good friend of my father's. I told him the same thing I'd told Torren Bramm. As he walked off, I glanced again at the fiery glow in the night sky. It had grown. The stars and moon had disappeared behind clouds of smoke. Mull was being smothered from above and burned from within. I'd seen fires before, although not on this scale. I knew how fast they could spread. If it wasn't put out soon, it would reach my street.

I glanced westward, in the direction of the palace. Could they smell the smoke from there?

I was about to close the door when I spotted a shadowy figure moving in the window opposite. Mistress Ashmole, perhaps, keeping an eye on me, or on the long queue that was growing restless as they waited to be seen by her husband.

Torren was waiting for me in the kitchen when I reached it. I helped him to drink a tankard of water then set a large pot to boil on the stove, adding a pinch of amani spice I found in Mistress Diver's larder. The steam would help clear his airways. Then I unwrapped the bandages around his hands. They were blackened and swollen, the skin blistering.

"There's nothing to do except wait for the pomfrey sap," I said. "Until then, try to relax and steady your breathing.

My second patient arrived, bringing with him the smell of smoke. I gave him a drink and bade him to stand near the boiling spiced water to allow the steam into his airways. I instructed Meg's sisters to block gaps in the window frames and around the external doors. The air inside needed to remain as fresh as possible.

I wanted to ask both men how bad the fire was, how many were helping and if people were trapped, but I didn't want them talking too much. Their throats would be raw and their breathing still sounded labored.

Meg returned, out of breath, a jar of sap in hand and rolled cloths under one arm. "Did anyone see you come in here?" she demanded of my two patients.

They both shook their heads.

She handed me the jar of sap and began tearing up more cloths. "There'll be more sap soon, but I thought it best to bring back what we had now."

I gently spread the sap over the burns then wrapped cloth

strips around Torren's hands. "The sap needs time for its healing properties to work. Be sure to keep the bandages on as long as possible before changing them."

Both men stood when I finished and headed for the door.

"Where are you going?" I demanded.

"To The Row," Torren said. "We have to help."

"But your injuries!"

"We have to," he said again. He opened the door, letting in the smoky air, then left.

It wasn't very long before another patient arrived. Mistress Grinsten, a neighbor, also returned with more sap and linen. By the time I finished bandaging his burns, another man showed up at the kitchen door, then another and another. They all had burns, but more worrying was their breathing difficulties.

They couldn't speak without a coughing fit taking over. They were also exhausted and agitated in equal measure. The fire must be out of control.

"I'm going to check," Meg said after another patient arrived. "I need to know."

She was gone a long time. More patients came. The kitchen filled with the coughs of a dozen of Mull's able-bodied men, and the smoke they brought with them. The spiced steam helped their breathing but it made the enclosed space very hot. Sweat dripped down my back as I worked, applying the sap and trying to alleviate sore throats and coughs.

Women from the street came and went with sap and bandages, but the elderly were beginning to show signs of breathing problems too. I assured them we had enough sap and sent them home.

Meg finally returned, a scarf wrapped around her nose and mouth. Her eyes streamed and she coughed incessantly. I directed her to stand near the boiling pot and waited until her breathing steadied before asking my questions.

"How bad is it?"

"Real bad," she said. "From what I can see, there'll be nothing left by dawn."

"Nothing left of The Row?"

Her worried look gave me the answer I dreaded. The entire village was under threat.

"The line outside Doctor Ashmole's house?" I asked.

"Long."

"Did you tell anyone that I can treat them?"

"Are you mad? Of course not."

I pressed the back of my hand to my hot forehead. It came away damp from sweat. "This is ridiculous. I'm going over there—"

She grabbed my arm. "No, you are not. Do what you can for those who come to our back door."

I huffed out a frustrated breath, not sure whether to defy her or listen to her counsel.

"The captain's here with most of his men and lots of servants from the palace," she said. "They've set up a human chain from the harbor to The Row, passing pails of water along it." Her grim face told me it wouldn't be enough.

One of her sisters cried as she came into the kitchen; the other tried to hold back her tears. Meg ushered them out again. "We're going to pack a few things," she told them. "Just what we can carry."

Some of the men left to return home and prepare their families to flee. Others left to fight the fire, while the ones sporting the worst injuries remained with me. More arrived, and the kitchen became crowded again. It was an ongoing fight against smoke and fire—one I couldn't win.

All night, they came and went. The hours blurred together. I immersed myself in my work and the fear of discovery was forgotten. Meg was an invaluable help, and despite her own fears, she managed to calm many nerves, including those of her sisters.

Until a badly burned and unconscious guard arrived, carried in the arms of Max. Meg sent her sisters out of the kitchen.

"Lay him down on the table," I instructed.

"You've got to help him," Max said before he succumbed to his coughs.

I quickly assessed the injuries, noting the burns on the man's face, hands and arms. Patches of his uniform were burned too.

But it was his ragged, shallow breathing that worried me the most.

"Meg, help me remove his clothing."

"No," Max said.

"You need to rest," I told him. "You can hardly breathe. Get yourself a drink and take a seat."

It wasn't until Meg gave him a little shove that he moved away and allowed her to get close to the guard. I didn't know his name, but only yesterday he'd nodded at me as I passed him at the gate.

I set to work with Meg's assistance, applying the sap to the burns. Once they were bandaged, there was nothing more to do. The steam would help his breathing, but only if he hadn't inhaled too much smoke already. There was no way of knowing.

Max studied him from beneath heavy lids. "When will he wake up?"

"I don't know," I said.

Max coughed again, his chest and shoulders heaving with the effort to breathe through the fit. Meg watched on, nibbling her lower lip until it bled. We both felt utterly helpless.

When Max finally suppressed the cough, he headed for the door.

"Where are you going?" Meg said, hands on hips.

"I have to get back. They need help."

"You're not fully recovered. Tell him, Josie."

"She's right," I said. "If you breathe in much more smoke, you'll be unconscious too."

His fingers touched Meg's before dropping away. "I'll be careful."

We watched him go. Another three patients left with him, all of them sporting injuries, none of them fully recovered.

When she turned back to me, Meg's eyes were full of tears. "What's the point in bandaging their burns when they'll just get more?"

I didn't tell her that they were in danger from the smoke more than the flames.

Mere hours later, the guard became my first casualty. He passed away as I watched on helplessly, willing his breathing to return to normal, yet listening to it dwindle away to nothing. When Meg realized, she burst into tears.

One of the other patients helped me move the guard's body onto my bed, out of the way, then he too left to go fight the fire again. I didn't try to stop him, even though I knew he might soon be back, struggling to breathe. They needed every man they could get out there or we could be in danger, even here. Meg's sisters sat with a bag each near the door, dolls cradled to their chests, waiting for instructions.

As I closed the door after yet another patient arrived, I realized the hazy glow in the east signaled the rise of dawn, not our entrapment by fire. It offered no comfort, however. The village still burned in the west.

Every newcomer looked grim, as sick with worry as they were with the pain of their burns.

Then finally Mistress Diver returned, exhausted and coughing, but with good news. "It's contained," she managed to rasp out. "It won't spread further."

I almost cried with relief.

"How?" one of the patients asked.

"Someone had the idea to pull down the houses around the fire and clear away the rubble so it had nothing to burn. The gap was wide enough for the fire not to cross."

"How far has it spread?" I asked.

She shrugged as another coughing fit overtook her. I directed her to sit down and gave her a cup of water.

"It's light now," Meg said, returning to the kitchen. She'd been outside in the street, gauging the number of injured across the road at the Ashmoles'. "We can't accept any more patients."

"We have to," I said. "Now that the fire is contained, there'll be more."

"They'll be seen coming here."

"This is an emergency, Meg. No one will care if I help. No one is that cruel, not even Mistress Ashmole."

"What about the Deerhorns?"

I concentrated on applying sap to my patient's hands.

"Meg's right," Mistress Diver said. "You can't take any more patients in, Josie. Meg, go outside and direct any newcomers to Doctor Ashmole."

I blinked at her. She'd been my ally last night. What had changed?

As if she'd read my mind, she said, "It's daylight now. It's too easy to see the injured coming and going. I'm sorry, Josie, but I can't risk my family."

I felt ashamed for not thinking of them. Of course she would worry about the consequences for her family. They might be punished for allowing me to work in their house. I wasn't the only one taking a risk.

Most of my remaining patients left when their breathing improved. Four remained, too injured or ill to leave. Once we cleaned up, there was little more to do. I snatched some sleep on a stool in the corner while Mistress Diver went to bed.

Mr. Diver and Lyle returned around midday. They drank deeply then sat beside the steaming pot of spiced water until their ragged breathing improved. Their exposed skin was blackened from soot, but neither sported burns, thank Hailia.

"Well?" I asked, when they seemed recovered enough to speak. "Is the fire out?"

Lyle nodded. "The sheriff's men and the palace guards are keeping watch to make sure there's no flare ups, but it's mostly embers and ash now."

"How far did it spread?"

"The Row's completely gone."

"The people?"

They exchanged glances. "There are several dead, and they'll find many more when the rubble's cleared away," Mr. Diver said.

I sat heavily and buried my face in my hands. It was too awful to contemplate.

"And outside The Row?" Meg asked. I hadn't heard her come in. She looked tired, her face pale from the strain of the night, her eyes red from smoke and crying.

"Some homes in the streets nearest The Row were destroyed," Lyle said. "I think everyone got out though. We'll know more soon."

I couldn't wait for news to reach us, however. I needed to know if Dane and the other guards were all right.

Meg joined me, telling me she wanted to see the damage done to Mull, although I suspected she was more interested in news of Max. We pulled a barrel of water on a cart behind us, past the patients leaving Doctor Ashmole's house. There were more leaving than arriving, thankfully, many with bandaged limbs, all covered in soot.

Smoke hung in the air, but a sea breeze worked valiantly to disperse it. There was no better healing agent for smoked lungs than fresh air.

We stopped behind a group of people, mostly women, blocking the way forward on a street that led to The Row. Some wailed, others begged to be let through. I pushed my way past and saw why they could advance no further. Four guards on horseback, all blackened from soot, wouldn't allow anyone beyond that point.

"Josie!"

"Quentin?" I hardly recognized him. He was covered head to toe in soot and ash. "Thank Hailia, you're all right. Do you have any injuries?"

"Not much. Not like some," he added heavily.

My heart surged into my throat. "The captain?"

"And Max?" Meg asked.

"Both unharmed. They're helping the sheriff's men look for survivors." He glanced over his shoulder toward The Row. I followed his gaze and suddenly realized why they weren't allowing anyone through.

The dead had been arranged in rows, with more being carried out and added to their number. Meg gasped and covered her mouth.

"Let us in!" one of the women cried. She was dressed in rags and wore no shoes. Her hair was black from soot and wild with tangles. Her hands were wrapped in cloth. "Let us in to see our men!"

"No," barked Zeke, one of the guards. "When the dead are all brought out, then you can look for your loved ones amongst them."

49

One of the women burst into tears.

"Zeke," I said. "Have some compassion."

"Sorry, Josie."

"Can they not see if those already brought out are their menfolk?" Meg asked. "One of you could go with them, ensure it's done in an orderly manner. Perhaps you could record names."

Zeke and Quentin exchanged glances. "Not me," Zeke said. "I don't want to look at them. Besides, I ain't no good with grief."

"I'll go," I said.

Quentin dismounted. "Me too." He handed the reins to Zeke. "But I've got no paper to write names on."

"I've got paper," came a voice from behind the group of mourners.

Zeke frowned and rose up in the saddle to see over the heads. "That you, Balthazar?"

The group parted and Balthazar limped his way through. "I'll record the names," he said, waving a small book. His clothing was clean, his face and hands free of soot, but he looked just as tired as the guards.

"How did you get here?" Quentin asked.

"Some of the maids came in to help where they could," he said. "I arrived with them on a cart." He glanced past Quentin to the bodies and leaned heavily on his walking stick.

"I'll do it, if you like," I said.

"No. But I would appreciate your help with the mourners." To Zeke, he said, "Allow one in at a time."

"Only one?" someone shouted.

"This must be managed. No mistakes can be made. You may come first."

"So we're just supposed to wait?" asked another.

"Is that water?" said another of the women.

"It is," Meg said. "Please, have some."

"Thank Hailia for your mercy," Zeke said, dismounting. "I'm parched."

I headed along the street with Quentin, Balthazar and one of the women. The closer we got to the burned buildings, the harder my heart pounded, and the deeper it sank. I hardly recognized the area. Where before there'd been derelict houses, lean-tos and crates used for shelter, now there was nothing but the occasional brick chimney standing guard over the rubble and smoldering ash. The fire had ravaged the whole area.

No, not entirely. Wide spaces on both sides of the street leading to The Row were untouched by fire. There was no rubble there, no fuel for the flames. The fire had nowhere to go. If not for these fire breaks, Mull would still be burning.

"Whose idea was that?" Balthazar asked Quentin.

"Captain's," Quentin said. "Sheriff wasn't so sure it was a good idea to destroy perfectly good homes, but Captain Hammer convinced him. We pulled the buildings down with hooks and ropes and carted the rubble away. It was hard work."

"But well worth it," Balthazar said. "If not for those breaks, the fire would have spread through the entire village."

The woman surged forward upon reaching the first of the charred bodies. She covered her mouth as she made her way along the rows of the dead. When she reached one near the end, she suddenly fell to her knees.

I did my best to console her, but my words had no effect. Somehow we managed to extract a name from her, and I helped her back to the gathered crowd. There were more than before, and not all of them the ragged poor from The Row. I recognized some women I'd known all my life. Their husbands had probably helped to fight the fire and not yet come home.

We let the mourners in, one by one, and took down the names of the dead. I counted twenty-eight, a smaller number than I'd first feared, but far greater than I ever wished to see.

As the hazy sky turned darker with dusk, the bodies were all accounted for, and no new ones were brought out of the rubble. There was no sign of Dane. Lyle arrived, leading some neighbors with carts, all laden with barrels of water.

"We should get this to those still working in there," I told Balthazar.

He leaned both hands on his walking stick and slumped forward. He nodded.

"Go and sit on the back of the cart," I said gently. "There's little to be done here now."

He was joined by some of the palace maids. They'd been giving out food, water and clothing to those in need, offering words of comfort. Among them was Dora. Her distressed gaze connected with mine. She would probably know some of the dead.

"I want to find the captain," I said to no one in particular.

"You can't go in," Zeke said. "Sorry, Josie, but it's too dangerous. Captain'll have my head if I let you in."

I sighed and sat on the back of the cart with Balthazar.

"You look exhausted," he said. "You were up all night, weren't you?"

"I got some sleep this morning."

He cast a glance along the street towards the burned buildings. "Did anyone see the wounded coming to you?"

"No," I said with more confidence than I felt. While Meg had sworn everyone to secrecy, we couldn't be sure they hadn't been seen, despite the darkness.

"He won't like it."

"Who?"

He nodded toward the soot covered figures picking their way out of the rubble. I immediately recognized Dane from his physique and the way he walked, all confidence but no swagger. He'd stripped down to his shirt. Some of the men were bare chested altogether, their jerkins nowhere to be seen.

I jumped off the back of the cart and almost ran to him, but checked myself.

Balthazar fought back a smile. "Take the water," he told me. "It won't look so obvious if you have a reason to go to him."

Meg liked his idea just as much as I did. We dragged the cart together and filled up cups with water from the barrels. I handed one to Dane then poured another and handed it to the sheriff. Meg passed a cup to Max and offered him a weak smile. He thanked her and drank deeply. They all did.

"How do you feel?" I asked Dane when he handed back the cup.

"Fine," he said, his voice husky from the smoke.

He didn't look fine. The only clean part of him was his

eyeballs and they were red-rimmed from exhaustion and the smoke.

"Are you having difficulty breathing?" I asked in my best professional voice.

"A little."

"Is your throat sore?"

Sheriff Neerim coughed. "You wouldn't be giving out medical advice, would you, Josie?"

I bit my lip and shook my head.

He grunted and walked past. Balthazar met him and they spoke in quiet tones.

"Have you retrieved everyone?" I asked Dane.

"I doubt it, but there won't be any survivors. It's no longer a rescue; it's a recovery." He glanced past me to the crowd of mourners. "You've been supervising them?"

"Balthazar took down names of the dead where they could be identified. Some are beyond recognition."

He closed his eyes. "I could have stopped this."

"How?"

He opened his eyes and pinned me with his familiar, deep stare. "I know where the gem is, and Brant claims he has the remaining wishes. I could have forced him to use one to end the fire before it was too late."

"He wouldn't have done it. He wants those wishes for himself."

"But—"

"No, Dane. No. This is not your fault. You *stopped* the fire from burning the rest of the village." I cupped his jaw and stroked my thumb along his cheek, smearing the soot. I wanted to do more, to embrace him and comfort him, but…

Forget all that. Forget what was right, that we didn't know if he had a woman somewhere. He needed comforting after witnessing the harrowing events of the night, and I needed it too.

I drew him into my arms and held him. He circled his arms around me and buried his face in my shoulder. I could hear his shortness of breath and feel the rapid beat of his heart. His shudder was unexpected.

We clung to one another. It wasn't until that moment of shared despair that I realized I *did* feel despair, and I *needed* to be wrapped in his arms. The outcome could have been worse. One guard was dead; other rescuers, too. It could so easily have been Dane, yet he was alive. Holding him, and being held by him, made me realize just how lucky we were.

The embrace was over too briefly, however, as we both pulled away from the other at the same time.

"I have to speak to my men," he said with ominous foreboding. "Some are missing."

I clutched him, bunching his shirtsleeves in my fists. He lowered his gaze to mine and I saw the heartbreak in them before I'd even uttered a word. "I have some terrible news." The words came out as a whisper. "One of your guards died last night. I don't know his name."

His throat moved with his swallow. "How do you know?"

"He's in Meg's house."

"How do you know?" he asked again. "Who brought him there? Who brought him to you?" His vehemence surprised me. Of course he wouldn't want me performing a medical task under normal circumstances, but this was an extraordinary situation.

"It doesn't matter," I said.

"It does to me. Whoever took him to you, endangered you. If he was seen—"

"He wasn't."

He looked as though he was going to ask more questions, but changed his mind. I was grateful. I was too heartsick to disagree with him.

He limped off toward his men.

"Your foot," I pointed out. "I forgot about it."

He glanced down. "I'll use that salve on it as soon as I get back to the palace."

I joined Max, Meg and the other guards while Dane headed towards Balthazar and the sheriff. He made slow progress. People kept stopping him to shake his hand or slap him on the back. He looked uncomfortable receiving their gratitude.

"Don't tell him it was you who brought that guard to Meg's house," I whispered to Max.

He frowned. "Why?" Then his brow cleared. "Right. I ain't going to hide, Josie. I made a decision, and I'll own up to it."

"You will not," Meg said, crossing her arms. "I forbid it."

Max arched his brows. Quentin snickered.

"How is he?" Max asked me.

I bit my lip and shook my head. "He didn't survive. I'm so sorry."

Quentin stumbled backward, his hand to his stomach. Zeke groaned and lowered his head. Max strode off, pushing through the crowd of mourners as Meg and I watched on helplessly.

"We should follow him," I said. "He's probably heading to your house."

Meg didn't need prompting and trailed after Max. Quentin fell into step alongside me in their wake. He swiped at his eyes with the back of his hand even though he was too dry to shed tears.

Dane caught up to us as we entered Meg's house. Her mother was in the kitchen, cleaning. She placed a finger to her lips for quiet.

"Everyone is asleep," she whispered. "You should go back to the palace and get some rest too."

"After we take our friend," Max whispered back.

"Not yet. Not until it's dark."

"But—"

"No."

Dane placed a hand on Max's shoulder. "Mistress Diver is right. We must wait until nightfall. I won't risk Josie or the Divers."

Max shrugged him off. "No one will blame Josie for helping last night. She was needed. Doctor Ashmole couldn't fix them all."

"We'll come back later." Dane turned to Mistress Diver. "Thank you to you and your family for your assistance. I'll see that there are no repercussions for you."

"The villagers would riot if there is," she said.

After they left, Meg and I helped Mistress Diver until the kitchen showed no signs of the night's activity. Not even the scent of amani spice hung in the air. Then we rested. Meg and I slept on the kitchen floor, neither of us wanting to share a room with a dead man.

I awoke some time later with a stiff neck. It was dark inside except for a single flame flickering by the door. When my eyes adjusted to the dimness, I realized someone held a candlestick but I couldn't see who.

"It's just us," came Quentin's tired voice. He lifted the candle to his face. It was still black from soot. He had not been back to the palace yet.

Other shadows emerged, and I recognized Dane and Max's silhouettes. They moved silently through the house and returned, moments later, with the body carried between them. They took it outside and Dane returned alone.

"It's on the cart beneath a pile of rubble we're removing from the site." He whispered so as not to wake Meg.

"Will you go to the palace now to rest?" I asked.

"Yes."

"Promise me."

"I promise."

"If I find out that you've broken that promise, I'll come to the palace and sneak a sleeping tonic into your ale. Don't think I won't find out, either. Balthazar and Theodore will spy for me."

His teeth momentarily flashed white in the dark. "The three of you make a formidable team." Before I knew it was happening, he rested his hands at my waist and pressed his lips to my forehead.

"Thank you," he murmured, drawing away.

I didn't know what he was thanking me for, and I didn't ask. My emotions swelled, surged, the good tangled with the bad so that I couldn't separate them—the thrill of being the recipient of his affection and the sorrow of recent losses. My heart felt as though it would explode with the intensity of them.

"Goodnight," he murmured. Then he was gone.

CHAPTER 5

A new day brought with it an overwhelming sense of relief that the fire hadn't caused more destruction. But it also brought absolute despair to those who'd lost everything, including loved ones. It was a difficult time, yet I was proud of my village. A skeleton crew operated at the harbor to process incoming and outgoing ships while everyone else joined the operation to clear away the debris left from the fire. Even the elderly women helped by doling out food and ale to the workers. Clothing and shelter was given to those who'd lost homes, no matter if they were not Mullian-born.

The cleanup was slow, however. The enormity of the task seemed insurmountable. At times, the amount of rubble looked like it would never get smaller. But every day it did. At the governor's request, Dane took charge of the operation. The governor had asked the sheriff first, but Sheriff Neerim said the captain was better suited, being used to mobilizing a large group of men.

I saw the proof. It wasn't so much that Dane was used to being in command, it was more that the men respected him. All the men, no matter if they were Mullian locals, immigrant Vytillians or palace servants. All accepted his authority.

There was no sign of the Deerhorns, although the governor's

speech after the mass burial of the victims referenced them frequently and without humility.

"Lord and Lady Deerhorn have promised to rebuild the village!" he declared from where he stood on the back of a cart just outside the graveyard. Most of the mourners had remained to hear what he had to say, although none seemed enthused by his bombastic speech. "This is an opportunity to make Mull even better than it was before! A grand center of commerce, fit for its new and magnificent status as The Fist Peninsula's most important harbor."

Most of the listeners remained silent. Most were too heart sore after the burials to think about rebuilding already. Only one brave soul near the front asked, "What do you mean by a better Mull?"

"An improvement." The governor gave the sort of encouraging smile one gives to a child attempting a new task.

"Who smiles at a time like this?" Meg muttered.

"The council will reveal plans for the vacant land as soon as it has been decided," the governor went on.

"It's not vacant yet," someone called out.

"Will the new houses be affordable?" someone else asked.

The governor put up his hands for calm. "All will be revealed soon."

Discontent rippled through the group.

"Who will fund the rebuilding?" Meg asked.

"Good question," someone said.

The governor's smile tightened. He gazed longingly at the village road. "The Deerhorns," he said as one of the sheriff's men helped him down from the cart.

"At what cost to us?" asked Torren Bramm.

The governor mounted his horse. "All will be revealed as soon as the details are settled." He rode off, leaving us staring after him.

"Turd," someone behind me spat.

"Heartless, that's what he is," said Meg. "How can he discuss making a new and better Mull just after we've buried those who gave their lives to save *this* Mull?"

"Aye," said Tammara Lowe. "He made it sound like it was a

stroke of luck the slum was destroyed so Mull can be *improved*, as he calls it." She spat into the verge. "He's scum."

"Him *and* the Deerhorns," Meg said. "I'll wager the rents will be too high for even us to afford, let alone those who were living in The Row before the fire."

"What will happen to them now?" Sara Tolly asked.

"We'll take care of them," Meg said.

"How? We've got nothing to give."

No one had an answer for her.

I stopped listening after that. Tammara's words niggled at me like woodworm. The Row's destruction was convenient for the Deerhorns. Now they could implement their plans to replace the slum. No doubt the agreement they came to with the council over the land would benefit the Deerhorns more than Mull. It was too neat a solution for my liking. I had to tell the sheriff.

I spotted one of his men at the feeding station the women had set up near the edge of the burned zone. "Have you seen the sheriff?" I asked him.

"He's in there, talking to the captain," he said.

Tracks had been made through the rubble and ash for access. The gaping expanse that had once teemed with life now looked like a barren wasteland. Men threw blackened bricks and timbers into carts while women sifted through the ash for possessions. It was dirty, back-breaking work.

I found the sheriff and Dane talking in a clearing. Dane glanced up as I approached and nodded a greeting. He looked little better than the morning after fighting the fire all night. His clothes were filthy, his boots and gloves gray from ash. Clearly he wasn't merely standing about and supervising the clearance.

"Everything all right?" he asked. "Has anyone…bothered you since the night of the fire?"

"Nothing like that," I said. "I wanted to speak to the sheriff about something that just occurred to me. You should listen too."

"Go on," the sheriff said.

"Do you know how the fire started?"

He looked to Dane and folded his arms. "That's confidential information, Josie."

"I'm going to assume that means you think it wasn't started by accident."

His arms fell to his sides. "I never said that."

"Sheriff, if this fire was started deliberately, I need to know."

"Like I said, it's confidential. I can't discuss it with you."

"Why?" Dane asked me. "Do you know something?"

"I might," I said. "I'm not sure. The governor spoke at the burial just now, and something he said got me thinking."

The men looked at one another. I had the distinct impression they'd just been discussing the same thing.

"He made it sound like the fire was a benefit to the village," I went on. "It cleared away the slum, which is exactly what the council and the Deerhorns wanted, yet they get none of the blame. The villagers were angry with them after the meeting when the idea was first mentioned. They shelved their plans, but what if they started the fire so that they can go ahead after all?"

Dane checked the vicinity but no one stood close enough to eavesdrop. He stepped toward me and lowered his voice. "Do not say that to anyone else. Do you understand, Josie? It's dangerous to even think it."

"I think you should investigate, Sheriff."

The sheriff rubbed his jaw. "It just so happens that I was telling the captain my own suspicions. Captain Hammer suggested the possibility that this is the work of the Deerhorns to me yesterday. I refused to believe it. But after listening to the governor just now, I think it's worth looking into."

"I've already started," Dane said. "The greatest concentration of burned material is in the middle of what was The Row. We recovered most of the bodies from there too."

"So the fire started there," the sheriff said.

"I found witnesses who were in that area before the fire broke out," Dane went on, "and two have reported seeing someone pouring out the contents of a barrel alongside several houses. One thought it was ale, but another claimed it was thicker."

The sheriff groaned and turned tired eyes to the sky. "Pitch," he muttered.

I felt sick. Pitch was abundantly available in Mull. Ship

builders used it to seal hulls. When it was wet it performed its task admirably. When it was dry, it was flammable.

But that wasn't what troubled me. "I saw Ned Perkin offloading barrels the day before the fire broke out."

The sheriff went still. "Are you sure it was him?"

"Yes."

"Where?"

I told him the street and which door. "It's a small storage facility."

"Did he see you?" Dane asked.

I nodded.

"Then we have to tread carefully. I've seen Perkin since the fire. He's helping clean away the rubble. He doesn't know someone was seen spreading pitch in The Row, so he thinks he's safe. As long as he thinks he's safe, he won't worry that Josie saw him offloading the barrels."

"But as soon as he knows we suspect him of starting the fire, he'll come for her to keep her quiet," Sheriff Neerim added. "I'll look through the storeroom to see if there's any evidence he stored pitch there."

"I'll do it," Dane said. "You're too conspicuous."

"As are you."

"I'll go," Dane insisted.

"Very well. I have another idea, anyway." The sheriff walked off without telling us what he meant.

Dane and I returned to the feeding station together. He began to warn me to be careful, but he was interrupted by villagers who wanted to thank him or shake his hand.

"You're a hero," I said, nudging him with my elbow.

He merely grunted.

We were met at the feeding station by one of his guards dressed in a clean uniform and mounted on a palace horse. "Balthazar wants you back at the palace, Captain."

"Is something wrong?" Dane asked.

"He didn't say."

"Does it seem as though something is wrong?" Dane pressed.

"No. The lords are all meeting behind closed doors. More leave the palace every day. There ain't much to do."

Dane dismissed him and watched him ride away, his brow furrowed.

"You'd better see what Balthazar wants," I said.

"I know what he wants." He helped himself to the bread and jam one of the women offered him. "He wants me to rest."

"You make it sound like a bad thing."

"There's too much to do here."

"Have you considered that you'll get more done if you're refreshed?"

He picked up a cup of ale. "Is this the point where I have to worry about you slipping something into my drink to make me sleepy?"

"This isn't a joke. Go back to the palace and get some rest. The men can work in shifts without you for a few hours."

"You're bossy."

"I wouldn't have to be if you weren't stubborn."

He drained the cup and set it down again. "And what about you? Will you go home and rest?"

"I'm fine."

"And you call *me* stubborn."

I didn't have an opportunity to give him the full force of my withering glare because two women dressed in low-cut gowns came up to him and planted kisses on his cheeks.

"Seems we've got you to thank for putting out the fire," one cooed.

Her friend draped herself over Dane's shoulder, trapping his arm. "We're so grateful. You saved the whole village."

"That deserves another kiss," said the first. She cupped his cheek and turned his face towards her. She planted a kiss on his jaw as he jerked his head away.

"You'd think he did it alone," grumbled a man watching on.

I tried not to smile as Dane attempted to politely extricate himself from the two women. We both failed. The women stuck to him like leeches, and his hapless effort was the funniest thing I'd seen in days.

"Better be careful or you'll find you owe them an ell," Max said, chuckling.

I giggled behind my hand. Dane shot me a glare and became

more insistent with the women. They finally backed away. One trotted off, blowing him a kiss over her shoulder.

"Shame on them," Deeta said, setting down a tray of clean cups. "They shouldn't be soliciting out here."

"I don't think they were," I said.

"Where can they solicit now?" asked Oona Dwyer. "Their homes are gone and the streets where they worked, too. Sheriff won't let them ply their trade at the dock."

Arrabette Fydler smacked one of the cups down on the table, hard. "They shouldn't be soliciting anywhere. Disgusting *whores*. They ought to be rounded up and put in prison."

"And then what?" Oona asked. "They can't afford to pay a fine and they can't be kept in prison forever. When they get out, they'll just do it again. What else can they do when there aren't enough honest jobs for women in the village?"

Arrabette sniffed. "Begging is better than whoring, surely."

"Not to everyone," I said.

Arrabette screwed up her nose. "You say the oddest things sometimes, Josie. One would think you were considering taking up the profession."

"I don't have to. I have friends in the village and a skill I can sell. Those women have no one and no skill. I'm lucky, as are you, Arrabette. You have a family and a husband with work."

"Not many friends though," Oona muttered as she passed me.

Arrabette turned away, also muttering, but not loud enough for me to hear what she said. I stormed off, only to be joined by Dane.

"If you let her rattle you, she wins," he said.

"Thank you for your wise counsel, oh hero of the village." I regretted my sarcasm the moment it was out. "Sorry, that was horrible of me."

"It's all right. The way they're treating me makes me want to be sarcastic too. It's as if I had no help. All I did was suggest the buildings be torn down to create a fire break. It's not even that clever an idea."

"No one else came up with it."

"If I'd fetched the gem—"

"Don't say it. Don't even think it. You know Brant wouldn't have agreed to use a wish."

His lips twisted to the side. "Are you going home?"

"Yes. Are you?"

"Balthazar won't let up unless I do. Allow me to escort you first."

"I'll do it," Max piped up. "I'll see she gets safely to the Divers' house, then come back here."

"I will take her," Erik said, standing behind Max. I hadn't seen him arrive. He was covered in dirt and sweat and held a cup of ale in each hand. "I wish to see the pretty girl, Meg."

"I said I will escort her," Max ground out. He grabbed my arm and marched me off.

I waved at Dane. He stood there, an amused look on his face.

Erik caught up to us. "I will come too." He offered a cup to Max. "Drink?"

Max focused forward and didn't respond. Erik shrugged and drained the cup then placed it atop a bollard as he passed.

"You are jealous of me," he said to Max. "That is not necessary. We can share her."

Max and I both stopped and stared at him.

"You do not like to share?" Erik asked.

"No!" Max cried.

"You are like Hammer. He does not like to share either. Me, I am happy to share with good men. I am not selfish." After a few more steps, he added, "It must be because I am from the Margin and that is what we do there. Share."

"It's not a Margin thing, it's an uncivilized thing," Max growled.

"You do not know this." Erik threw his arm around Max's shoulders and hugged him.

Max's face ended up near Erik's armpit. He shoved Erik away. "Get off, you big peacock."

"If you do not want to share, we must decide who gets her," Erik said. "We will fight. The prize is Meg."

Max made a sound of disgust. "I like you, Erik, but you're a barbarian, sometimes."

It was time to end their spat before Erik decided to fight Max anyway. "Meg is not interested in you, Erik. Sorry, but she only has eyes for—" I cut myself short as we rounded the corner and I almost smacked into Mistress Ashmole walking briskly in the opposite direction.

She stiffened, which was quite a feat since her back was already straight as a pole. "I've been looking for you," she said. "Mistress Diver said you were out."

"Good day to you, Mistress Ashmole." I refused to sink to her level. My mother would always want me to be civil, even to the likes of the Ashmoles. "What did you want to speak to me about?" I asked, already knowing the answer.

"Did you take in patients on the night of the fire?"

"That would be illegal."

"Did you take in patients or not?"

"She didn't," Max said.

Mistress Ashmole turned her icy stare onto him. "Of course *you* would say that. She's having a liaison with your captain."

Erik bent forward so that his face was level with hers. Mistress Ashmole stepped back and clutched her basket in front of her with both hands. "She is not," Erik said. "And Josie does not fix patients now. If you think I lie, tell your warrior to meet me at the garrison with his weapon."

"My what?"

"A warrior to fight for your honor. I will fight for mine. It is a good way to decide an argument, yes?"

"I—I have no warrior." She gave him a wide berth and hurried on her way.

"She has a husband, yes?" Erik asked me.

"Yes," I said. "But he's not a fighter. He's the new doctor."

"Pity."

Max slapped Erik's shoulder. "She won't worry Josie again."

I doubted Mistress Ashmole would be warned off so easily. Next time she confronted me, she'd make sure I was alone.

Erik and Max both left the house disappointed. Meg wasn't at home. I made sure to tell her they'd both called on her when she returned, however.

"They almost came to blows over you," I said.

She laughed. "They did not, Josie. Don't tease me."

"It's true. Erik was very keen."

She winced. "Did you tell him I'm not interested in him? He's very...er...intriguing, but I find him rather frightening."

"Erik isn't at all frightening when you get to know him. He's sweet, in his way."

"But did you tell him?"

"I did. We didn't get a chance to discuss it further, though. We came upon Mistress Ashmole, and Erik challenged her warrior to a fight."

She laughed until I explained why he'd challenged her. Her laughter quickly dwindled. "Merdu. She knows what you did."

"She doesn't know, she suspects. There's nothing she can do about suspicions without proof. Besides, even if she does tell Sheriff Neerim, he'll disregard it. He's a sensible man."

We women dined frugally on weak soup and bread that night. Mr. Diver and Lyle returned after we'd finished. They washed up in a pail of water outside but were still filthy when they came in.

"Sit, eat," Mistress Diver said, setting bowls in front of them. "Meg, slice some bread. Josie, pass the cheese."

"There isn't any," I said, checking the larder.

"You gave the last of it away at the feeding station, Mama," Meg said. "I'll get some tomorrow at the market." She opened the earthen jar on the shelf where they kept spare coins only to sigh and close it again. "We'll have to wait until after you're paid, Pa."

"Never mind," he said cheerfully. "There's bread enough to fill our bellies."

Lyle plunged his spoon into the soup bowl with more vigor than required. "Might not even have bread soon. The bakers say they've cooked up almost all the grain they had and gave the bread away at the feeding station. The council promised to compensate them, but they say it won't matter if they can't get hold of more grain."

"That's good of the council to offer compensation," Mistress Diver said.

"If they didn't, the bakers couldn't afford to give it away," her husband told her.

"And the villagers would blame the council, not the bakers," Lyle added. "The governor had to pay up or there'd be a riot."

Meg surveyed the meager fare on the table with a sad shake of her head. "Can we not get more grain?"

"It's coming," her father told her, "but it won't get here for a week, maybe more. Depends on the weather."

Lyle ripped his slice of bread in two and pointed one half at his father. "You heard what I heard today. There *is* more and it can be here within the day, only it's going to cost us."

"Where is it coming from?" Mistress Diver asked.

"The Deerhorns. They store some for lean times."

"Which this is," Meg said. "Are you telling us they won't donate it to the village?"

"I am."

She threw her hands in the air. "I don't believe it! That family are cruel beyond words. Did the council tell them where to shove their grain?"

"Meg," her mother scolded.

"Calm yourself," Mr. Diver snapped at his daughter.

Meg sat with a huff and slumped into the chair, her arms over her chest.

"The council claim it is negotiating to buy the grain but won't reveal the cost," Lyle said. "No doubt it's another debt the village owes the Deerhorns."

"A debt that will only grow bigger once the houses are rebuilt," Meg said. "Houses regular people can't afford to rent."

Her father shook his head but didn't scold her again.

* * *

Meg and I ventured into the market for gossip instead of supplies in the morning. We'd just arrived when Bridie Sellen parted the candles hanging by their uncut wicks above her head and beckoned us to her cart. "Did you hear about the thefts?"

"What thefts?" I asked.

"Someone broke into Penny's shop overnight and took some knives and cups." She nodded across the way at the cheese seller's stall where three members of the Fallon family worked. "The

Fallons' stall was also broken into and most of the cheeses they were going to sell today were stolen. They're lucky their aging room is at the farm or they could have lost everything. The sheriff has already asked around but no one saw anything."

"Who would do such a thing?" Meg asked.

"People from The Row," Bridie said.

"We don't know that."

"Who else would it be? They're sleeping in the streets at night, and temptation's right in front of their noses." She indicated the market with its dozens of stalls, many of which were permanent fixtures. Their owners locked them up overnight, but the locks couldn't keep out a determined thief. "I see them in the mornings when I come here." She tapped one of the hanging candles, sending it swinging. "I'm just lucky they don't need what my Pa makes."

"I thought villagers took in those whose homes had burned down," I said.

"Only for a night. No one wants strangers in their house longer than that, Josie."

"They *should* be housed in the temple or the hall," Meg said. "Until proper shelter can be built."

"Tell that to the governor and priests. Are you two going to buy something?"

"Not today."

Bridie began her story all over again as a new customer arrived. Meg and I joined some friends who'd stopped to gossip. They already knew about the thefts. Like Bridie, they blamed the displaced people from The Row.

"The whores are working in these very streets," said one. "My husband passes them on his way home, and the children can see them. It's disgusting."

"My daughter asked me just this morning why people are sleeping in doorways," said another. "It's not right."

"We can't build new homes overnight," Meg said. "They have to sleep somewhere."

"Imagine what it'll be like when the weather turns," said Yolanda. "The council's got to do something for them before winter."

"The council don't care," Meg said. "It'll solve their problems if the people from The Row die from the cold."

Meg and I moved on, listening in to snippets of conversations. All focused on the fire and its aftermath, and what needed to be done for the village to recover. The tension around the market felt as dense as the smoke on the night of the fire, with everyone grumbling about the council's decisions—or lack thereof.

After the king's death, talk had been about Glancia's future. It had not been as earnest as this. That had been politics and wars, something for the lords to worry about, and a distant threat. This directly affected ordinary Mullians, and it affected us now.

In the afternoon, we served drinks and bread at the feeding station. Many of the guards had come to help clear away the rubble. According to Quentin, Dane was on the far side, working with a team of guards and servants. We loaded up a small cart with supplies for him to deliver to them.

Gossip was just as rife at the feeding station as it was at the market. The content was little different until the arrival of Lola Ives. Lola worked as a maid in the Camley household, and the Camleys owned the largest boat building business in the village.

"You'll never guess who came to the house last night," she said. "Sheriff Neerim."

"What's Mr. Camley done?" asked Deeta.

"Nothing. The sheriff wanted to ask him if some pitch had gone missing from the boat yard."

Meg and the others gasped. "Does the sheriff think pitch was used to make the fire spread faster?" Deeta asked.

"Seems so," Lola said.

"But that means the fire was started deliberately. Who would do such an awful thing?"

"We can't be certain it wasn't started accidentally," Meg said with authority. "Let the sheriff investigate. It might be him just ruling it out. For all we know, no pitch was stolen."

"It was," Lola said firmly. "Mistress Camley told me later that her husband and the sheriff went to check the storerooms, and sure enough, four barrels of pitch were gone."

"It could have been a mistake," Meg said. "The barrels might have been misplaced, or already used and Mr. Camely merely forgot."

"He ain't forgetful," Lola said. "He's real careful with his things, too. He don't misplace them."

Deeta pressed a hand to her stomach. "Who would start a fire deliberately where people live?"

"We know who," Lola said darkly. "The people who wanted The Row replaced with fancy houses."

We all looked north east, in the direction of the clifftop estate of the Deerhorns. No one mentioned their name.

"You knew, didn't you?" Meg whispered in my ear after Lola left. "You didn't look surprised when she mentioned the sheriff questioning Mr. Camley about pitch."

The arrival of the sheriff himself gave me an opportunity to avoid answering. "I need to speak to him," I said, rushing off.

The sheriff wasn't too pleased to see me, however. "I have to update the captain," he said, not stopping when I caught up to him. "Alone."

"I was the one who told you about Ned and the barrels. I should hear how the investigation is progressing."

"No, you should not."

"I already know Mr. Camley told you he is missing barrels of pitch."

He eyed me sideways. "Gossip in this village spreads faster than any fire."

"What else have you discovered?"

He sighed. "At least wait until we reach the captain to save me from repeating myself."

We found Dane working alongside eight of his men, tossing bricks into wheelbarrows. They were all shirtless, their chests and shoulders glistening with sweat. Their clothes hung over a clean bench that had been set up for the purpose.

Dane straightened upon seeing us. He moved away from the others and rolled his shoulders and stretched his neck from side to side. I watched the movement of muscle and sinew beneath his skin with professional admiration that was quickly quashed by admiration of a baser nature.

"Josie? Are you listening?" the sheriff prompted.

"Yes, of course." I cleared my throat. "You were telling the captain about the theft."

Dane smirked and crossed his arms, making his chest look even more muscular. I swallowed and forced myself to focus on the sheriff.

He frowned back. "I was telling him that you refused to be left out of this discussion and followed me like a stray animal follows a butcher."

"Right, I did hear that, I was just… er…"

"I know what you were doing. I have grown daughters." To Dane, he said, "The barrels of pitch were stolen from Camleys' boat yard. He wasn't aware of the theft until we checked his store room."

"So he says," Dane said.

"I don't think he would be involved in something like this. He's a good man."

Dane glanced at me. I nodded.

"Glad I brought you along, Josie," the sheriff said tightly. He turned to Dane. "I also found out who owns the store room. You won't be surprised."

"The Deerhorns?" I asked.

"Governor Wainwright."

CHAPTER 6

*E*ven though I'd suspected the governor or the Deerhorns were behind the fire, hearing his name still shocked me. He was supposed to be the father of the village, our leader and protector. Yet he had almost destroyed it. And for what? To help the Deerhorns gain even more power and wealth? It was almost impossible to fathom the depths he'd plunged to, but the evidence was damning.

"That links Ned Perkin and the barrels to the governor," I said. "All we need now is to question them and find out if the Deerhorns are involved too."

"We?" the sheriff echoed.

"You won't question the governor yet, nor Perkin," Dane said. "Not until we find something else to link them. If you tell Perkin he was seen moving barrels into the store room, he'll know it was Josie who told you. It's too dangerous for her."

"That's one problem," the sheriff conceded. "The other is proving there was pitch in those barrels. Perkin can claim they contained ale and, with the barrels destroyed, we can't prove otherwise. He also wasn't identified as the one pouring out the contents of the barrels on the night of the fire."

"Did you find anything in the store room?" I asked Dane.

"It was empty," he said.

The sheriff scrubbed a hand across his jaw. "Then Josie's evidence is all we've got."

"Give me time," Dane said. "I'll find something else."

The sheriff cast a look at the guards tossing bricks and debris into the barrows. "You have until tomorrow. I can't wait longer than that. Gossip is already spreading through the village, and it has potential to do more damage than the fire."

The sheriff left, but I waited until he was out of earshot before speaking to Dane. "How will you find other evidence?"

"I don't know, yet."

I narrowed my gaze. "You won't place something in the store room that will implicate Ned, will you?"

He shifted his stance and looked over at his men, just as the sheriff had. "I'll do whatever is necessary."

I heaved a sigh as I followed his gaze. "Be careful, Dane. If you break the law, the sheriff will have to arrest you."

"Only if he can prove I broke the law."

"Sometimes you are far too cocky for your own good."

He smirked. "Only sometimes?"

I left him to the hard work of clearing away the rubble, knowing he'd ignore any advice I gave to take frequent breaks. There wasn't much daylight remaining, so they would be forced to stop soon, thankfully.

That evening, one of Lyle's friends visited to urge him to go to The Anchor. "I heard something down at the docks this afternoon, and I want to find out if it's true," he said. "Apparently they know something about the fire."

"They?" I echoed.

But he wouldn't answer me. I went to grab my shawl to follow them, but Meg stopped me.

"It's too dangerous," she said. "Particularly now."

"She's right," Mistress Diver chimed in. "Neither of you are going anywhere." Her lips flattened as she glared at the door through which her son had just left. "I wish Lyle wouldn't go."

Her husband passed her as he pulled on his jacket. "I'll make sure he stays out of trouble."

"You'd better!" she called after him. "Or I'll serve your privates to the pigs."

"We don't have pigs," said Tilly, one of Meg's sisters.

"Serve them to the baby chicken," said little Meena, rubbing my downy chick over her cheek.

I did as Mistress Diver wished and remained at the house. The men still weren't home by the time we went to bed, and I couldn't sleep. I stared up at the ceiling and listened for the front door.

I heard something else instead.

"Down with the governor!" came a distant shout from outside.

It was repeated by a much louder chorus of voices.

"Down with the council!" the leader shouted again.

"Down with the council!" dozens of voices echoed.

I leapt out of bed and opened the front door to see a swarm of men marching towards us, torches lighting the way. Up and down the street, doors opened and neighbors emerged to see what was happening. Most were like me, still dressed in their nightgowns, jackets or shawls hastily thrown on. At each door, someone split off from the pack and spoke to those watching on. Across the way, Doctor and Mistress Ashmole stood as still as statues.

"What's going on?" Meg asked from behind me.

"A march," I said. "Against the council, and the governor in particular."

"Why?"

I didn't answer. I knew why, but no one else *should* know.

"Arrest the governor!"

"Arrest the governor!" the leader's shout was repeated by the mob.

Mistress Diver joined us in the doorway. She looked like thunder as she crossed her arms beneath her bosom. I expected her to tell them to be quiet lest they wake the girls, but then I saw who her glare was directed at. Her husband and son marched near the front, right behind the leader.

Mr. Diver broke away from the group to speak to us. "Don't look at me like that, Wife," he chided. "We're calling for action. Something has to be done about the governor. He's the one responsible for starting the fire."

"What?" Meg said on a gasp.

Mistress Diver covered her mouth with her hand. Her huge eyes stared back at her husband.

"How do you know?" I asked.

"Someone at the council office says he let Sheriff Neerim look at the records of building ownership. The sheriff was particularly interested in one store room. It's owned by the governor. The sheriff also asked Camley about some stolen pitch. It doesn't take much to put two and two together."

"You can't be certain the governor started the fire," I said.

"It does sound damning," Mistress Diver said. "I can't believe it. How could he do such a thing?"

My gaze connected with Meg's. It was obvious she knew that I already knew, but she didn't accuse me. She simply looked sad. As sad as I felt, probably. The governor wasn't a good man, but to think that he was almost certainly behind the fire... It was unfathomable.

"We want the sheriff to arrest him," Mr. Diver said as Lyle joined him, flushed from the excitement.

"Then shouldn't you be talking to the sheriff instead of marching through the streets?" his wife asked.

"We have," Lyle said. "He says he's still gathering evidence. It's not good enough. We want justice *now*."

"You should let the sheriff do his job," Meg said. "It will take time—"

"He has had time and he found evidence of the governor's guilt. We know it."

"Maybe his evidence isn't enough for him to be certain," I said quickly. "It might be just enough to give him an inkling. Meg's right, you should wait. Sheriff Neerim is a good man. If the governor is guilty, he'll arrest him."

"If he waits, he gives the Deerhorns time to intervene. We can't allow that. We want justice and we want it *now*!" He punched his fist into the air and rejoined the crowd as it marched past.

"It's too late to stop this anyway," Mr. Diver said. "Everyone's angry. We've been at the governor's mercy too long. It's time we stood up to him and let the Deerhorns see what we're capable of."

He ran after the group with more vigor than a man half his age. The mob wasn't made up of just young men, but villagers of all ages, both men and women. The group was larger by the time it turned the corner and left our street. It would be larger again after passing down the next street. The people were angry. They were tired and hungry, anxious and hurt.

I, however, felt guilty. The sheriff had waited to accuse the governor because Dane asked him to, to protect me. This protest could have been stopped before it started if the sheriff arrested Ned Perkin and the governor this afternoon.

"The Deerhorns won't sit idly by," Meg said as she closed the door. "They'll see this as a setback to their plans for The Row."

"They'll see this as a slap in the face," I said.

"But what can they do about it?" Mistress Diver asked. "There'll be riots if they don't agree to alter their plans, and not even the Deerhorns want rioting."

I tugged my shawl up as the back of my neck prickled. "They could hire a private army to quash any trouble."

Mistress Diver clutched her daughter's hand. "Let's hope it doesn't come to that. This might all blow over once the men have sobered up."

Neither Meg nor I spoke. We knew it wouldn't blow over unless the Deerhorns were forced to change their plans.

* * *

MISTRESS DIVER GOT her wish only hours later when her husband and son returned and announced the mob had dispersed.

"Everyone went home after the sheriff spoke to us," Lyle said, hovering by the fire where his mother cooked eggs.

Mr. Diver dipped a spoon into the pot of tea warming over the coals and tested it. "Hot enough," he said, picking up the pot and pouring some of the liquid into a cup.

"What did the sheriff say?" I asked, trying to keep the edge of worry out of my voice.

"He arrested Ned Perkin for starting the fire," Lyle said.

I plopped down on the chair and pulled my cup of tea close to my chest.

Meg and her mother stared at Lyle. "Merdu," Meg murmured. "Why did Ned do it?"

"He wouldn't say, according to the sheriff," Mr. Diver said.

Lyle accepted the plate of fried eggs from his mother and sat beside me. "But we know he was working for the governor, and the governor is probably working for the Deerhorns. Ned stole the barrels of pitch from Camley and hid them in the governor's store room until the night of the fire."

"But the sheriff hasn't confirmed that's what happened," I said carefully.

"He told us he can't arrest anyone else because there's no evidence the governor knew his store room was being used," Mr. Diver said.

Lyle snorted. "So he claims."

Meg pulled her brother's plate away to get his attention. "Sheriff Neerim wouldn't lie about that. If he hasn't arrested anyone else, it's because he hasn't got proof. You know that, Lyle. Stop being a rouser."

Lyle snatched his plate back and circled his arm around it to protect it.

"That was enough to disperse the crowd?" Mistress Diver asked. "Seemed to me they were calling for the governor's blood and nothing would stop them until they got it."

"Wiser, older heads reassured the youngsters we couldn't ask for more," Mr. Diver said with a stern look at his son. "Meg's right. The sheriff can't arrest the governor without proof. *Some* of us know that."

Lyle shoveled eggs into his mouth and didn't meet his father's gaze.

Mistress Diver and Meg seemed satisfied, but my heart raced faster. "Why Ned Perkin? What evidence did the sheriff have against him?"

"A witness saw him," Mr. Diver said.

My stomach dropped.

"He was seen pouring pitch from a barrel in The Row that

night," Lyle said around his mouthful of egg. "Right where the fire started, so the witness reckons."

I cocked my head to the side. "In The Row?"

Lyle nodded.

"The witness identified Ned?"

"Saw his face as he poured out the pitch."

I blew out a measured breath. Either a new witness had come forward or the sheriff had lied. The witnesses who'd spoken to Dane hadn't seen the face of the person pouring the pitch. If the sheriff had lied, he'd done it to save me from being identified as the witness who'd seen Ned with the barrels. Dane had influenced him, I was sure of it. The sheriff didn't know the trouble I would be in if the Deerhorns learned of my involvement, but Dane did.

"Thank the goddess it's over," Mistress Diver said as she served eggs to her husband.

"It ain't over," Lyle said. "We don't know if the Deerhorns were involved, but we're sure Ned worked for the governor. Until he's arrested, we ain't giving up."

His father shook his head.

"But the sheriff already told you he can't arrest the governor without proof," Meg cried. "Honestly, Lyle, you and your friends are just looking for trouble."

"We want justice," he snapped back. "People died in that fire. The village could have been destroyed. Don't you want to see those who did it pay for it?"

"Of course I do, but Sheriff Neerim can't do more. Stop being bullish and see reason."

"I am seeing reason! The governor did this. We all know he did."

"But without proof—"

Mr. Diver brought his fist down on the table, causing all the cups and plates to jump and rattle. "Enough! You'll wake the girls."

Brother and sister glared at one another until Lyle looked away.

He held out his plate. "More eggs, please, Ma."

Meg snatched it off him and shoved it into his chest. "Get them yourself." She marched off to the bedroom.

I followed in her wake but we didn't speak as we both lay on our beds, trying to fall back to sleep.

* * *

I WENT OUT mid-morning to check on an expectant mother. The streets were quiet, and I assumed most men were helping to clear the rubble left from the fire. I was wrong. A large group of men stood on the village green, talking in hushed tones. Several cast glowering looks at the nearby council building where two constables guarded the door.

Two more constables watched on from the base of the steps, and six mounted palace guards were positioned at intervals around the green. I spotted Max and lifted a hand in a wave. He nodded stiffly then his gaze scanned the vicinity. Either he was looking to see if Meg was with me or he was simply keeping watch.

More men joined the group as I left the village green behind. I hurried to see my patient. Fortunately she had a few weeks to go and, as an experienced mother, she knew what to expect at this stage of the pregnancy. I left her with reassurances that all was as it should be.

I could have avoided the village green and gone the long way home, but I wanted to see what was happening. I stopped short before I reached it, however. Up ahead, the small group of men had swelled to the same size as the mob that had marched down our street.

Like last night, they shouted "Down with the governor!" over and over, but this time, they focused their anger on the council building.

"Come out!" one of the men shouted. "Answer to the people!"

More and more joined the group, pouring in from the surrounding streets. The guards were vastly outnumbered, their horses skittish from the noise and activity. The constables stood where I'd seen them earlier, but they looked worried now, their hands hovering near their swords, ready to draw.

"Come out, coward!" shouted a man at the front of the mob.

A roar of "Coward!" erupted. Fists punched the air. Some of those fists held clubs, and some even clutched burned bricks. These men had been working to clear away the rubble only yesterday. Today, there must be only the palace guards and servants working there. Most of the villagers seemed to be here, and more came with each passing moment.

As the crowd increased in number, their voices grew in volume, their chant of "Coward" filling the village green. Then a roar erupted as a face appeared at an upstairs window of the council building.

"Come out!" they shouted.

"Coward!"

"Fire starter!"

"Murderer!"

Merdu and Hailia. This wasn't going to end swiftly or quietly.

"Josie!" Lyle emerged from the crowd, his eyes bright and beads of sweat dotting his forehead. "Join us. We're trying to get the governor to come out, to answer for his crimes."

"It's going to turn violent," I said. "You know it is."

"We're voicing our anger, that's all. If the governor comes out, there'll be no need for violence."

"And if he doesn't?"

He answered by punching his fist in the air and shouting, "Show yourself!" along with the rest of the mob. He rejoined the crowd. I saw many people I knew in the group, including good friends. Ivor Morgrain was among them. So much for his assurance that he would stay away from trouble.

"Josie!" Max called out as he rode up to me. His hand rested on his thigh, not because it was a casual pose and he was not worried, but because it meant he could quickly draw his sword. "Go home and stay there!"

While I didn't like being told what to do, I'd been about to head off anyway. I wouldn't admonish Max. He must be anxious. They were vastly outnumbered.

"Keep Meg and her sisters safe too," he said.

"I will if you promise to keep an eye on Lyle." I nodded at Meg's brother. "She will appreciate it."

"I'll try."

I hurried off as the crowd roared again. I didn't head home, however, but to The Row to warn Dane that he needed to send more men to help Max.

He was a step ahead of me. He rode towards me with no less than twenty of his men riding behind. The men wore armor, but Dane did not. He slowed and fixed a glare on me when he saw me.

"I'm going home," I told him before he gave me the order. "But you should hurry. It's volatile."

"Stay indoors. Do it for me," he added. He rode off before I could assure him I would.

I ran all the way to my street, stopping abruptly when I rounded the corner. A carriage laden with trunks strapped to the back and roof waited outside Meg's house. Two palace guards wearing armor and mounted on armored horses stood guard.

Merdu, what now?

A blonde head popped out of the window. "There you are," Miranda said. She opened the door and stepped out to embrace me. "Thank goodness you're here. We were just about to leave. My mother is worried and didn't want to wait much longer."

"Your mother is right to worry." I looked through the open door and bobbed a curtsy to the elegant woman clutching a closed fan in both hands. "Lady Claypool."

"Miss Cully, please tell my daughter we must hurry. The guards say we need to leave the village immediately."

"We arrived at the same time as the captain and his men," Miranda told me. "He says there's a mob forming in the village, demanding the governor be arrested for starting the fire. Is it true? Did he start it?"

"The sheriff doesn't have any evidence that he did, but many in the village are convinced he orchestrated it."

"How awful."

"Miranda," Lady Claypool barked. "Say your goodbyes. I don't want to get tangled up with the protestors."

Miranda clutched my hands and blinked back tears. "I have to go."

I indicated the trunks. "You're not returning to the palace, are you?"

Her lower lip wobbled as she shook her head. "My father is sending us home. We heard about the trouble last night in the village and he's worried it's going to get worse."

"He's wise."

"Surely the palace is safe. It's miles from here."

"Possibly, but with the king gone, who knows what will happen there, too?"

"You're always so practical." She suddenly threw her arms around me. "I adore you so much. I wish I didn't have to go. I want to stay here with you and Kitty."

I put my arms around her and kissed her cheek. "I'm going to miss you both too."

She pulled away. "Kitty isn't leaving. The duke isn't sending her away."

"Why not? I know things aren't very good between them, but surely he's worried about her safety."

She leaned forward to whisper. "Not if he wants to kill her. Don't look so shocked, Josie. You also thought the Deerhorns and the duke might plot her demise so Violette can marry him. I'm quite certain Kitty has reason to worry now."

"What's happened?"

"He has been more awful to her than usual. He constantly tells her how much he despises her, how she has failed him as a wife, how stupid and hopeless she is. I've told her to ignore him, that he's saying those things in the hope she'll fall into despair and end her own life."

"As horrible as that is, it's not really proof he wants to…" I lowered my voice. "…murder her."

"He told her to go drown herself yesterday."

"What a snake!" I spat. "Poor Kitty. Is she holding up?"

"Barely. I wish I didn't have to leave her at a time like this. She's lonely and frightened. She suspects everyone of trying to murder her at her husband's or Violette's order."

"She can trust the palace servants," I said. "They wouldn't

jeopardize their positions for the duke."

"You ought to tell her that. If you can get to the palace to reassure her, that would be the best thing you can do right now." She took my hands again. "There's one other thing," she said, voice low. "If things get very bad, if it seems as though there's no other way, I've urged her to take drastic measures and leave her husband."

I squeezed her hands. "I'll help her. She can take shelter here until the danger passes then I'll take her to the priestesses. She can live in the goddess's temple—"

"No, Josie, you don't understand." She glanced over her shoulder at the carriage. "The only way she can be free is if the duke and the Deerhorns think she's dead. If they know she's alive, they'll keep trying to kill her. Violette can't marry the duke if he's still married to Kitty. She has to die."

"What are you saying?" I hissed.

"I told her she should make it *appear* as though she died."

"You want her to fake her own death?"

She nodded. "Will you help her if the time comes? She's not particularly bright. To make it look convincing, she's going to need help."

Lady Claypool peered out of the carriage. "Miranda," she snapped. "It's time to go."

Miranda drew me into a fierce hug. "Be careful, Josie, here and at the palace." When she pulled away, her cheeks were damp.

My eyes welled with tears. "I will. And don't worry about Kitty. I'll see that no harm comes to her." I wished I felt as certain as I sounded.

"Write to me often," Miranda said with a wobbly smile.

Lady Claypool leaned out of the carriage. "Come, Miranda. I want to be out of the village before the riots start."

Riots.

Hopefully it wouldn't come to that.

But as I watched them drive off with their armed escort, my heart felt heavier than ever with the weight of all our problems.

* * *

THE DAY DRAGGED ON. There was little to do in the house but perform domestic duties, my least favorite thing to do. I tried to keep Tilly and Meena occupied with games but found it hard to be cheerful.

Meg and I stepped outside frequently and listened to the shouts brought to us on the breeze. The only news we had was when a neighbor, Mr. Grinsten, returned for the club he kept under his bed.

"The governor still hasn't come out," he told us as he paused outside his house to catch his breath. "Everyone's riled. Some are talking about storming the council building and dragging him out." He thumped the club into the palm of his hand. "Everyone needs to protect themselves."

"Don't you use that unless you have to!" Mistress Grinsten shouted at him as he ran off. He brandished the club in response before turning the corner.

Meg and I returned inside, only to rush to the door again when someone pounded on it moments later.

"Miss Cully," said the frightened girl on the doorstep. "Miss Cully, you have to come now."

"Is it your mother, Kirrin?" I said, bending to her level.

She nodded. "Mama says the baby's coming but she can't catch her breath."

"Where's your father?"

"He said he was just going out real quick to see what all the fuss was about in the green, but then Mama felt the baby coming and she couldn't breathe properly." She grabbed my hand. "Let's go."

"Wait," I said. "My bag."

"You can't go," Meg said, following me into the bedroom. "It's too dangerous."

"I'll take the long way," I assured her. "We won't go near the village green."

"Didn't you just see her this morning?" she said. "Surely she can't be in labor already. You would have noticed the signs."

"Kirrin said her mother's having difficulty breathing. That's worrying enough."

She blocked the doorway, arms crossed.

I leveled my gaze with hers. "Meg, she sent her twelve-year old daughter here when she knows there's trouble in the streets. She wouldn't have done that if she wasn't very worried. Let me through, please."

She squeezed her eyes shut and emitted a frustrated growl. Then she stepped out of the way. "Just be careful."

"I will."

I ordered Kirrin to remain with the Divers and set off, taking the long route that bypassed the center of the village. Even so, I was close enough to hear the mob's shouts as clear as day.

They called for the governor's execution.

I hugged my bag to my chest as I hurried down streets that were empty of people but filled with the echoes of the mob's cries. Late afternoon shadows kept the air cool, but even so, I sweated as I ran. I didn't dare slow. Kirrin's mother must be terrified, all alone with her four year-old son and a baby on the way, worrying if Kirrin had arrived at her destination.

I kept my wits about me, listening for any movement of the crowd in case they decided to march through the streets this way. Despite my heightened awareness, I wasn't worried when I saw the horses and cloaked riders up ahead. It was probably some lords from the palace come to see what all the fuss was about.

The riders had their backs to me. They were not advancing or retreating, but simply seated in the saddles. They must be listening to the mob too, from the safety of these quieter streets.

One of the riders was in advance of the others, peering around the corner. From there, he should be able to see the village green. He turned to rejoin his friends and spotted me.

"You there!" he shouted. "Get going."

The other five riders turned as one. I recognized two of them, despite their hoods.

Lady Deerhorn and Lord Xavier Deerhorn.

"Well, well, isn't this fortunate," Lord Xavier said with a slick smile. "And she's all alone, too."

I turned and ran.

"Get her!" Lady Deerhorn commanded.

CHAPTER 7

*H*ooves thundered behind me, drawing closer, closer, until I was sure the horse would run me down. I didn't dare waste precious moments and glance back. I jumped into a recessed doorway and flattened myself against the door.

Lord Xavier rode past, the horse's momentum propelling him along the street, just far enough away for me to escape.

I ran, but he chased me again. Behind him rode his mother and their armed escort, black cloaks billowing behind them like pirate flags, warning of the advancing danger.

My breaths came hard and fast.

I turned a corner, checked left and right for an open doorway that I could dive into, but there were none. It was all brick walls and high fences.

Hailia, save me.

I pretended to turn into a narrow lane I knew was a dead end, but instead I dodged into another street. My efforts were in vain, however. They kept coming and coming. Lord Xavier was almost on top of me, his huge beast of a horse snorting like a creature from the underworld.

I stumbled and lost my balance, but somehow I managed to dive to the side, stilling holding my pack. My left hand and arm scraped against the cobbles. Searing pain tore up my arm as the flesh scraped off and my bones jarred.

I backed up as the six horses surrounded me, blocking all escape routes.

Lord Xavier sneered, his mouth twisted into a satisfied grin. He licked his lips, as if he could taste my fear. He was the sort of man who relished the thrill of the chase, no matter that his prey couldn't possibly win.

Lady Deerhorn urged her horse forward. I scrambled away until my back slammed against a wall. Blood pounded in my ears and rushed through my veins so fast that I felt sure my heart would give out.

"What do you want?" I asked.

My trembling voice seemed to delight Lady Deerhorn. Her sneer matched her son's. "You tried to ruin us, so I will ruin you."

"I don't know what you mean. I've done nothing to you. I wish you no ill."

"Ha!" Lord Xavier barked. "I like your pluck, but we know you're lying."

I glanced around, searching for an escape route. But there was none. I couldn't get past the horses.

"There is no one to save you now, Miss Cully," Lady Deerhorn said. "The captain and guards are occupied. You are friendless."

"Is it the gem?" I asked. "Because I will get it for you. I just need time. As you say, the captain is busy. I haven't had the opportunity to ask him about it."

"Liar," Lord Xavier snapped.

"Get her," Lady Deerhorn ordered.

"Wait!" I cried as her man dismounted. I licked dry lips and scrambled to think of something to say, to try to talk my way out of this predicament. If that didn't work, I still had the scalpel in my skirt pocket. But I couldn't stab all of them if they came at me as one. "If you kidnap me or harm me in any way, the captain will know. Not only will the guards come looking for you, but he'll never give you the gem."

Lady Deerhorn smiled. "He will if he wants you back."

Lord Xavier's tongue flicked over his top lip as he eyed me hungrily. "The longer he takes to rescue you, the more time I get with you."

Hot, bitter bile surged into my throat.

"You deserve everything you get," Lady Deerhorn said as her man advanced on me. "It was you who started the rumors that we set the village on fire."

"No!"

"I know you did. The governor's man said he saw you when he offloaded the barrels."

So they *were* behind it.

Her guard, a giant of a creature with an ugly scar where his left ear should be, grabbed my scraped arm and hauled me to my feet. I hissed in pain. Satisfaction flashed in the icy blue depths of Lady Deerhorn's eyes.

"But it was the captain's threats that truly annoyed me," she said in a deadly calm voice.

The guard's grip tightened around my arm. "I—I don't know what you mean. What threats?"

"Don't play the innocent. I know you sent him."

"He warned us to stay away from you," Lord Xavier said. "Or he'd make us pay." He snorted. "As if that would scare us."

Lady Deerhorn signaled for her guard to put me on the horse. "No one threatens my family. Especially nobodies like you."

I shifted my pack and slowly, slowly slipped my hand into my pocket. My fingers wrapped around the slender scalpel. I would have only one attempt to stab my captor. If I missed, he would overpower me.

I whipped the scalpel out and dug it into the hand holding me. He cried out and let go, but only to pull the scalpel out. It happened so quickly, I didn't even get a chance to run off. He grabbed me again and threw the scalpel on the ground with a growl.

My heart sank, just as a chorus of shouts rose from the direction of the mob. Something had antagonized them further. The chorus did not diminish but kept going and going. It echoed in my head and plucked at my already frayed nerves.

It disturbed the horses too. They shifted and jerked their heads up and down. The riderless one jostled the horse of the guard holding both sets of reins. It was towards this horse that I was pushed. I struggled, hitting out with my fists and feet.

It was useless. I was too weak. All I managed to do was anger the guard when I kicked his leg.

"Stop fighting or this won't go well for you," he snarled in my ear.

I squeezed my eyes shut against a wave of hopelessness washing over me. There were six of them, all armed. I would not get out of this.

Lord Xavier's brittle chuckle echoed off the walls until it was drowned out by another eruption of shouting then a sudden, booming crash.

Two of the horses reared in fright, their hooves thrashing the air. The riderless one bolted, dragging the guard that held its reins off his own horse. He let go, but fell to the ground with a bone-crunching thud.

I swung my free arm in an arc and smashed my pack into the head of the guard holding me with as much strength as I had left. He loosened his grip and I slipped free.

I took off in a sprint through the gap left by the fleeing horses. Lord Xavier, Lady Deerhorn and their other guards struggled to control their frightened mounts, leaving the one on foot to chase me.

I was mere steps ahead of him. I hardly knew in which direction I ran, I just knew it had to be forward.

"Get her!" Lady Deerhorn screeched, sounding closer.

I glanced back to see her and Lord Xavier advancing rapidly on the guard chasing me, their horses once more under control. The guard reached out. His fingers grasped the back of my skirt, flapping behind me.

I gathered up the skirt and jerked hard, tearing the fabric. I was free and up ahead was a way out. The village green. Instead of trying to avoid the mob, I ran to it.

Their voices rose as one, baying for the governor's blood. Their numbers had swollen so much that the green couldn't contain them all. They filled the nearby streets, swarmed the council building, sat in tree tops and on walls. The low brick wall enclosing one side of the blacksmith's yard had fallen. That must have been what caused the crash that frightened the horses.

I felt my skirt tug again, just as I reached the edge of the mob. Without pause, I plunged through, squeezing between sweating bodies. I didn't stop moving forward and did not look behind me as I ducked and wove through the throng, never following a straight line.

When I thought myself somewhere near the middle of the crowd, I took stock. No one followed me. I couldn't see the horses above the heads of the villagers nor the Deerhorn lackey who'd chased me. Either I'd lost them or they had simply not followed me, knowing they couldn't attack me here.

The mob had swallowed me, enclosing me in its seething, tempestuous mass, and kept me safe.

I clutched my pack to my chest and concentrated on catching my breath. As my blood calmed, I felt the rise of the tempers around me. The mob was angry. They'd been here all day, calling for the governor to answer for his crimes, and they'd been left unsatisfied.

From my vantage point, I couldn't see any of the palace guards or constables. They would be near the council building, protecting the occupants. Not that the governor deserved protecting.

I prayed to Hailia that no one would get hurt trying to keep the governor safe. Then I prayed to the goddess that my patient and her unborn baby were all right. I couldn't risk leaving the village green while the Deerhorns might still be out there, waiting.

Suddenly the shouted chants of the mob changed from calling for the governor to come out to a cry of, "Storm the building!"

The crowd surged, taking me with it. I was forced forward, towards the council building. I tried to move against the tide, but it was pointless. We moved as a single entity, a hotbed of anger and vengeance, all directed at one man.

I was jostled, my feet trod on, my chest elbowed as I was hustled forward. My arm hurt and my palm stung. I could see nothing around me anymore. The bodies were too close, many of them taller than me. I could only look straight up at the sky, darkening with a brooding dusk.

"Storm the building!" the crowd roared as one.

Between the chants, I heard voices calling for calm. They sounded distant, small. Much too small to have any effect. A horse whinnied. Dane was an able horseman, but Quentin wasn't. If his horse reared in fright, he would fall.

"Please, stop this." My voice was lost amid the cries of the people. I was ignored, even by those closest to me.

Then someone near the front of the crowd screamed. Shouts erupted. Not the organized calls for justice, but the chaotic, indistinguishable bellows of fighters. The crowd around me no longer moved forward as one, but became individuals, trying to scatter in all directions.

"What is it?" I asked the tall man next to me. "What's happened?"

"They're trying to storm the council building. Guards won't let 'em pass." He roared in protest and used brute force to push through the crowd ahead to get to the front.

Others followed in his wake, but many tried to flee. They could not. Like me, they were trapped in a human prison that was slowly but surely inching forward. Advancing towards Dane and his men. The guards and constables couldn't hold them off for long. They were vastly outnumbered. The mob had no issue with them except that they stood in the way of their prize.

The more we moved forward, the more panic settled into my bones. Dane should call his men back. He should retreat. I hoped he would, that he didn't foolishly try to protect the governor.

But Dane was stubborn and put honor above all else. If he saw it as his duty to hold the mob back, he would do it.

Somehow I managed to move to the side through the crowd, while still being forced forward. I must have been close to the edge because I caught glimpses of the guards, mounted on their horses, pushing people back from the steps. They hadn't drawn their swords.

I searched for Dane and found him standing on one of the

lower steps of the council building. He put up a hand to signal the crowd to stay back.

They did not. They surged forward.

He fell.

Just like that, he disappeared from view.

"No!" My scream was swallowed by shouts.

Seeing their captain go down, the guards drew their swords and began slashing at the mob trying to pass. It was like swatting a swarm of flies. For every one they felled, another ten replaced him.

The steps of the building were completely invisible now. The crowd had surged up it, brandishing axes, bricks and bats. The constables guarding the door dove over the sides of the steps to get away, and the mob slammed into the thick wooden door. Finding it locked, they pushed.

I no longer cared if they broke it down. If the governor's head on a spike could stop this madness, then I would happily present it to them. All I cared about was getting to Dane.

He was somewhere beneath the feet of the mob.

Miraculously, the door held, but it wouldn't for long. The crush of bodies was denser near the council building. I elbowed my way through and earned bruises for my efforts. I ignored the pain in my grazed arm and hand and used every last piece of strength I had left to forge a path for myself.

But the closer I got, the more difficult it became. The crowd had stopped edging forward, the way blocked by the bolted door.

"Captain!" I couldn't even hear my own voice over the angry shouts.

I managed to force my way to the base of the steps, almost tripping over the lowest one. I searched through the legs, kicking when I had to. He must be here somewhere, but it was dark and there were so many people.

Then I spotted something near the side of the stairs. I inched forward, my gaze focused on it, trying to see what it was, if it moved.

Then the crowd roared again, growing impatient with the door that continued to withstand the efforts of the men pushing against it. It must be barred from the inside, and without a battering ram, they didn't have enough strength to force it open.

These thoughts flittered through my head, but meant nothing to me. Only Dane mattered.

"Josie!" came a shout.

"Max?" I shrieked, standing on my toes. I could just see him through the crowd, standing at the edge of the stairs. Blood poured from a gash on his forehead but he was otherwise unharmed.

"He's with me!" he shouted back. "He's fine, just dazed. Get out of there. Go home!"

I wished it were that easy. The bodies pressed in on me, sucking up all the air. I tried to steady my breathing as I pushed through, not back the way I'd come but to the side, to where Max stood.

But it was useless. I hardly advanced, and breathing became more and more difficult as my energy was sapped. Running from the Deerhorns had been exertion enough, but pushing my way through this dense forest of sweating flesh was too much. My chest ached and my head felt light.

I grasped around, searching for something to hold on to, to keep myself upright. If I fell unconscious here, I would be crushed.

I caught a glimpse of Dane's ashen face, looking back at me. Blood streamed from a cut on his cheek. He said something to Max and he plunged into the crowd toward me.

He beat back those trying to stop him, using fists, elbows and the hilt of his sword.

I slumped against someone's back, battling to keep my eyes open, and focused on Dane moving relentlessly towards me.

He reached out and I slipped gratefully into his arms.

"Stay awake," he ordered. "You're not a fainter."

Not a fainter. It was almost amusing.

I tried to walk, to make it as easy as possible for him to get me to safety. He used his sword arm to push through the crowd. But for every step forward, he was shuffled back further and further. We would not make progress like this.

Dane grunted as someone's elbow hit his cut cheek. My grip

tightened around his waist as I searched for the best way out. But there was none. We were trapped.

Shouts burst out from the edges of the mob. Women screamed. Then the crowd pulsed, surging and receding in all directions.

"Who are they?" I heard a man near me say. He stood on his toes, neck craned.

The pause in the surge from those on the steps allowed Dane to forge a path to Max. He wasn't looking at us, however, but over the crowd below, and the newcomers on horseback.

Dozens of armed soldiers wearing helmets and armor over brown tunics beat back the crowd. As with the palace guards, they did not use their swords except to brandish them in a show of might.

The mob stopped as the soldiers kept coming, pouring in from the west in two orderly columns. They spread out, one column going left, the other right. No one had given the order. They'd simply done it calmly and efficiently until they completely circled the quieting crowd.

"It's about time," Max grunted.

"Who are they?" I asked.

"Warrior priests from Tilting," Dane said. "I sent for them thinking there might be unrest after the king's death."

With the crowd calm, Dane and Max were able to make their way through. I followed, wanting to get out of the horde as quickly as possible in case this calmness didn't last.

"Go home!" the sheriff shouted from where he stood on a low brick wall. "It's over for today. Let justice take its course." At the crowd's rumblings, he added, "These are Merdu's Guards! If you disobey them, they will retaliate in the god's name!"

Bringing Merdu into it was enough to quieten the crowd but not disperse them. Some of the women left, but the men stayed. They eyed the warriors with a mixture of awe and caution. Some tried to restart the chants, calling for the governor to come out, but their voices dwindled when few joined in.

As Dane made his way towards the sheriff, one of the warriors rode up. "Sheriff? Are you in charge here?"

Sheriff Neerim nodded at Dane. "Aye, along with Captain Hammer of the palace guards."

The warrior removed his helmet. He was a young man with short brown hair, damp with sweat, and a clean shaved jaw. Strong features made him handsome but would have looked out of place on a man with a smaller build. He sat tall on the horse, his broad shoulders made wider by the armor. His gaze quickly took in the sheriff, Dane, Max and then me, trailing behind. I felt as though I ought to bow beneath the imperial appraisal.

"And you are?" Dane asked.

"Brother Rhys Mayhew, at your service." He gave a half-hearted bow.

"*Master* Rhys Mayhew," corrected one of the warriors with a smirk.

The leader pressed his lips together. I wasn't sure if he was trying not to smile or trying not to admonish his man.

"You're young to be master of the warrior priests," said the sheriff.

The four nearest priests gave him arched looks. I suspected this was a contentious issue among them.

"Nobody else wanted the job," was all the master said.

"Thank you for your assistance," Dane said.

The master dismounted and extended his hand. "It's good to meet you, Captain."

Dane shook it and introduced Max.

I left them and headed off through the crowd. My patient still needed attention, perhaps urgently. I didn't have to push and force my way through this time, but it was still slow going. At least the people weren't surging toward the council building anymore. They still grumbled, however, and I doubted it would be long before they took up their cause again.

Those priests had better be as good as their reputation claimed. The numbers were still greatly in the mob's favor.

I scanned the faces but saw no sign of the Deerhorns. Even so, I didn't want to venture into the streets alone. To my relief, I spotted my patient's husband, also making his way through the crowd. Together, we headed to his cottage.

Thankfully, the expectant mother, Posey, was all right. She breathed normally and she no longer felt any contractions.

"They were false ones," I said after checking her. "Sometimes they happen."

"And the breathing problems?" she asked.

"Brought on by panic. When you felt the contractions and your husband wasn't here and you could hear the mob, you grew worried."

"I'm sorry I bothered you."

"It's always safest to fetch me," I assured her with a smile.

She indicated my arm. "You look as though you've been in a war."

My smile fell. "Do you mind if I stay overnight here? I don't fancy going home in the dark, and I think it best if I'm nearby so I can monitor your condition."

She welcomed my suggestion. Knowing Kirrin would be fine with the Divers, she settled into a deep sleep that lasted all night. I managed a few hours too and awoke early in the morning, feeling a little stiff but otherwise satisfied. Posey was still breathing normally and didn't have any pains.

I left with her husband but we parted at the village green. He went on to the Divers' cottage to fetch Kirrin, while I wanted to see Dane and reassure myself that the danger was over.

The early morning air felt cool on my grazed skin. I ought to put something on the injury, but I didn't have any salves and it boiled my blood to have to buy some from the Ashmoles.

The overnight presence of the warrior priests must have dampened the spirit of the crowd. Most had dispersed. Some slept on the council building steps or under trees. The numbers of the priests and guards had also thinned. They must have returned to the palace for rest. The sheriff was still there, however, as well as Dane and Master Rhys. Despite their casual stances, they seemed watchful, alert. They kept to their own kind, the remaining guards together, and the warrior priests in groups surrounding the green.

Dane strode towards me. "Josie!" His pace quickened.

I smiled, pleased he was so eager to see me. My own pace

quickened, only to slow again when I caught sight of his thunderous face.

"Why were you here last night?" he snapped.

"I had to see an expectant mother. It was an emergency."

"She was giving birth right here in the green, was she?"

"I ended up here through no fault of my own."

He folded his arms over his chest and arched a brow.

I hiked my pack up my shoulder. "I met the Deerhorns on my way. They chased me here."

He lowered his arms and his lips parted with his expelled breath.

"As you can see, I'm all right," I assured him.

He indicated my bloodied arm. "That doesn't look all right to me."

"It's just a graze."

He stepped closer and tucked my hair behind my ear. "You're disheveled," he murmured.

"You look in need of a bath and a good sleep yourself."

I glanced up as Master Rhys approached on foot. "One of my men just rode in," he told Dane. "Reinforcements from the palace are on their way." He frowned and cast a glance over his shoulder. "He seemed...strange."

"Strange how?" Dane asked.

"Excited."

"The palace can be overwhelming at first," I said. "Perhaps he's excited for you to see it."

Rhys shook his head. "Brother Vizah told me I'll want to speak to someone they met there. They're bringing him now."

Dane and I exchanged a glance.

Dozens of mounted guards and warrior priests arrived from the western road. Reinforcements, as promised.

"Master Rhys!" shouted one of the warrior priests with a grin that split his face. "Come see who we found at the palace! You'll never believe it."

Master Rhys set off, and Dane fell into step beside him, hand resting on his sword hilt. I trotted to keep up.

All the priests who'd arrived from the palace beamed like boys who'd won prizes at the fair. The smiles looked odd on their fierce, scarred faces. The warriors who'd remained on duty all night frowned back at their brothers, intensely curious.

But it was the guards who'd just come from the palace that I couldn't tear my gaze away from. They sported odd looks on their faces. It took me a moment to recognize they were expressions of hope.

The priests at the front of the pack moved aside, revealing a cloaked figure on horseback. He sat awkwardly, his back bent. A walking stick was strapped to the saddle.

He pushed back his hood.

"Balthazar?" Master Rhys cried, rushing forward. "Brother Balthazar, it *is* you!"

CHAPTER 8

"*B*rother Balthazar?" Max echoed.

"We need to talk," Dane said to Master Rhys. "But not here. In the palace garrison."

"Why not here?" Master Rhys asked. "Balthazar, what are you doing in Mull? Why didn't you write to us?"

Balthazar blinked at him. He looked uncertain, frail, as if his age had finally caught up to him.

It was Theodore who spoke with authority. "The captain's right. We'll talk at the garrison. There's something you need to know, sir. Er, Master."

"Rhys will do," Master Rhys said. "Very well, we'll leave some men here and come with you to the palace. I admit I'm curious to see it, although I want to hear your answers even more, Bal." His gaze softened. "You've worried us, Brother."

Balthazar swallowed. His gaze had sharpened again as he took in the figure of the broad shouldered master in armor that bore the dents and scratches of battle.

I was concentrating so much on Balthazar that I didn't notice Dane turn to me until he touched my fingers. "Put something on that wound," he said. "I'll see you later."

"I'm coming with you," I said.

"Your arm needs attention."

"It's fine."

"Let her come, Hammer," Balthazar said. "She'll expire from curiosity if she doesn't."

"And I'll be safer with you," I told Dane.

It was a winning argument. I sat behind Dane on the ride to the palace. Balthazar seemed to have recovered his wits, and he observed the priests closely. Our procession moved swiftly but slowed as the palace came into sight. Rhys and the brothers who'd not yet seen it stared open-mouthed. I smiled, recalling my own amazement upon first spying the magnificent building.

"Merdu's bollocks," muttered the priest named Vizah.

It was such an odd thing to hear from a priest's mouth that I laughed. Brother Vizah winced sheepishly. It made the scar bracketing the corner of his mouth lift so that it looked as though he smiled.

"My apologies, Miss Cully," he said. "I've never seen anything so beautiful or so grand."

"It's all right, Brother Vizah. I understand perfectly."

"Just Vizah."

"Call us all by our first names," Rhys told me. "We prefer it."

"And I am just Josie."

"It's not like the castle in Tilting," said the serious looking priest named Rufus as we passed through the gate.

"No wonder everyone thought magic created it," said Andreas, the only one without any scarring on his face. He had thick, wavy hair and was the most handsome of the priests, though not the most striking. That title belonged to the master with his intense blue eyes and commanding presence.

"How quickly was it built?" Rhys asked. When no one answered, he prompted a response. "Captain?"

"I don't know," Dane said. "I wasn't here."

Rhys glanced at the other guards then turned to Balthazar. "Will no one answer?"

"We can't," Balthazar said. "None of us were here. Except Josie."

The priests looked to me, but I was saved from answering by Dane dismounting. He assisted me down and directed the guards to take all the horses to the stables.

"The garrison is this way," he said to the priests.

Thankfully they asked no more questions. They couldn't be answered truthfully out here with the nobles wandering about. I scanned the faces, but Kitty wasn't amongst them.

They were all very curious about the priests strolling with us across the outer forecourt. Two noblemen even greeted Brother Rhys and he greeted them in return, giving them shallow bows and assuring them that the protestors had been dispersed.

Dane suggested his remaining guards take all of the priests except Rhys to the commons to enjoy a meal, but Rhys wanted Vizah, Rufus and Andreas with him. They seemed to be his most trusted men, all speaking their mind without worry of censure from their master.

Vizah gazed longingly at those who headed to the commons. He licked his lips as if he could taste the food he wouldn't get to enjoy with them, then, with a heaving sigh, dutifully walked with us to the garrison.

Erik and Quentin were both in the garrison with two other guards. They sat, booted feet on chairs or the table itself. All but Quentin looked to be asleep. My medical book was open on his lap.

He slammed it shut when we entered, waking the others, and jumped to his feet. "Finally! We've been waiting and waiting, wondering what this is all about. Vizah recognized Balthazar this morning," he told us. "But he left with Balthazar before I could ask questions. So where do you know Bal from?"

Rhys frowned. "From home, of course."

"And where's that?"

"Tilting," said Andreas.

Quentin gave him a blank look.

"In the temple," Andreas added as if Quentin were stupid. "Bal didn't tell you?"

"It's not as simple as that," Max said, pouring ales at the sideboard.

Vizah gathered four tankards in his big hands and passed them around. "He lives there with us. Or he did, until a year ago when he vanished overnight."

"Without a word," Rufus added with a stern glare for Balthazar.

"Your temple is for warrior priests," Dane said. "Are you saying Balthazar is one of you?"

"He didn't tell you?" Rhys asked, frowning.

Quentin, Erik and the two other guards burst out laughing. "Balthazar is a warrior?" Quentin said, still grinning.

Rhys looked to Balthazar, brows raised. "Tell him, Bal."

Balthazar sighed. "I think we need to start at the beginning. Hammer, there's no getting away with it. We have to tell them."

"Agreed." Dane indicated that everyone should sit.

"Tell us what?" Rhys asked as he sat.

While he directed his question at Dane, his cautious gaze flicked to Erik. The gazes of his men did too. Erik eyed each of them in return, taking in their battle scars and armor, and most likely comparing his physique to theirs. While he was taller than all of them, Rhys and Vizah were broader in the shoulders.

"Merdu," Andreas murmured. "You're a Marginer, aren't you?"

Erik crossed his arms. He frowned, and I could see that something troubled him about these men. "Aye. And you are a priest. You work only for Merdu."

"Our lives are dedicated to the god. We defend his realm and our faith."

"I've never seen a Marginer before," Vizah said. He looked impressed, but not at all afraid of Erik, as most were.

Erik didn't seem to hear him. He simply stared back, his forehead tattoos almost disappearing into the creases of his frown.

"So," Rhys said, setting down his tankard. "Bal, will you tell us what's going on? Why are you here? Why did you leave the temple without telling anyone?"

Balthazar accepted a tankard from Max. "I can't answer your last question. I wish I could, but I don't remember why I left."

Rhys sat forward. "You've lost your memory?"

"We all have."

The priests went very still. "I don't understand," Rhys said. "How can you *all* lose your memories? That's absurd."

"Not all of us," Quentin piped up. "Only the servants. Josie's from the village. She has her memories."

"It's true," I said. "What you're about to hear will sound absurd. I thought them all mad, at first. Then I saw the sadness and confusion in their eyes and heard it in their voices. Look and listen to what they have to say and you'll believe them too."

Balthazar told them everything he could, beginning with the first day of waking up in the palace, knowing his name, his role, and the names and positions of all the servants. He finished with an account of the king's death and his admission that he used magic to become king, but he left out any mention of the gemstone.

"Merdu's blood," Andreas murmured. "What a prick."

"How did he perform the magic?" Rhys asked. Of the four of them, he seemed to suspect something had been omitted from the story.

"We don't know," Balthazar lied. "He died before giving us more information."

"He never explained why he chose us," Dane said, "We don't know where we came from, what our lives were like before coming here. We don't even remember our families."

"Josie told me I am from the Margin," Erik said, tapping his forehead tattoos.

"And now I know where I come from too." Balthazar looked down at his hands. "I wouldn't have guessed I was a warrior in my younger days. I bear no scars."

Rhys shifted his weight in the chair. "You are a priest, but you were never a warrior."

"Merdu's Guards are a soldiering order."

"I thought you lost your memory," Rhys shot back.

"I can read." Balthazar waved his hand to encompass the four walls. "The library here is extensive. In those early weeks, we spent a lot of time reading. I read all about the god and goddess, the temples, priests and priestesses."

"Reading is what you liked to do most," Rufus said with a knowing nod.

Vizah smirked. "And order people about."

Quentin snorted. "He still does."

I smiled and tried to catch Dane's gaze, but I suspected he was avoiding me. The comments about Balthazar reminded me of something I'd said to Dane, that much of our character was ingrained deep within us and didn't change. The servants might have lost their memories, but their basic nature would remain. A good man would always be good, and a man who liked to kill would always want to harm others. Dane hadn't been convinced of my theory. It was another reason he didn't want to start a relationship with me without knowing his past. He worried that he was not a good man.

"How could I be a priest but not a warrior and still live in your temple?" Balthazar went on. "Isn't it specifically for your order?"

"It's true," Rhys said. "We are a specialized order, created for a single purpose. Our day is dedicated to training and becoming as disciplined as possible. Without discipline, a soldier gets distracted. A distracted soldier is a dead one in battle." He spoke as if he were reading the words.

Andreas rolled his eyes. "We do have time off in the evenings after prayers. It's not all sword play and exercise drills."

"What do you do in the evening?" Quentin asked.

"Drink," said Vizah. "Play cards."

"But not for winnings," Rhys cut in. "We have no possessions, no money."

"What else?" Erik asked.

"Not much," Rufus said. "We read or talk."

Erik screwed up his nose. "So it is true?"

"What?" asked Rufus.

"That you cannot be with a woman."

Max groaned. Theodore covered his mouth with his hand, but I suspected he was trying not to laugh. Quentin flushed to the roots of his hair.

"Quiet, Erik," Dane barked.

"No, it's all right," Vizah said without blinking. I got the distinct feeling he was staring straight ahead so as not to glance unwittingly at someone. "It's true. We're a celibate order."

"Discipline," Rufus said, somewhat blandly.

"No distractions," Andreas added.

Erik looked horrified.

Dane took the opportunity of his shocked silence to ask more questions. "Tell us what you know about Balthazar. If he wasn't a warrior, what did he do in your temple?"

"He was the Keeper of the Temple Archives," Rhys said. "Every temple has a scholar priest who dedicates himself to keeping the archives safe, and expanding them as history unfolds. He records important events as well as stores accounts of others from within the order."

"Events important to the temple or to Glancia?" Balthazar asked.

The question seemed to unnerve Rhys as he took a long moment to answer. Or perhaps it wasn't the question but the fact Balthazar needed to be told. It must be slowly sinking in that Balthazar truly lacked a memory.

"Both," Rhys said. "Indeed, anything that matters to The Fist Peninsula."

Balthazar and Theodore exchanged glances. "So I would have recorded the earthquake event that became known as The Rift?"

"I suppose. I haven't checked."

"Elliot would know," Andreas said. "He was your assistant, Bal. He took over your role when you disappeared."

"Tell us about his disappearance," Dane said. "Do you know why he left?"

The priests shook their heads. "He didn't tell us he was leaving," Rhys said. "He simply went to bed one night and the next day, he was gone. He didn't even tell Elliot, and you two were close, Bal. That was the oddest thing."

"No, the oddest thing was how he behaved that day," Rufus said. To Balthazar, he added, "You were distracted. Something worried you, but you wouldn't tell us what."

"Did you look for him?" Dane asked.

"We looked for him everywhere," Rhys said. "We sent messages to other temples in Glancia asking if they'd seen him. All we learned was that he left on horseback with provisions for several days, accompanied by one of the other priests of the order."

"Another priest?" Balthazar said. "Did *he* return?"

"He's still missing."

Balthazar and Theodore exchanged glances again.

"He was assigned to stable duty," Rhys went on. "Since two of the horses were missing, we assume he escorted you."

"Describe him," Dane said.

"Gray hair, about fifty years old, a mix of Glancian and Vytill blood. About Rufus's height. He has a limp from a broken leg that never healed properly. Like many of our veterans, he can no longer fight. They're given other roles in the temple. Amar worked in the stables."

"Amar," Balthazar murmured. "We have a gardener by that name. Theo?"

Theodore rose. "I'll fetch him."

"Meet us in the commons," Dane said. "It's time the other servants were informed."

"You remember none of this?" Andreas asked Balthazar as Theodore left.

Balthazar shook his head. "What did I do in the days leading up to my disappearance? Did I go anywhere? Did someone come to see me?"

Rhys looked to his men, but they all shrugged. "Elliot would know."

Silence weighed heavily as we all considered that information. Balthazar had not even told his assistant where he was going that night. The question was, why?

"Do you receive visitors at the temple?" I asked. "Can people call on you, or on Balthazar?"

"Of course," Rhys said. "We're not closed off from society. We welcome visitors."

"Women?" Erik asked.

"Only priestesses."

Erik saluted them with his cup and a wink.

"Do you know what King Leon looked like?" I asked. "The man who called himself King Leon, that is."

The priests shook their heads.

"If we show you pictures of him, perhaps you'd recognize him." I said it more to Dane and Balthazar than the priests.

They both understood my meaning. "Quentin, fetch one of the paintings of the king," Dane ordered.

"The one hanging above the fireplace in the Rose Salon," Balthazar added.

"He hated that painting," Quentin said.

"It's the closest likeness. Meet us in the commons."

Quentin left with one of the other guards as the painting was too large for one man.

The rest of us made our way to the commons, walking slowly for Balthazar's sake. The priests continued to look up at the palace as they had done on the way in. I wondered what they'd think if they saw the opulent furnishings and the manicured gardens.

"Who else knows about your memory loss?" Rhys asked.

"No one," Dane said. "Only Josie."

"None of the noblemen?"

"No." It was a lie but neither Balthazar nor I corrected him. It might not be wise to tell anyone that a Vytill spy knew their secret.

"This is all very…strange," Rhys said. "I'm overwhelmed by it, to be honest. I came here expecting to suppress unrest and I discover an old friend who can't explain why he left us." He gave Balthazar a grim smile. "I know the order can be trying for new recruits, but you were not a new recruit, and you never had to endure the same tests anyway."

Andreas put his arm around Balthazar's shoulder. He towered over the frail old man. "You'd been there longer than everyone. You've been a father figure to many of us."

Balthazar removed Andreas's arm. "I find that hard to believe."

"A grumpy father," Rufus pointed out.

"And controlling?" I asked.

Vizah snorted. "Definitely."

Balthazar narrowed his gaze at us. "You two are cut from the same cloth, I see."

Vizah grinned at me, a big smile within a tanned face.

"Are you part Zemayan?" I asked.

He shrugged. "Maybe. I don't know. I never met my parents.

The order and the temple have been my life. I came to them at the age of thirteen, straight off the streets of Tilting's slums. Balthazar taught me my letters and numbers." He chuckled, a robust sound that came from the depths of his chest. "He'd curse me by the end of our sessions. I wasn't a good student. Lucky for me, a temple dedicated to defending the honor of the god values strength and fighting over cleverness."

"We don't value stupidity," Andreas said. Vizah punched him in the arm.

"Vizah is battle smart," Rhys told us. "He can read and write as well as any of us. Balthazar liked telling stories of how difficult a student Vizah was, but he wasn't one to let the truth get in the way of a good tale."

He smiled at Balthazar. Balthazar merely frowned back.

"And he likes everyone to think he had a difficult time of it teaching Vizah," Rufus added. "He wants us to think he has the patience of Hailia and the tenacity of Merdu. The truth is, he liked Vizah. They used to play games together."

"Then I grew up and wanted to become a fighter, not a scholar," Vizah said. "He hasn't let me forget that I owe him my education."

I linked my hands around Balthazar's elbow. "That sounds familiar."

Balthazar grunted. When I went to remove my hand, he crooked his elbow to keep it there.

We dropped behind the others. Dane and Rhys spoke quietly at the front, while Erik positioned himself with the remaining three priests just ahead of us.

"I do not understand," Erik said. "Vizah was rescued by the priests, so he owed your temple service. But you, Rufus, Andreas? Why do you serve a god who does not want you to use your cock for what it is made for?"

I pressed my lips together to suppress my smile.

Rufus cleared his throat. "I—er... We've used it."

"*Before* we entered the priesthood," Andreas stressed.

Rufus looked past Erik at Andreas and Vizah. Andreas shrugged and mouthed "What?"

Vizah's gaze drilled into his master's back.

Erik was lost in thought and didn't seem to notice the exchange. "I believe Balthazar was a priest," he finally said. "He is not handsome and is a small man. But you…" He grasped Rufus's shoulder. "You are all strong men with appealing faces. The women like you. Yes, Josie?"

"I suppose," I said.

Up ahead, Dane turned ever so slightly, but he could have simply been listening to Rhys.

"So it must be a lie," Erik said with a satisfied nod. "You tell the people you do not have women, but you do, in secret. Yes?"

"No," all three priests said.

Erik wagged a finger at them. "You meet with the priestesses of Hailia?"

"No!"

"Erik," I warned.

"We will talk later." Erik clapped Vizah on the back. "I will tell you all about women and you will never want to go back to your temple. There are maids here who will show you what to do with your cocks. I can give you one of mine."

"One of your what?" Andreas asked.

Erik looked at him as if he were stupid. "Maids."

Rufus's brows flew up his forehead and Andreas stumbled over his own feet.

"Oh, look," I said. "We've arrived at the commons. You must be starving."

"Thank the goddess," Vizah muttered. I wasn't sure if he was thanking her for the food we could smell or for the interruption.

I ate with the men in the vast dining hall. We had hardly begun when Quentin and his fellow guard returned carrying a painting of Leon framed in thick gold. The man depicted standing on the palace forecourt was taller than he had been in life and broader in the shoulders. The face was a good likeness, however.

"I don't recognize him," Rhys said. He turned to his men, but they shook their heads.

My heart sank and I resumed eating. I was joined by Dora, wringing her hands in her apron. "How is the cleanup operation going?" she asked.

"Slowly."

"Where have the survivors gone?"

"Some were taken in by families in the village who have room to spare. Others are on the street, unfortunately. Hopefully something will be built to house them over winter."

She looked as though she believed that would happen as much as I did. "They say the governor started the fire so that the Deerhorns' plans for the land could be implemented. Is that true?"

I took her hand in mine. "It's likely."

"How could someone do such a thing to other human beings?"

I shrugged, too heart sore to tell her the Deerhorns and governor probably didn't see the people in the slum as human beings. To people of their ilk, those in the slum were something less, lower even than their horses and hunting dogs because those animals had a use.

I looked up and noticed the hall had filled with servants. Word had got around, and there was great interest in the warrior priests.

Andreas suddenly shot to his feet, tipping back his chair. "Amar!" He rushed towards the gardener Theodore ushered in. He was about to embrace him, but the forbidding look on Amar's face warned him not to.

The other priests crowded around, speaking over each other at Amar. His startled gaze darted from face to face.

"Amar, you are one of us," Rhys said. "You and Balthazar. Your home is in Tilting in the temple of Merdu's Guards."

"I'm not a guard," Amar said. "I'm a gardener."

One of the priests laughed. Amar took another step back. This time his limp was pronounced.

Balthazar ordered everyone to give him space. "Don't over-whelm him. Amar, come sit with us. It seems you and I knew one another, once. We knew these men too."

Amar hesitated before joining Balthazar and the priests at the end of one of the long tables.

I left the dining hall to go in search of Kitty. As I crossed the commons courtyard, a figure sitting on the edge of the fountain looked up.

Brant.

I hesitated. If I kept going, he might follow me outside. With everyone inside the dining hall, I would be alone, vulnerable.

Brant bared his teeth in a sneer. He understood my predicament. He was an expert at hunting prey and sensing fear.

CHAPTER 9

"*R*un along, little Josie. I can't attack you today." Brant pulled up his right shirtsleeve to reveal a bandage wrapped around his forearm. "Your lover did this after the last time you were here. Hammer," he bit off.

"Are you surprised? You used me to try to force him to give you the gem. Is it broken?"

"What do you care?"

"If it is, the bone needs to be set so it can regrow properly. I can do it for you."

"It's not broken."

"And your leg where I stabbed you?"

"It was just a prick." He looked away. "Leave me alone."

I hurried out of the commons and entered the palace through the door the servants used. The flames of the wall torches danced in the drafts of the service corridor. I thought it empty, but a maid nodded a greeting as she passed me on the stairs. When I reached the door leading to the ducal corridor, another maid carrying a blue silk dress stopped me.

"I heard Theodore was looking for one of the gardeners," she said. "What's going on?"

"The warrior priests recognized Balthazar and suspected the gardener was their missing brother."

Her breath hitched. "And?"

"He is. It's Amar."

"I know Amar. Handsome fellow. Not as handsome as the priest called Andreas, or Master Rhys." She flashed a grin, revealing a chipped tooth. "I wish I could go to the commons now, but the Duchess of Gladstow's maid asked me to clean one of her gowns." She indicated the dress. "She spilled wine on it."

"Did you see the duchess?"

She shook her head. "Just her ladies' maid. She's a mean cow. I don't know why the duchess keeps her."

I knew the woman she spoke of, and she was indeed mean. It would seem Kitty hadn't managed to remove her from her entourage. "Can you do something for me?" I asked. "Can you lure the maid out so I can speak to the duchess alone? I'm worried about her."

"I'll try."

We passed through the hidden door. I continued to the far end of the corridor where I pretended to rearrange flowers in a vase. The palace maid knocked on the duchess's door.

"The duke wants to see you by the inner forecourt fountain," she told the person who answered.

"Why?" came Kitty's maid's voice.

"Don't know. I didn't speak to him. The message was passed to me by one of the other maids, just now. I said I'd deliver it to you since she had to get to the other side of the palace in a hurry. She told me it was urgent."

There was a pause before the door clicked closed. I glanced over my shoulder to see both maids walking away. When they were gone from sight, I knocked on Kitty's door.

"Who is it?" she asked from the other side.

"Josie."

She opened the door, grabbed my hand, and dragged me into her apartment. "Thank goodness it's you. I thought it might be one of Lady Deerhorn's men come to murder me now that Prudence has gone."

"She won't be gone for long," I said. "When she discovers the duke doesn't need her, she'll come hurrying back. Is she your jailor?"

"Not quite." She glanced at the door. "But when I go out,

Prudence escorts me unless my husband is with me. They think I'm going to run off, which is ridiculous. Where would I go?"

"Miranda visited me after her departure," I said. "She told me to look in on you. She's worried."

Kitty squeezed my hands. "That's so sweet of you both, but I'm all right." She nibbled her bottom lip and glanced again at the door. "Miranda said not to trust anyone, particularly the Deerhorns."

"There are people here you can trust, Kitty. The captain of the guards, for one. If you become truly worried that something will happen to you, you must send word to him. Any of the palace servants will take your message."

"But my husband or the Deerhorns could buy their loyalty."

"They cannot be bought. They all need to continue working here and the Master of the Palace would dismiss anyone he couldn't trust."

She continued to nibble her lower lip. It was unnerving to see this noble, elegant woman so afraid, and I desperately wanted to reassure her. Shrugging off the differences in our social classes, I threw my arms around her.

"Trust me," I said. "Trust the captain and his men."

She clung to me. "I will." She drew away and frowned at my dress. "What happened to you? You're filthy. And your arm looks sore."

"There was trouble in the village, but it's all right now. My arm is fine." I'd not thought about it for some time but the abrasions still stung. I needed to clean and bandage it.

I left Kitty and returned to the commons. The excitement had faded and many of the servants had left. Rhys and his three closest advisors sat talking to Balthazar and Amar with Dane and Theodore listening in. Dane spotted me as soon as I entered. I gave him a flat smile and scanned the faces for Quentin. He and Erik were talking to two priests.

"Can you help me with this?" I asked Quentin. "I can't do it one handed. My pack is in the garrison."

He puffed out his chest. "Of course. I'll clean it first and apply some Hollyroot for the pain then bandage you up good and proper."

We stepped away from the others and made our way back to the garrison.

"How was my diagnosis?" he asked.

"Excellent," I told him. "Save the Hollyroot. I don't need it."

"Not even a little?" He sounded disappointed.

"Just make sure you clean the area properly before bandaging it. If it gets infected I'll have to buy anneece off Mistress Ashmole, and I'd rather face another angry mob than her."

Some of the guards had made their way to the garrison where it was quieter than the dining hall. They all slept where they sat, exhausted after being up all night in the village.

Quentin picked up my medical pack and I signaled for him to follow me through the internal door. "We'll go to Balthazar's office," I whispered once the door closed behind us. "I don't want to wake them."

"They should be in their beds, but none want to look weak in front of the priests. The priests are impressive, don't you think? Did you see them beat back the crowd? They made it look effortless."

"The guards make it look easy too," I said as we rounded a corner into another corridor. "You're all excellent swordsmen. Even you have come a long way with all the training."

"Not like them. They worked as a neat unit. Rhys hardly had to give orders; they just seemed to know what to do. He's masterly, isn't he? Master Rhys?"

"They all were, but they've been in the temple for years, following a strict training regimen. You would all be just as good if you did nothing but train and pray every day for years."

He chuckled. "Can you imagine Erik as a warrior priest? I think he'd rather die than give up women."

Balthazar's door was unlocked. I poured water from the jug into the basin while Quentin rifled through my pack.

"What is this for?" he asked, holding up a pair of forceps.

"Pulling out babies that can't come out on their own."

He made a face. "Glad I ain't a woman." He removed the roll of bandages and set it on the desk. "Why have you got these in your midwifery bag anyway? What do you need to bandage up down there?"

"They're not for birthing." I put a finger to my lips. "Don't tell anyone, but I just like to keep other equipment on hand."

He set to work. The position of the graze was awkward for me to see and I reminded him to make sure he cleaned it thoroughly.

"You said that already," he said. "You don't want to get an infection. I know, Josie. I have cleaned wounds before. The men are always scraping themselves in the training yard."

He finished, patted the area dry with a cloth, and wrapped the bandage around my arm. The door opened as he was tying the end.

"This is not the infirmary," Balthazar said as his walking stick stamped into the floor with a regular beat. Dane and Theodore followed him in.

"We don't have an infirmary." Quentin wagged a finger at him. "We should get one. We could turn one of the unused salons—"

"No." Balthazar sat in his chair with a groan.

"You look tired," I said. "You should go to bed."

"I'm not tired from lack of sleep. This has been a long day and it's not yet midday."

"It's been overwhelming," Theodore said gently. "You need time to take it all in and to think about what to do next."

I eyed Dane, standing silently by the door. He watched Balthazar closely.

"You're lucky," Quentin said to Balthazar. "You know who you are, now."

"Knowing that I worked in Merdu's Guards' temple isn't the same thing as knowing who I am." Balthazar indicated the wine on the sideboard. "Pour me a drink, Theo."

"Quentin," Dane said. "Leave us."

Quentin wordlessly did as ordered, and Dane closed the door behind him.

Theodore passed Balthazar a cup of wine. "It seems drinking wine is allowed in the order."

"Were you going to deny me this if it was banned?" Balthazar asked.

"No, but you'd have to keep it a secret from the brothers.

Speaking of which, you'd better not go chasing any of the maids in the priests' presence."

Balthazar grunted. "Very amusing."

"At least we know the maids are safe from them," I said.

Balthazar sipped his wine. He was about to put the cup down but thought better of it and drank again, deeper this time. Theodore sat beside me and Dane leaned against the wall by the sideboard.

"Why didn't you tell them about the gem?" I asked. "And everything we know about magic?"

"It's not wise to trust them completely," Balthazar said.

Dane agreed, but Theodore wasn't so sure. "They're honest men dedicated to the god."

"Are they honest? I don't know that. They said themselves that I left the temple without telling anyone where I was going. If I trusted them, why would I do that? Why not confide in someone?"

Theodore looked to Dane. "You don't trust them either?"

"They seem trustworthy," Dane said. "But Bal is right. He had a good reason for leaving in the middle of the night without telling anyone except Amar. Until we regain our memories, and find out what that reason is, we don't tell them everything. The gem is too important."

It was a sobering thought that plunged us into thoughtful silence.

Theodore finally broke it. "How long will they stay?"

"Not long," Dane said. "If the village remains calm tomorrow, they might leave the following day. Rhys said he'll stay as long as they're needed, but he doesn't want to be absent from Tilting for long at the moment."

"Why not?" I asked.

"There's considerable lawlessness in the capital. Ever since the lords came here upon Leon's summons, the governor has been running the city as he wishes. It seems he's taking advantage of his newfound power."

"Governors are the same everywhere," I muttered.

Balthazar picked up his cup, drained it and set it down with a thud on the desk. "Rhys asked me to return with him.

Amar, too. He says we belong at the temple in Tilting, not here."

Theodore's swallow was the only sound in the ensuing silence.

"He begged me," Balthazar went on. "I told him no."

"And what did Amar say?" I asked.

"He didn't give an answer. He wanted to think about it."

"You should too," Dane said.

"This is my home now. It's the only place I know." Bleakness edged his tone and clouded his eyes.

I reached across the table and touched his hand. He offered me a flat smile.

"You should consider returning with them," Dane said again. "Our situation here at the palace will become increasingly precarious."

"You'll keep it safe," Theodore said. "You and your men."

Dane fixed his gaze on his feet.

I stared hard at him, but he did not look up.

"Hammer's not referring to the physical safety of everyone at the palace," Balthazar said. "He means we won't be able to stay here much longer. When the last of the lords leaves, a skeleton staff is all that is required. The rest will be told to go home or find work elsewhere."

There was no work in Mull for the servants, and they had no homes to go to. If they were forced to leave, they would disperse throughout the kingdom.

"It might be a good thing," Balthazar said. "Perhaps some of us should have left months ago in search of our pasts. If I'd gone to Tilting, someone probably would have recognized me."

Theodore's eyes lit up. "Perhaps we're all from Tilting. Bal, I think you should return and find out more about your life there. You might learn something that could help the rest of us."

Balthazar's eyes closed as if they were too heavy to keep open. When he did open them, he looked straight at Theodore. "Very well. I'll go. But you have to come with me."

Theodore drew in a deep breath then let it out slowly. "I will. Like Hammer said, we'll probably be told to leave here soon anyway. The first one to lose his position will be the king's valet."

They both looked to Dane.

"I need to remain here," he said. "The situation in the village is too volatile. The guards will stay."

"The guards can remain under the sheriff's leadership," Balthazar said. "I know you want to find out more about your past, Hammer. This is your opportunity to do so. Come with us to Tilting and investigate."

Dane hesitated then shook his head. I felt hot and cold all at once as the gazes of Theodore and Balthazar settled on me.

"Josie could come with us," Theodore said.

Dane shook his head again. "Her home is here. Her friends are here and her work."

Was that why he was staying? For me? I suddenly felt as overwhelmed as Balthazar. I blinked watery eyes back at Dane, but he wasn't looking at me. He was once again staring down at his boots.

Balthazar made a shooing motion. "You two go. Talk, but not here."

Dane picked up my pack and we left the office. We exited the palace on the forecourt side and walked toward the gate in silence. Bright sunshine warmed my skin but my heart remained numb. I didn't know what to think, only that Dane wanted to be with me.

But not at that moment. He strode quickly, as if he couldn't wait to be rid of me. He headed towards the stables and coach house, no doubt to send me back to the village.

"You have to go to Tilting with them," I said.

"No."

"You *want* to go."

"Don't tell me what I want," he growled.

"Listen to me." When he didn't slow, I grabbed his arm.

He finally stopped but wouldn't look at me. Very well, I would speak to his profile.

"We both know you won't find answers here. Not now that Leon is gone. You have an opportunity to learn about yourself through Balthazar, and you *have* to take it." When he didn't respond, I tugged on his arm. "Say something."

"I can't go," was all he said. "You're too vulnerable here in

Mull. You need me here."

I cupped his jaw. "I am not going to stand in the way when you have the perfect opportunity to find out more about yourself. So I'm coming with you."

He finally looked at me, his eyes narrowed to slits. "No."

"I will see my friends again when I return. As to my work... I'll talk to Mistress Ashmole about taking over midwifery duties. She'll require some training, but she has my books and she seems smart. She'll pick it up."

"No, Josie. If I go, you won't be coming with me."

I dropped my hand away. "You don't want me with you." I hated that I sounded forlorn. I wished it didn't bother me that he didn't want my company as he rediscovered his life, but it did.

"It's not that. What if I find out I have a wife? If you're with me, it will hurt you deeply. Hurt us both."

And his wife, too.

"I'll stay in Mull until the village is safe and I can be sure the Deerhorns won't trouble you again," he added. "Only then will I leave."

"And how are you going to ever be sure of that?"

The corner of his mouth flicked up. "Trust me."

The impish look on his face was almost my undoing. I wanted to throw my arms around him and beg him to take me with him. The thought of being separated for weeks, possibly months or years, was unthinkable.

But I knew tears wouldn't sway him. When he thought he was doing something for a good reason, he wouldn't be diverted from his path.

I snatched my pack off him and walked away before I changed my mind and begged to go with him.

* * *

"Are you sure it's what you want to do?" Meg asked. We sat on her bed, side by side, our legs outstretched. It was the only room where we had any privacy. We didn't have long to be alone. Mistress Diver would soon ask for our assistance in preparing the evening meal.

"It is," I told her. "If the captain leaves, I'm going with him." I'd made my decision to ignore Dane's wishes the moment the palace carriage in which I rode turned into my street. Mistress Ashmole stood on the porch of what had once been my house, and I entered a house which was not mine to be with people who, while kind, were not my family.

"But your life is here," Meg said. "Everyone you know is in Mull."

"You're the only reason I want to stay, and as much as I love you, it's not a good enough reason." I took her hand. "You'll be fine without me. But the captain needs me. He won't admit it, but he's worried he'll learn something about himself that he won't like. I want to be there for him if he does."

Meg blinked rapidly. "I can't believe you're going to leave. Mull won't be the same without you."

"Mull has already changed beyond recognition."

She wiped her damp eyes. "Sad but true."

The door burst open and Mistress Diver poked her head through the gap. "Riccard is here. The baby's coming, and Posey's in a bad way."

I snatched up my pack and met Riccard at the front door where he paced back and forth, clutching his cap in both hands.

"She's in a lot of pain," he said. "More than the last two times. And her breathing is bad again."

The pain was causing her to panic, just as the riots in the village had, and panic constricted her chest and throat. I checked my pack for the jar of Mother's Milk. "I'll give her something to ease the pain," I told him. "That should calm her enough for her breathing to return to normal." Once Posey was stable, I could concentrate on the baby. It was possible she was experiencing false contractions again, or the baby might really be on its way this time.

He slapped on his cap and strode down the street. I didn't immediately follow, however.

"I need to speak to someone first," I said.

I pounded on the Ashmoles' door until Mistress Ashmole opened it. She frowned at me, taking in my pack and Riccard, standing in the middle of the street, looking stricken.

"You're still here?" she asked, her frown deepening.

"Of course I am." I dismissed her odd remark. There was no time to ask what she meant. "I'd like you to be the village's new midwife. There's a baby on the way. Come with me and I'll show you what to do."

Her lips parted with her silent gasp. "Why? What trick is this?"

"No tricks. I might be leaving Mull soon, and the village will need a midwife. It's customary for the women in the doctor's family to take on the duty."

Mistress Ashmole stared at me then her attention was diverted to a commotion at the end of the street. Her spine stiffened. "I'll get my shawl."

"Josie!" Riccard barked. "Come, please."

"Wait for Mistress Ashmole. She'll act as my apprentice." I joined him just as three riders rode up, led by Lord Xavier. Behind him was the sheriff and one of his constables.

They headed straight for me. Lord Xavier's smile and Sheriff Neerim's furrowed brow told me everything I needed to know. I hugged my pack to my chest and tried not to show my fear.

"Miss Cully!" Lord Xavier called. "You are under arrest for performing medical tasks without a license."

"That is not how we agreed to do this," the sheriff growled.

"When did I perform medical tasks?" I spat, all defiance. Anything else would be taken as an admission of guilt.

"The night of the fire," Lord Xavier said. "You were seen. The sheriff was informed but his failure to act meant the witness came to my father instead. My father sent me to remind the sheriff that your second offence is to be taken seriously."

"I've had more important things to do than arrest a girl for helping the injured in a time of crisis," Sheriff Neerim snapped.

Mistress Ashmole emerged from her house, shawl in hand. She met my gaze, her chin jutting forward, her gaze sharp. *She* had been the witness.

"For Merdu's sake," the sheriff went on. "How many would have suffered if Josie hadn't helped? She should be commended, not condemned."

Lord Xavier looked as though he wanted to draw his sword

on the sheriff for his insolent tone.

"My husband would have helped them," Mistress Ashmole declared.

"Only those who could pay," the sheriff shot back.

"Miss Cully saw patients who were able to pay. Those payments could have come to us."

"I wasn't paid," I told them. "Doesn't that make me innocent? I was simply a concerned citizen helping out."

Lord Xavier's mouth twitched from side to side as he tried to think of a counter argument.

"You robbed my husband of those payments," Mistress Ashmole said. "Theft is a crime, is it not?"

My heart sank. She had thought of everything.

"My lord, don't do this," Riccard begged. "Josie's needed at my house. My wife's having a baby but there are problems."

The sheriff swore under his breath. "My lord, let Miss Cully deliver the baby first."

"And give her a chance to escape?" Lord Xavier's nostrils flared. "Absolutely not. She's slippery."

"She's not a danger to anyone."

"She most certainly is! Constable, tie her hands together." Lord Xavier tossed the end of a rope to the constable. The other end was tied to his saddle.

"I'll stay with her while she attends Posey," Sheriff Neerim said quickly. "I'll make sure she doesn't escape."

Lord Xavier ignored him. A slick smile stretched his lips as the constable approached me.

I inched backward. "My lord, have compassion. I'm needed. I promise to present myself to the jailhouse when I'm finished."

"You're not going to the jailhouse. You're going somewhere you can never escape. Somewhere the jailors can't be bought."

"Where?"

His smile widened. "Get on with it, Constable."

Riccard grabbed Lord Xavier's reins. "My wife and child need her! Have mercy, please."

Lord Xavier kicked him in the stomach. Riccard grunted and doubled over.

"You there!" Lord Xavier said to Mistress Ashmole. "You're

the doctor's wife. You attend to the mother and her brat."

"She has no experience!" I cried.

"She can take her husband."

Mistress Ashmole threw her shawl around her shoulders. "My husband has been called away to a patient on one of the ships in the harbor."

"Her husband also doesn't have specialized knowledge of midwifery," I said. "They don't teach it in the medical colleges."

Mistress Ashmole held her hand out. "Give me your equipment, Miss Cully. I'll attend to Posey alone."

Riccard eyed her up and down. "Have you delivered babies before?"

"Babies are born all the time, often without a midwife in attendance. You're worrying unnecessarily. It's no wonder your wife has gone into early labor if you fuss like this."

He stared at her, speechless.

I closed my eyes and prayed to Hailia that Posey would be all right. I opened them again when the constable removed my pack from my hands and passed it to Mistress Ashmole. She snatched it from him and held it away from her body as if it had been dragged through the mud.

"Sorry," the young constable said to me. "I've got no choice."

I allowed him to tie my hands together and waited for Lord Xavier to untie the other end of the rope from his saddle. He did not.

Riccard lunged at me and scrabbled at the knot. "Let her go!"

Across the road, the Divers' front door opened. Meg and her mother spilled out and rushed over.

"What is this?" Mistress Diver commanded. "What are you doing with Josie?"

"She's under arrest for performing medical tasks," the sheriff told her. "You should return inside, Mistress Diver. Please. I don't want anyone else arrested."

His warning was clear. He knew they'd aided me that night of the fire, but so far, I was the only one in trouble for it. That could change.

"Do as he said," I told her. "Go inside. I'll be fine."

Meg's face crumpled. Her mother slipped her arm around her

daughter's shoulders and hugged her.

Lord Xavier turned his horse around, jerking me with it. I stumbled, as the rope tightened, but caught my balance before falling.

Riccard grabbed at the rope near the saddle. "Let her go! You can't do this!"

Lord Xavier struck him across the head, sending him tumbling to the ground.

He got right back up and stabbed his finger at Lord Xavier. "This isn't right! You can't just take her! We won't stand for it!"

Lord Xavier struck him again. He gave a snarl of satisfaction as Riccard fell to the ground, bleeding from the temple. "Shut up or I will go to your house and rip the baby from your wife's belly myself."

He rode off at a trot, and I had to sprint to keep up. With my hands tied, running was awkward and I was quickly out of breath. I stumbled but thankfully did not fall. I couldn't keep this up for long, however.

Where was he taking me?

Sheriff Neerim rode up alongside me. With one arm, he scooped me up and positioned me on the saddle in front of him, facing sideways. I slumped forward, sucking in huge breaths.

The sheriff sliced through the rope connecting me to Lord Xavier's horse with a knife.

Lord Xavier turned in the saddle, teeth bared. "You had no right to do that!"

"Do you want another riot?" the sheriff growled. "The villagers won't stand to see her paraded through the streets like a dog."

Lord Xavier's jaw hardened, his nostrils flared, and I thought he would overrule the sheriff. But he faced forward again and rode ahead.

"Thank you," I whispered to the sheriff.

His haunted gaze shifted away from mine. "Don't thank me," he said bleakly. "I can't help you where you're going. No one can."

"Where am I going?"

"The dungeon in Deerhorn Castle."

CHAPTER 10

$\mathcal{T}$he dungeon beneath Deerhorn Castle felt too small, the walls too close, despite the enormity of the castle itself. Lord Xavier seemed to fill the cell, and he wasn't a big man.

He shoved me in the back so hard that I fell to my knees. With my hands still tied, I couldn't catch myself, and I slammed onto the stone floor with a bruising thud. The arm that sported grazes burned with fresh pain. I groaned as I rolled over, only to be faced with his descending boot.

I screamed and scrambled away until my back hit the wall.

He chuckled, the brittle sound echoing off the bare stone walls. "Screaming will do you no good down here. These walls are thick. And nobody here cares about you, anyway."

I bit my tongue. I would not rise to his bait, would not put myself in further jeopardy by lashing out. He wanted a reason to hit me, but I wouldn't give him one.

Then again, Lord Xavier required no reason. He could hit me if he wanted to, whenever he wanted to. I was at his mercy.

He crouched before me, just far enough that he was out of range of my foot. I wouldn't kick him. Not unless I could be sure of hitting him hard in the head and rendering him unconscious.

I curled my legs up, partly in readiness to strike out if the opportunity arose, partly to get as far away from him as possible.

"You're afraid of me." His tongue darted out and moistened his lip. "That will make it more enjoyable." When I didn't respond, he edged closer. "Come now, Miss Cully. Josie. You always have something to say. Don't you want to tell me how cruel I am? How beastly I'm being to you?"

I clamped my mouth shut.

"Since you no longer like to speak, perhaps I'll cut out that tongue of yours." His eyes brightened. "I'll send it to your lover in a box, tied with a pretty bow made from a lock of your hair. Isn't that what captors do to torment their enemies? My mother used to tell me stories about an ancestor doing something similar to a priest who betrayed him. It would be rather a fitting punishment for the girl who's arrogant enough to talk back to her betters."

My scalp prickled and I shivered.

"Don't fret, Josie. I won't cut out your tongue yet. My mother needs you to use it. The thing is, I don't think you'll do what she wants without an incentive. Now, what could I possibly do to you that would make you do as she asks?" He pursed his lips and tapped his chin in mock thought. "It would have to be something I enjoy, or what's the point." His hand whipped out and caught my ankle. "Don't you agree?"

I swallowed but my fear remained, lodged in my throat with my heart.

His hand squeezed my leg and I bucked in response. His fingers pinched hard and I cried out. "Stay still, Josie. I can't say that you'll enjoy this, but I'm sure you'll enjoy it less if I have to leave you black and blue."

His other hand pushed up my skirt above my knee while the one on my leg continued to press and squeeze my flesh. His gaze dipped to my leg as he pushed my skirt higher, exposing my thigh. His hand followed, cold and hard as a blade. His breath quickened as more of my flesh was bared, and he shifted his weight.

My stomach rolled, revolted by his touch, by the cruel desire in his eyes. It was all I could do not to throw up.

Then realization struck. He was drunk with the power he had over me and with the desire to hurt me, to have me. A drunken man was a stupid man, slow and vulnerable. It was a weakness I could exploit. Maybe.

The higher his hand crept, the closer his face drew to mine. I watched him from beneath lowered lashes, my own breaths quickening as I saw my opportunity draw ever nearer.

I balled my bound hands into fists. I tensed.

"Lady Deerhorn has requested you, my lord." The voice at the dungeon grill startled me as much as it did Lord Xavier.

He stood and whipped around. "Now?" he bellowed.

The guard, the one with the scar who'd captured me in the lane, held Lord Xavier's gaze. "Aye, my lord."

"Have you told her I have the midwife?"

"Aye, my lord."

"She doesn't want to see her for herself? To question her?"

"She has requested your company in the southern salon, my lord. Immediately."

With a growl, Lord Xavier strode out. The guard locked the grill behind him and walked off.

I listened to their footsteps recede. Once the dungeon was silent, I lowered my skirt and breathed again. I got to my feet and checked the grill, but it was definitely locked. I checked all the bars but they held firm. There were no windows, and the only light came from flickering wall torches outside my cell.

"Is anyone there?" I said. When no one answered, I tried again, louder. There was no response.

Hailia, help me.

I inspected every inch of my cell for a way out. I kicked the stones on the floor to see if any were loose. I scrabbled at the stones on the walls and hammered them with my bound fists. There was nothing to use as a weapon, not even a spoon or bowl to throw at Lord Xavier. They hadn't even given me a pan to relieve myself in. The cell was relatively clean and smelled as though it had been closed up for a long time. I must be the first prisoner to be thrown into the dungeon in years.

I sat on the floor and tried to untie the rope around my wrists but it was no use. I couldn't even bend my fingers enough to touch the knot.

I tipped my head back against the wall and allowed fear and hopelessness to overwhelm me.

But just for a moment. Then I gathered my nerve and thought about what I'd say to the Deerhorns when they asked for the gem.

I waited. It felt like an age, but in truth, I couldn't tell how long they left me there. Without a view of the sky, I couldn't even see if it had gone dark outside. The waiting was almost as horrible as Lord Xavier's touch. Perhaps that was the entire point of Lady Deerhorn summoning her son away. The longer I waited, the more desperate I became, the more afraid and lonely. The more likely to tell her what she wanted.

The echoing footsteps set my heart racing. I stood, my back to the wall, my bound hands in front of me, and kept my gaze steady. I refused to show the fear that Lord Xavier craved, even though it seized my bones.

The guard with the scar unlocked the grill and my cell suddenly became full with Lord and Lady Deerhorn and Lord Xavier. My interactions with the head of the family were almost non-existent, although he probably remembered me from the village meeting where I'd spoken against his plan for The Row. He was not a potential ally.

"This is what all the fuss is about?" he said, eyeing me up and down. "Hardly seems worth it."

Lord Xavier smiled. "She will be, I'm sure of it."

Lady Deerhorn's hard gaze chilled the room. "You'll have to wait, Xavier. That's your punishment for bringing this to our door."

Waiting gave me more time to escape or for help to arrive. My heart lifted a little with hope.

"It's not all bad," Lord Xavier muttered. "We have her, don't we? If we can get the gem—"

"Quiet," she snapped. "You've done and said enough already."

"Xavier did the right thing." Lord Deerhorn's praise saw his son's face brighten, but his gaze remained wary.

A muscle in Lady Deerhorn's jaw bunched as she clenched her teeth. She whipped around to face me. Even though her anger seemed directed at Lord Xavier, I suspected I would be the one to bear the brunt of it.

I steeled myself for the first blow.

It did not come.

"You have one last chance to tell me where to find the gem," she said, teeth still clenched. "Or my son will break you in."

"I told you before, I don't know."

She struck me across the head. I slipped down the wall as pain flared and my vision blurred. I struggled to sit upright, and fought through the fog of light headedness. I focused on Lady Deerhorn, keeping her in my sight, until my wits fully returned. My temple throbbed and I felt blood trickle down my hairline to my ear.

"You didn't let me finish," I said. "I was going to tell you I can guess where it is."

A distant sound caught Lord Deerhorn and Xavier's attention. Lady Deerhorn's eyes narrowed, but whether she heard it or not, I couldn't tell. "Where?" she said on a rush of breath.

"Do you remember when the captain said it is somewhere unexpected?"

"Go on."

"There's a pond he likes to swim in on hot days. It's in the forest on the palace estate, just off Grand Avenue. The king used to have trysts there sometimes."

"I know it," Lord Xavier said. "Violette told me about it."

"Where at the pond?" Lady Deerhorn asked me.

"I saw him throw something in the water. He wouldn't tell me what it was, but it was the right size to be the gem." I held her gaze with a steady one of my own.

I should have blinked.

"You lie," she said.

I shrank away. "It's the truth!"

Her husband rocked on his heels as he regarded me. "Why do you think she's lying?"

"It was too easy," she said. "She put up no resistance."

"You've struck her, kept her prisoner, and threatened her with violent rape. Are those not reason enough for her to tell us everything?"

"Not for her."

"It's the truth!" I cried. "Please, my lords, you both believe me. Why would I lie? What do I possibly gain?"

"Come, Mother," Lord Xavier said. "We can look for it in the pond and if we don't find it, we'll come back here and beat her until she tells us the truth." He strode off, his father at his heels.

Lady Deerhorn didn't move. "We don't have time. You made sure of that, Son," she bit off.

Lord Xavier swallowed.

She caught my jaw and squeezed so hard I thought the bones would shatter. "You were telling the truth the first time, weren't you? You don't know where it is. Only the captain does." Her lips twisted with her smile as she let me go.

"Then we no longer have a need for her," Lord Deerhorn said. "Good. Keeping prisoners is costly. Xavier, she's yours. When you're done, kill her. I'll see that the captain is brought here for questioning."

Lord Xavier grabbed my arm and wrenched me to my feet. He licked his lips as he pulled me against his chest. "Finally," he whispered.

Everything inside me recoiled. Not just because of his fetid breath, his cruel sneer, but from the thought of Dane being questioned. What would they do to him to get him to confess?

My savior came in a surprising form. "Let her go," Lady Deerhorn said with strained patience. "For Merdu's sake, think, both of you. The captain won't tell us anything if she's not alive. He's no fool. He'll want to see her and make sure she's safe before he confesses the location of the gem."

Lord Xavier pouted. His grip tightened momentarily before he obeyed his mother and released me. "Doesn't mean I can't leave my mark on her." He raised his hand to strike.

I ducked my head into my shoulder but the blow never came.

"My lady!" said the guard with the scar. He was out of breath from running, his sword drawn. "My lady and lords, they're here. They've broken through the gate and are marching on the castle."

"Fuck." Lord Xavier glanced at his mother.

She looked worried.

Her husband did not. "Order them to keep their distance," he said.

The guard's gaze flicked to his mistress then back to his master. "My lord, ordering them will do no good. They won't listen and we can't fight them. There are too many."

Lady Deerhorn looked at her son as if she wanted to throttle him.

Lord Xavier cleared his throat. "They won't get inside."

Lord Deerhorn agreed. "They wouldn't dare try."

"Who's to stop them?" Lady Deerhorn spat. "Vierney said there are too many for his men to hold off."

"They're just villagers with clubs. Vierney's men are well trained and armed." Lord Deerhorn shooed his man, Vierney, out of the cell. "Stand your ground."

"It's not just villagers," Vierney said. "The palace guards are with them."

"How many?" Lady Deerhorn asked.

"All of them."

"This is outrageous," Lord Deerhorn snapped. "They can't come into a nobleman's home and demand the release of a prisoner!"

"There's no king to command his guards not to do so," his wife said, her voice shrill. "The dukes are holed up in the palace, too scared to get involved. They won't give the order, and I don't think the captain will listen anyway."

"He will be executed for treason!"

"Who will capture him?"

"Aren't Merdu's Guards near?" Lord Deerhorn said to Vierney. "They will take up arms for me."

"They won't fight for a cause that doesn't directly affect them or their order," Lady Deerhorn told him. "They will protect Glancia from unrest, but—"

"Is this not unrest?" her husband screeched. He glared at Lord Xavier. "This is *your* fault. Why did you arrest her in full view of everyone? If you'd let her deliver that baby then arrested her during the night, we wouldn't be in this predicament now."

Lord Xavier paled. "But you said—"

"Don't put the blame on me."

Lord Xavier took a step back beneath the glares of both parents.

"My lady, what should we do?" Vierney asked.

They all looked to Lady Deerhorn.

"We must use the only weapon we have." She jutted her chin out at me. "Show her to the people. They won't burn the castle down with her in it."

Lord Xavier pushed me towards Vierney. The guard grabbed my elbows from behind and marched me out of the cell.

"And then what?" Lord Deerhorn asked.

"Then we tell the captain we'll kill her unless he gives us the magic gem."

CHAPTER 11

*V*ierney presented me on one of the castle balconies like a new bride. Down below, no one noticed.

It was chaos. The splintered wooden gate hung from its hinges and villagers streamed through, brandishing clubs and knives, shouting incoherently. Mounted palace guards struck down the Deerhorn guards without hesitation. In the village, they had used the hilts of their weapons. Here, they used the blades.

Blood soaked the ground. No amount of straw strewn over the earth could soak it up. Almost all of it came from the bodies of Deerhorn men.

"Merdu," Lord Deerhorn muttered in wonder. "So many."

"Get their attention," Lady Deerhorn barked at Vierney. "Show them the midwife with your blade at her throat."

Vierney's knife pressed into the flesh beneath my ear. I struggled, but my attempts were pathetic, useless. His strong arm across my chest locked me in place.

"Stop or I'll cut her!" His shout drifted on the wind, drowned out by the battle cries of the villagers.

I searched the palace guards, but none of the figures was Dane's tall, commanding one. He wasn't among them.

I started to chuckle but it quickly swelled and became a throaty, hearty laugh. "He outsmarted you," I said to my captors.

"He knew you would use me to force him to tell you where the gem is, so he stayed away. You can't manipulate him if he's not here. There's no point threatening to kill me."

"Perhaps," Lady Deerhorn sneered. "But we can actually kill you."

My laughter died. "Then you won't get the gem."

"We'll get it another way. Vierney, slit her throat."

"No!" I screamed.

The point of the knife bit into my flesh.

Thud.

Vierney jolted and shoved me forward, into the balustrade. His blade scratched my throat, but not enough to draw blood. His push, however, propelled me onto the balustrade and over it.

I screamed again. Far below, people looked up. I could just make out their horrified faces as I teetered on the edge.

I tried to maneuver my body and grasp the stone balustrade but with my hands tied and my position awkward, I couldn't get purchase.

I felt myself falling.

A hand wrapped around my bound wrists and pulled me back then an arm caught me around the waist.

"Merdu, that was close," Quentin said.

It wasn't Quentin who held me, however, it was Dane. He looked utterly relieved.

"Too close," he said, voice trembling.

I gripped the doublet at his chest and let my tears flow unchecked for a moment. I was giddy with relief and my body shook uncontrollably. With a steady breath, I swiped my damp cheeks on my shoulder and offered Dane a smile.

"Thank you," I said, lamely.

He returned my smile with a fleeting one of his own. Then he turned to my captors.

Three palace guards pointed their swords at the three Deerhorns. Vierney lay dead on the balcony floor, a knife buried in the middle of his back. Rhys planted one booted foot on each side of Vierney's body and withdrew the knife. He wiped it on Vierney's sleeve and sheathed it.

"You have to teach me how to do that," Max said to him.

He, Quentin and Erik held the Deerhorns at blade point. If we weren't in public I would have hugged each of them. Rhys too.

"Put down your weapons," Lord Deerhorn commanded.

Dane nodded at his men and they lowered their swords.

"This is outrageous," Lord Deerhorn spluttered.

Lord Xavier puffed out his chest but kept his gaze on Quentin's sword. "You can't do this! There will be consequences."

"Call off your guards before they're all killed," Dane said.

Neither Lord Deerhorn nor Lord Xavier moved. It was Lady Deerhorn who called over the balustrade for her men to surrender. To Dane, she said, "You have what you came for. Leave and take everyone with you, including the villagers."

"I don't command them. They can do as they please."

"This is outrageous!" Lord Deerhorn spluttered again.

"What is outrageous is your kidnap of an innocent woman."

"Innocent?" Lord Xavier blurted out. "She was impersonating a doctor!"

"In a time of emergency, the law states that a midwife can use her skills to assist the injured."

Lord Xavier looked as though he would argue, but then caught sight of his mother's thunderous face.

There was a crash down in the courtyard as the gates were torn from their hinges. Several men dragged them into the center of the courtyard and threw them on top of a pile that was composed of doors, wheels, carriage parts, and anything else that might burn. A victorious cry erupted as it was set alight.

Lady Deerhorn paled.

"You can't do this!" Lord Deerhorn ordered. "Get out! Leave at once!"

"My men will go," Dane said. "As to the villagers…they're angry. They blame the governor for the fire, and they know you're behind the governor. They want revenge."

Lord Xavier swallowed. "What sort of revenge?"

Dane just looked at him.

"Mother?" Lord Xavier whispered.

She took his hand and squared her shoulders. "We must go."

"They can't do this!" her husband cried. "We're noble born."

"Who will stop them?" Rhys said. "Your men are outnumbered and the palace guards are under the authority of Glancia's co-rulers. The Duke of Gladstow is prepared to order the guards to assist you but the Duke of Buxton is not. Both must agree. If I were you, I'd leave immediately."

"Leave?" Lord Xavier said weakly.

"But *you* are here, Brother," Lord Deerhorn said, just as weakly. "Merdu's Guards *must* fight for us, for your noble lords. You will be handsomely rewarded."

Rhys smirked. "Bribery doesn't work on us. Nor do we get involved in local squabbles unless it's a direct threat to the faith."

"This *is* a direct threat! If one noble house falls, what will stop the people overthrowing the others? Or…or the temples? It is just a small step from there to anarchy. Brother, I beg you. Help us."

"It's Master." Rhys strode back inside and disappeared from sight.

Dane untied my hands. We followed Rhys, with Erik, Max and Quentin behind. We exited the castle and crossed the courtyard to where the horses were being held by one of Dane's men. The animals were becoming agitated from the fire now blazing in the middle of the courtyard. Villagers continued to throw anything they could carry onto it—chairs, tables, and even window shutters—cheering with each flare of sparks.

They looked in no mood to stop, and most of the Deerhorn guards had vanished. The Deerhorns were all alone amid the wild, lawless mob. I felt no sympathy for them.

Not all of the villagers were bent on destruction. Some crossed the courtyard carrying sacks of grain across their shoulders. They'd found the Deerhorns' storehouse. When the others saw, they abandoned the fire and helped.

"Ride with Quentin," Dane said as he assisted me onto the saddle. "He'll take you to the cottage on the estate. Do you still have the key?"

"Around my neck," I said. "Why there?"

"Few know about it. The Deerhorns may come for you yet, and the Divers' house is not safe. Nor is the garrison. They have friends at the palace. If the Duke of Gladstow demands your immediate arrest, I don't want you easily found."

"Is it true the law says a midwife can use her medical knowledge in an emergency?"

He patted the horse's neck as it shifted uneasily at a loud noise. "I made it up. Which is why you need to get to safety. When they discover the lie, the Deerhorns might come for you." He looked back up at the balcony on which we'd stood moments before. Two villagers threw a bed over the balustrade. There was no sign of the Deerhorns.

"Are you going to try and disperse them?" I asked.

"They can do what they want here." He mounted and gathered the reins. Lightning was the most jittery of all the horses, but seemed to calm a little with Dane on his back. "I have to go to the village. There's rioting again and the sheriff has requested my assistance."

"Be careful."

He gave me a small smile that wasn't at all reassuring before ordering Quentin to set off. We rode out of the castle first, passing beneath the sharp points of the portcullis that no one had thought to drop when the villagers approached. Dane and all of his guards filed out behind us, but many villagers remained to continue loading grain onto a cart.

Some left with us to return to the village. They carried swords taken from fallen Deerhorn guards. If they joined the riots in Mull, Dane would soon be fighting them. If he only used the hilt of his sword instead of the blade again, he would be at a disadvantage.

I looked around for Rhys, but he was nowhere in sight. "Where are Merdu's Guards?" I asked Quentin, perched on the saddle in front of me.

"Some are in the village, keeping the rioters from doing too much damage, and some are back at the palace to free us to come here. Rhys was the only one who joined us at the castle."

I glanced behind me to see thirty or so palace guards dressed in crimson uniforms, some also in armor. They had all come to rescue me.

The column of guards took the Mull road, but Quentin and I

diverted onto the palace road. I glanced behind, but no one followed, thank the goddess.

"What should we put on your wrists?" Quentin asked. "Is pomfrey sap for rope burns or just fire burns?"

"Just fire. I don't have any on me anyway. Oh! Merdu. My patient!"

"What?"

"Posey. Turn around, Quentin. We have to return to the village."

He shook his head. "Can't. Captain's orders."

"We won't go near the village green."

He hesitated. "Sorry, Josie. The captain'll blame me if anything happens to you."

"If something happens to me, it will happen to you too, and then he can't get mad." My attempted joke fell flat. "Quentin, please, I have to go back. Posey was having difficulty and I left her in Mistress Ashmole's hands. She has no idea how to deliver a baby."

"I can't, Josie. Sorry."

"Quentin," I said levelly. "You want to be a doctor, don't you?"

"If I can get into the college."

"A doctor is obliged to do everything in his power to help a patient."

"You're not playing fair."

"You *have* to turn around or you'll have the death of Posey and her baby on your conscience."

He hesitated then sighed. "Don't tell the captain."

We turned around and took the village road.

We were almost there when Quentin muttered, "Merdu. Another fire."

I followed his gaze to the slender column of smoke rising from the center of Mull. It wasn't enough smoke to be a large fire, but small fires could spread.

The smoke appeared to be coming from the village green, as were the shouts. I couldn't make out individual words but the tones were angry and urgent. They were probably calling for the governor again, still hiding away inside the council building.

Two women ran by, their skirts held away from their feet. I knew them well and hailed them. They were pleased to see me. "We thought you were surely dead," one said.

"I got free," I told them. "What's going on here?"

"Chaos, that's why we're leaving. Most of the villagers we know went to the castle to rescue you. The ones who stayed are newcomers, Vytllians mostly. They didn't care about you and they don't care about the village. They just want to destroy. They're smashing down shop doors and pushing over market stalls, stealing whatever they can get their hands on."

"The guards will stop them," Quentin assured her.

"Aye, and the priests are coming back now too, but they don't want to use their swords."

"They might have to," I said.

They headed off and we continued to Posey's cottage. I offered a prayer to Hailia as I barged in, not bothering to knock. The house was quiet. Too quiet.

"Posey! Riccard! It's me, Josie."

"In here!" Riccard's stricken face appeared around a door. "Thank the goddess. Come quickly, Josie. The baby is the wrong way and Posey doesn't look too good."

I pushed past him into the bedroom and took in the scene. Posey lay on the bed, her color as pale as the linen, her hair and clothes soaked with sweat. She was barely conscious. Mistress Ashmole knelt on the bed, trying to get the exhausted Posey to draw up her knees.

Posey's face suddenly contorted in pain as a contraction wracked her body. She whimpered. It sounded far too weak.

I knelt alongside Mistress Ashmole and inspected Posey. The baby was indeed breech. We had to move quickly. I hoped it wasn't too late.

"How did you get out?" Mistress Ashmole asked, lips pinched.

"The villagers and palace guards stormed the castle. Pass me the Mother's Milk. There's a jar in my bag."

"So it worked," Riccard said. "I told as many as I could what they did and how Posey needed you. Seems everyone was as angry as me."

"The Mother's Milk, Mistress Ashmole. Posey's in a lot of pain. She can't do what she needs to do if she's exhausted from the pain."

Mistress Ashmole's nostrils flared. "If the goddess didn't want us to experience pain in childbirth, she would have made it so. If Posey would just calm down and try to breathe through it—"

"Give me the Mother's Milk!"

Quentin fetched it from my bag and measured out a small dose according to my instructions. Under Mistress Ashmole's stern glare, he spooned it into Posey's mouth.

"The baby's going to come out bottom first," I told Posey once I gauged the Mother's Milk had taken affect. "You won't feel much pain, but you will need to stay awake to push. Do you understand?"

She nodded.

"Riccard, encourage her when I say so."

A bottom first breech was safer than feet first, but still made for a difficult labor. As much as I wanted to talk to Mistress Ashmole about the dangers and the importance of a speedy delivery, I didn't want to worry Posey and Riccard. I would have to tell her later that there was a higher risk of the baby being born dead or simple.

Despite her aversion to using Mother's Milk, Mistress Ashmole proved an able assistant. Her clinical, unemotional nature was an asset when the parents' emotions ran high. Riccard sat on one side of his wife and held her hand, while Quentin held her other. They both encouraged Posey to push when I instructed her to bear down.

The baby was born as dusk settled outside the window. His angry cry was the most wonderful thing I'd heard all day. He had a bruised hip, as expected for breech births, but otherwise seemed healthy. While a smiling Riccard lay the baby on Posey's chest, I showed Mistress Ashmole how to cut the cord, deliver the afterbirth, and stitch the mother.

Riccard paid me on the porch as we left. "Thanks, Josie. This doesn't seem like enough." He dropped the coins onto my palm.

"I should owe you," I said. "It seems you were responsible for sending the villagers to the castle in time."

"I can't believe they arrested you for doctoring on the night of the fire. Do you know who the witness was who told the Deerhorns?"

"I do," I said, very aware that the witness was standing right beside me.

She cleared her throat and held out her palm. "My work is not free."

"You're just learning," Riccard told her. "And you were no use until Josie showed you what to do."

"Even so."

He slammed the door, almost striking her fingers.

Mistress Ashmole plucked the pouch off my hand. "Half of that is mine."

Quentin drew his sword and pointed it at her chest. "Give it back to Josie."

She swallowed and gave me the pouch. "The sooner you leave this village, the better." She gathered her shawl around her shoulders and strode off.

Quentin sheathed his sword. "I feel sorry for the future babies of Mull, coming out and seeing that pinched face for the first time."

"Thank you for standing up for me, but I would have given her half. An assistant deserves to be paid."

"She deserves nothing from you except a slap across that sour, smug mouth."

I was pleased to see that smoke no longer rose above the rooftops. Quentin agreed to journey closer to the village green but when we saw the crowd throwing bricks and other objects at the warrior priests from behind a makeshift barricade, we quickly diverted.

He hailed one of the warrior priests riding past us into the fray. "Where are the palace guards?" Quentin asked.

"Called back to the palace by the dukes. They're worried for their own safety."

"Can the priests hold on here without help?"

"Against untrained villagers armed with a few rocks?" The

guard grinned. "It's going to be a dull evening. I'll try to stay awake."

"They're arrogant," Quentin said as we rode off. "But I like them."

"Thinking about becoming a warrior priest?"

"Merdu, no. Not now."

"What do you mean?"

I may have been sitting on the saddle behind him, but I could see his entire neck flush. "Nothing," he muttered.

Night fell quickly and I realized I was starving. Hopefully there would be something to eat at the cottage, or if not, Quentin could bring me food from the palace kitchens. I was about to ask him if there were any provisions prepared for my stay, when the thundering of hooves on the road behind had me swiveling in the saddle to see who approached.

"Get down and hide behind those bushes," Quentin said. "Just in case."

I crouched behind the low thicket that edged this part of the road. A group of riders approached rapidly, but it was too dark to see how many or who they were. In such low light, it was dangerous to move so quickly. The horses could step on a pebble, in a ditch, or on a fallen branch. Dane wouldn't let his men travel at that pace in the semi-dark unless it was urgent.

The riders slowed as they drew closer to us. If we could have hidden the horse, I would have urged Quentin to hide behind the bush with me. My pulse quickened.

Then it began to pound as the riders came into view. Four men sporting injuries rode at the head of the group, another four behind. In the center were Lord and Lady Deerhorn, Lord Xavier and his brother Lord Greville.

It was Lord Xavier who stopped first. He drew his sword and pointed it at Quentin. Quentin rested his hand on the hilt of his sword but didn't draw.

Merdu, no.

"Not so brave now, are you?" Lord Xavier snarled.

"Come." Lady Deerhorn glanced behind her. "We don't have time."

"The villagers are on foot, Mother," Lord Greville said. "They can't catch us." He drew up alongside his brother. "Is this one of them? He doesn't look too strong. I could've beaten him if I'd been there."

"There will be other guards traveling this road," Lady Deerhorn snapped. "We *must* get to safety."

"I don't like retreating," her husband grumbled.

"Knowing when to retreat is just as important as knowing when to fight. Our home has been taken over, our possessions burned, our men killed or injured. *Now* is the time for retreat, Husband, unless you want to see your sons' heads on spikes before you lose your own."

Lord Deerhorn shifted in the saddle. "We will continue on. Xavier, come."

"After I deal with this turd," Lord Xavier sneered. "He's one of the ones from the balcony."

"Where there's one, there's usually more not far away," Lady Deerhorn said.

Her words gave me an idea. I scraped up a small stone with a fistful of dirt and tossed it onto the road behind them.

Lord Deerhorn screwed up his eyes and tried to see through the murkiness. "I think someone's on the way. Come, Xavier, there's no time for that now." He ordered his men forward then rode off without waiting to see if his family followed.

Lord Xavier was the last to leave. "Next time I see you, Turd, you're dead." He sheathed his sword and rode away.

Quentin blew out a breath, but waited until the sound of hooves had disappeared in the distance before telling me to step out. "I hate him," he said, helping me up to the saddle. "I hate them all."

"She's the dangerous one," I said. "She's smarter than all of them. Lord Deerhorn and his sons are ruled by baser instincts."

"That makes them dangerous too, Josie. They're cruel. Lord Xavier reminds me of the prisoners in the palace cells. They like to see others suffer."

We didn't head to the cottage immediately, but detoured via the palace to pack food from the kitchen. Quentin wouldn't let me leave the commons until he'd scouted the area for Deerhorns. It was lucky he did. When he returned, he reported that the

Deerhorns had just been farewelled at the stables by the Duke of Gladstow and Lady Violette Morgrave.

"Lady Morgrave was crying, so the stable boy told me," he said as he gathered up the pack of food. "She begged the duke to do something about the siege at her family's castle, but he said his hands were tied. Unless the Duke of Buxton agreed to send the palace guards, nothing could be done."

"Buxton knows the Deerhorns are on Gladstow's side," I said. "He won't lift a finger to help them."

"Lord Deerhorn proceeded to complain about having a realm where two dukes rule and not one king." Quentin glanced around the commons courtyard then lowered his voice. "According to the stable boy, Lady Deerhorn took her daughter off to the side. He swears he heard them say 'duchess' and 'out of the way' in the same breath."

I felt sick. Kitty was in danger. It was precisely what we'd feared. "Promise me you'll keep an eye on the duchess, Quentin. A close eye."

"The captain already has a man watching her at all times," he said. "Except when she's in her apartments. It's too hard for us to think of excuses to get in. Her ladies' maid's a real dragon."

"Did the Deerhorns actually leave the estate?"

He nodded. "I saw them ride off myself, but Lady Morgrave didn't go with them. They're heading to Tilting, so the stable hand says."

"So I can return to the village."

"I ain't going against Hammer's orders. You're staying in the cottage until he says so."

"I will do as I please," I said, hand on hip. "And not what he tells me to do."

He looked uncertain. "But if I don't do as he ordered, *I'll* get in trouble, not you." He pouted. "It ain't fair."

I sighed. "Then I'll stay at the cottage until the riots end. I no longer have any patients in need of my midwifery services anyway. Please see that Meg and her family are informed so they don't worry."

"I'll ask Max to do it." He grinned. "He'll be more welcome than me. Let's go to the garrison to see if there's any news."

We entered the palace through the service door and followed the labyrinth of corridors to reach the garrison through its internal door. I counted some twelve guards lounging around the enormous table, plus Balthazar and Theodore, and several servants. One of them was Amar. All were questioning Balthazar and Amar about their encounters with the brothers in Merdu's Guards.

"Did they tell you how you got the limp?" Zeke asked Amar.

Amar rubbed his right leg. "I was part of a small group traveling from Fahl in Vytill when we were ambushed by bandits in the forest. My horse fell on me."

"And you?" one of the footmen asked Balthazar. "Were you a warrior when you were younger too?"

Yen snorted. "Are you blind?"

"I was the archivist," Balthazar said. "I didn't train to be a guard."

"But you're still a priest, right?" a maid asked.

"Apparently."

Erik entered from the adjoining dormitory, yawning and stretching his arms above his head. "Priests are strange," he announced. "They cannot sleep with women."

"What about men?" asked Deanne from the menagerie.

"That's illegal in Glancia," Theodore told her.

"It is? What about women sleeping with women?"

All eyes suddenly fell on me. "I suppose it is but no one has ever been arrested for it, as far as I know," I told them.

"Seems you broke your vows, Amar," Ray said with a chuckle.

Amar blushed. "I don't care. I'm not sure I want to go back to the temple anyway. I like it here."

"And you, Balthazar?" Zeke asked. "Do you want to be a priest again?"

"I want to find out more about my life," the Master of the Palace said. "I'll return to Tilting with Rhys and his men just as soon as the riots have ended. He's keen to get back to the city, so his men tell me."

"You're leaving us?" the maid muttered. "What will we do without you?"

"Go dancing in the ballroom," one of the footmen said with a wry grin. His joke fell flat. Everyone was staring at Balthazar. It seemed to be difficult for them to grasp that one of them was leaving.

"You can come to Tilting too, if you like," Balthazar said. "There's nothing keeping you here except each other. It's possible more of us are from Tilting, not just Amar and me."

"I don't think so," Theodore said. "We would have heard if a large number of people had gone missing from the capital. I can understand how we wouldn't have heard about two, but not a thousand."

Theodore's words put a dampener on the gathering and a weighty silence fell. I suspected every man and woman in the room was thinking about whether to stay or leave. Some might return with Balthazar to Tilting in the hope of learning about themselves through him, but many would stay at the palace. The fear of being separated from the only people they could trust frightened them.

Not even Balthazar could trust those he'd known before his memory loss. He'd left the temple without telling the brothers and, knowing Balthazar, his secrecy would have been for a good reason. He ought to be anxious about returning to Tilting with them, but he showed no sign of it. Perhaps he put on a brave face for the sake of his fellow servants. Or perhaps he expected Dane to keep him safe.

But I doubted Dane would be able to stay with him in the temple. I certainly couldn't, as a woman.

I eyed Theodore and Balthazar, wondering if I should tell them now about my plan to travel with them to Tilting, or if I should keep the news to myself until after I'd told Dane. I might need their support to sway Dane, but it was far from guaranteed. Indeed, I suspected they would align with Dane.

In the end, a distraction solved my dilemma for me.

CHAPTER 12

*T*he external door opened and a cloaked figure entered. His hood obscured his face but I knew it was one of the guards from his size.

"Where've you been?" Max asked.

The figure threw off his hood. Brant.

Quentin moved closer to me, but Brant was not a threat with so many people crammed into the garrison. Besides, he still favored his arm, holding it to his chest.

"Village," Brant said as he headed to the sideboard.

"You're not supposed to leave the palace."

Brant poured himself an ale then drank it all. "That order was for my own safety. If I want to take the risk, that's my problem. Besides, I wanted to see how things were." He poured another drink and saluted me with the cup. "I saw the captain, working alongside the priests. Why's he the only palace guard there?"

"We were ordered to return, but he decided to stay."

Brant didn't seem to be listening. He sported a smug look that settled on Balthazar. "I saw someone in the village," he said. "Someone who shouldn't be there."

"Who?" Balthazar asked.

"Lord Barborough. He was watching on."

"Did he see you?"

"Aye, and he chased me. He probably wanted to talk to me about the wishes."

Balthazar and Theodore exchanged glances.

"Don't worry," Brant said cheerfully. "I lost him in the graveyard."

"Why did you go into the graveyard?" Zeke asked. "It's not on the palace road."

"Seemed like a good place to lose him among the mess the rioters made in there."

"What mess?" I asked carefully.

His eyes flashed, as if he could sense distress and fed off it. "Some headstones were pushed over, branches pulled off trees, plants uprooted." He shrugged, as if it didn't matter.

"What about the southern corner? You would have passed my parents' graves to get to the gate. There's a riverwart growing near the headstone. The captain planted it after my father died. It's distinctive with a bright yellow flower. Did you notice it? Are those headstones still upright?"

Brant swirled the ale around his cup, taking his time to answer. I knew he was delaying simply to irk me and see my temper rise, so I bit my tongue to suppress my frustration.

"That area wasn't touched," he finally said.

Quentin took my hand and squeezed. "Don't worry. The riots will end soon, I reckon. Now that the Deerhorns are gone—"

"Gone?" Theodore asked.

Quentin nodded. "They fled, but not before making a stop here to speak to the Duke of Gladstow and Lady Morgrave."

Murmurs of "Thank the goddess" and "Good riddance" rippled around the garrison. Ray patted me on the back and congratulated me for driving them out.

"It wasn't me," I said. "It was all of you and the villagers. The Deerhorns are afraid for their lives."

"Everyone rose up because of you," he said. "Because they hated how the Deerhorns manipulated the sheriff into arresting you."

"They manipulated the governor into starting the fire too," I said. "Don't forget that. But I am relieved they're gone. They can't continue their corrupt rule over Mull anymore, nor can they harm anyone."

"I wouldn't count on that," Brant said, making his way towards me. "They're powerful people, and they have Violette Morgrave in Gladstow's bed." He drank from his cup then wiped his mouth with the back of his hand. "You should be worried. You and the duchess." He pushed the cup into my chest. "You both get in the way of their ambitions."

Quentin snatched the cup away. Brant raised himself to his full height, towering over Quentin. I heard the smaller, younger guard swallow.

"Stand down," Max growled. "And get out of here."

Brant sniffed. "You're all pathetic." He stalked off in the direction of the internal door.

"Wait," Balthazar said, rising. "You didn't seem surprised about the Deerhorns' sudden departure. Did you know they'd left? Did you see them go?"

He must have. The timing fitted. Brant had returned to the palace not long after the Deerhorns departed. He could have watched them leave.

"Go back to your temple, old man," Brant said. "And good riddance."

* * *

I AWOKE the following day in the large bedchamber of the cottage. I'd slept with the window open to air out the stuffy room and the bird chatter in the surrounding forest had begun early. I boiled some eggs for breakfast and put some of the palace kitchen's herbs in a pot of water to steep. Then I washed all the dishes and cups I could find and dusted from top to bottom. The cottage was so small that it didn't take long, but I was glad to move into the garden. It was a fine early autumn day and the leaves hadn't yet started to change color. The cottage and garden would be pretty in its autumnal glory, but I might not get the opportunity to see it this year. The journey I was about to set off on with Dane could take a long time.

I hummed as I collected herbs from the extensive range. For

the first time in a long time I felt completely safe. The Deer-horns had fled and I was far from the trouble in the village. The cottage felt like it existed in a different world to Mull and the palace. Perhaps that was the result of the magic that had created it. I imagined the sorcerer conjuring up this peaceful place for his own pleasure. But that wasn't right. The sorcerer was an entity, not a person, and did not perform magic for itself.

I looked around, admiring the sorcerer's fine work, and caught sight of a horse through the trees. I crouched behind the yellow rose growing at the side of the cottage as the rider came into view. I released a breath and stood up.

"Good morning, Dane. I hope you brought food with you because I don't have enough for—"

"Dane?" came a voice from beyond the trees.

I groaned and mouthed "Sorry" to Dane as he dismounted.

"It's all right," he said. "They were bound to find out sooner or later."

Theodore and Balthazar rode into the clearing, twin looks of thunder on their faces. Theodore dismounted while Dane assisted Balthazar to the ground.

"Why did you tell her your real name and not us?" Theodore asked. "Are we not your friends too?"

"He didn't trust us," Balthazar said.

"That's not it," Dane said.

Balthazar and Theodore glared at him, waiting.

Dane sighed. "I didn't trust you in the beginning, it's true, but later…I simply didn't see the point in telling you after so long."

"You didn't see the point?" Theodore threw his hands up with a huff. "I would like to have called you by your real name instead of that ridiculous moniker."

"Hammer isn't ridiculous," Dane said.

"It doesn't suit you."

"It does sometimes," Balthazar said.

It was Dane's turn to glare.

"When were you going to tell us?" Theodore asked. "Or were you never going to?"

"Of course I was going to," Dane said. "And soon."

Theodore crossed his arms. "You say that now that you've been caught."

"Let's go inside," I cut in quickly. "The tea will be ready." I hooked my arm through Balthazar's to help him on the uneven garden path. "Isn't it beautiful here? It's so peaceful. How is the village? Have the riots ended? Are Rhys and his men still there? Oh, and did you know the Deerhorns have left?"

Theodore glanced over his shoulder at me. "You don't have to be nervous, Josie. We don't blame you for not telling us. We know *you* trusted us." He punctuated the sentence with another glare for Dane.

Dane sighed again.

Balthazar's hold on my arm tightened. "Perhaps she did trust us," he said quietly. "Or perhaps she did not."

I stared straight ahead as Theodore pushed open the cottage door. He held it as we filed past him, his narrowed gaze tracking Dane.

Dane pulled out two of the chairs and slapped their backs with his palm. "Sit. Both of you. And drop the matter of the name. You can call me Dane from now on, if you prefer, or Hammer. It's up to you. If the others overhear, then so be it."

Theodore jerked a chair away from him. "So you put Bal and me on the same level as every other servant? Even the ones you've never had a conversation with? Nice to know where we stand."

I groaned. He was deeply hurt and I couldn't see any way to make amends. "Who wants tea?" I asked cheerfully.

Balthazar put up his hand. "Put some of those calming herbs into Theo's."

"And some truth-telling ones into his." Theodore jutted his chin in Dane's direction. "Whatever his name is today."

"There's no such thing as truth-telling herbs," I said lamely.

"Fine," Dane said to Theodore. "You want to know the real reason I never told you and Bal?"

"If it *is* the real reason," Theodore said huffily as he slunk into the chair.

Dane accepted one of the cups of tea from me and set it down with a thud in front of Balthazar. "I liked that Josie was the only one who called me by it." He deposited another cup in front of Theodore. Tea sloshed over the sides. "Satisfied?"

Theodore picked up his cup and saluted me with it. "Yes. Thank you. Why didn't you just say so before?"

"Why do you think?" Dane growled. He took the next two cups off me without meeting my gaze. Even when we both sat at the table, he wouldn't look in my direction.

I was glad of it. I didn't want him seeing my fierce blush. It was bad enough that Balthazar sported a small smile.

"Can we get down to business now?" Dane asked.

"Go right ahead, *Dane*." Theodore shook his head. "It's going to take some getting used to."

"What has happened?" I asked. "Are the villagers still rioting?"

"The riots have eased overnight and finally stopped this morning," Dane said. "Rhys is keeping some men there to make sure there are no more flare ups, but we both think the worst is over now that word has reached the villagers of the Deerhorns' departure."

"And the arrest," Balthazar added.

"They arrested the governor?" I asked.

Dane shook his head. "The sheriff refused, stating there isn't enough evidence."

"Which is true," Balthazar said.

"He's still guilty in my book," Theodore said.

"And mine," I chimed in. "But I can see why Sheriff Neerim won't arrest him without solid proof. He has already arrested Ned Perkin, so what is the new arrest you're referring to?"

"The two main leaders from The Row, the heads of each faction. They'd been at loggerheads before the fire and it was they who encouraged the looting and rioting in the village after-wards. If it hadn't been for them, there would still have been protests, but property would not have been damaged."

"They would have still stormed the Deerhorns' castle," I said. For me, I might have added. It was both incredible and humbling that the villagers had been willing to go to such lengths to save me.

"We didn't come here to tell you about the village," Balthazar said. "Although I understand your desire to know how your friends have fared."

"Then why have you come?" I glanced at each of them in turn. I didn't like the worried looks they gave me. "What's happened?"

"An attempt was made on the Duchess of Gladstow's life last night," Balthazar said.

My stomach dropped. "Hailia, no."

"It appears she has been poisoned, "Dane said. "She's ill but not as gravely as Lady Miranda was. I gave the duchess the same instruction your father gave Miranda to purge the poison from her body."

"She should rest too," I said. "But she's vulnerable."

"My men are watching her. I informed both dukes of my suspicion of poisoning immediately. Gladstow scoffed, saying it was just her delicate constitution and that she must have eaten a bad piece of fish, but Buxton instructed me to have men guard her. Gladstow couldn't refuse or he'd look guilty."

"He is guilty," I said. "He and Violette Morgrave."

"Quentin informed me of the conversation the stable hand overhead between Lady Morgrave and Lady Deerhorn. He should have informed me sooner."

"Give the lad his due," Theodore said. "He's been taking care of the duchess, making sure she purged up all of the poison and sitting with her, wiping her brow."

I rose, my hand at my stomach. "I have to make her some riverwart tea. If she doesn't drink it immediately…"

"The dose of poison mustn't have been very strong," Dane said. "She's not too sick."

Thank Hailia for that, but I still wanted to see her. "The danger to me is over now that the Deerhorns have gone," I assured him. "I'm going to see her."

"Not all of the Deerhorns have left," he pointed out. "Violette Morgrave is still here. If you are seen helping the duchess, she can report you to the authorities. The duke will support her, since he clearly wants his wife dead."

"It's just a tea," I told him. "I'm an apothecary." He hesitated so I added, "I'm allowed to dispense teas to ease a stomach ache."

He stood. "Then I'll fetch the water."

I'd picked enough riverwart in the cottage garden to make three cups of tea. I didn't make it as strong as the antidote given to Miranda after she'd been poisoned. By diluting the riverwart in the water, Kitty would gently expel the rest of the poison from her body rather than do it quickly and violently.

I poured the warm tea into a jar and joined the men at the horses. Dane assisted Balthazar into the saddle then held the reins of Theodore's horse. Theodore didn't mount immediately, however.

"What is it, Theo?" Balthazar asked.

Theodore's lips flattened. "I find it hard to believe the duke would murder his wife in cold blood. The duchess is a fine woman, very amenable. What can he possibly have against her?"

"She's not Lady Violette Morgrave," Balthazar said. "Make no mistake, that woman is her mother's daughter. She's manipulative and knows just how to make a vain, weak man like the duke do her bidding."

"He certainly is vain, but I'm not so sure about weak," I said. "He's too cruel to be weak. He tried to force himself on Lady Claypool in the garden one evening."

Theodore gasped.

"He also wants an heir," I went on. "Kitty hasn't fallen pregnant in two years of marriage. To him, that's too long. He's hoping Violette will give him an heir."

"But she has no children of her own," Theodore said. "How can he be sure she will fall pregnant?"

"She's manipulative," Balthazar said again. "No doubt she has convinced him she's fertile."

We rode to the palace, and Dane escorted me to Kitty's apartment. Her ladies' maid, Prudence, let us in, although her displeasure was written into every groove surrounding her pinched lips.

Kitty lay beneath the covers on the large canopied bed. Her eyes were two deep pits amid her pale face, but they were alert rather than glassy. She managed a smile upon seeing me.

"Josie." She lifted her hand and I took it. "I'm so glad you're here."

"How do you feel?" I asked. "Any nausea?"

"No medical questions," Dane warned.

"I feel better," Kitty said. "I think the poison has left my body." Her fingers tightened around my hand, and I was pleased to see she had a good amount of strength.

I glanced at the bowl on the floor beside the bed. "Let me empty this for you."

"Prudence will do it."

I picked it up anyway and took it into the bathroom where I sniffed the contents. Beneath the stink of stomach juices was the distinctive sickly sweet smell of cane flower, the same poison that had been used on my father. Thank Hailia the poisoner hadn't used enough to kill her.

I emptied the contents of the bowl into the small bath and flushed it down the drain with the entire pail of water. I took the bowl back into the bedchamber and met the maid's stern gaze with my own.

"I brought you some tea," I said to Kitty. I removed the jar from my pack and filled the cup by the bed.

Kitty sat up and sipped. I waited until she'd drunk all of it.

"You look as though you need some rest," I said, choosing my words carefully in the presence of Prudence.

"She does," Prudence said. "Please leave. Take your guards with you, Captain. There's no need for them to be here."

"She was poisoned," Dane said. "There is every reason to keep a watch stationed with the duchess."

She made a scoffing sound. "She merely has a weak constitution and a fanciful imagination. She wasn't poisoned, she just ate something that had gone off."

Kitty's lashes lowered and she sank into the pillows. She'd given up fighting this woman. Prudence was the duke's creature, and Kitty, for all her high status, had no power over her.

Prudence crossed her arms and regarded me coolly. "I ordered you to leave."

"You are the one who will leave," Dane said.

The maid bristled. "I will not. My orders are to remain with the duchess at all times."

"Leave," he said again. "Or my men will remove you."

The two guards moved up alongside her, hands on sword hilts. The maid's mouth worked but no sound came out. She turned quickly and marched out of the bedchamber. One of the guards closed the door.

Kitty expelled a long breath. "Thank you, Captain. I thought I'd never be rid of her."

"Do you know how the poison was administered?" I asked.

"It must have been in my meal last night. Prudence served it in here. My husband has banned me from joining the other ladies, you see. It was him, Josie. I know it. Prudence might have been the one to administer the poison, but it was done at his bidding."

I looked to Dane. "What can we do?"

"Without proof? Nothing," he said.

I rubbed my aching forehead. Poor Kitty. She deserved justice. "At least it wasn't a strong dose," I said. "But next time, they might not make the same mistake."

"Which is why you're going to leave the palace, Your Grace," Dane said. "Pack your things and return home."

"I wouldn't be safe there either," she murmured. "No, I won't leave the duke."

"But he's trying to kill you!" I cried.

"You misunderstand, Josie. I'm not staying because I still love him. I'm staying because I'm the Duchess of Gladstow. If I leave, it is an admission of defeat. I might as well just give Violette my title on a platter." She fussed with the bedcovers that had fallen to her waist. "I will show him, show them both, that I will not be set aside."

"Kitty, he's not trying to set you aside. He's trying to kill you. You're risking your life by staying."

"I agree with Josie," Dane said. "My men can only protect you so much. If the duke commands them to leave your chambers, they'll have no choice. You'll be vulnerable to another attack, particularly if your maid continues to work for him."

She nibbled at her lower lip. "I see your point."

"So you'll leave," I said.

"No."

"But—"

"I won't give in, Josie." She caught both my hands in hers. "I will be careful with my food. I won't eat a thing until Prudence has eaten half. Or I'll go to the kitchens myself and eat with the staff. I've always wanted to see how the servants dine."

I groaned. "This isn't an entertainment."

"You mustn't worry. I'll be very careful from now on."

I sighed. How could I get through to her?

"There is another way." Dane's voice sliced clear through the silence.

Kitty leaned forward, her interest piqued as well. "Go on, Captain."

"Do you remember the tea you made for Leon?" he said to me.

"To relieve his constipation," I said. "I remember. What about it?"

"Make some for the maid. Add it to her tea, her food, anything she consumes."

Kitty pulled a face. "I think I follow. You plan for her to be frequently absent in order to relieve herself. Actually, I don't follow. How will that protect me?"

"If she can't adequately perform her duties, the duke will dismiss her. We'll make sure she's replaced with someone we can trust. A palace maid, perhaps, or a woman from the village."

"Josie, can you make some of that potion?" Kitty asked.

"I'll have it ready this afternoon," I said.

"In the meantime, my men will remain here." Dane nodded at the two guards and they nodded back.

He opened the door and waited for me to exit ahead of him, but Kitty caught my hand. She waved me closer and I bent down to her level. "Your captain is both handsome and clever," she whispered, her warm eyes shining. "You're very lucky."

"He's not my captain," I whispered back.

"He could be, if you put in a little effort. It only requires you to use your femininity a little more effectively."

I had no idea how to do what she suggested but I smiled and thanked her for the advice, then realized what I was admitting by doing so. "He's not my captain," I said again so there could be no mistake.

158

"Of course." She winked.

It would seem I wasn't going to get through to her. Without telling her the full story of the memory loss, I doubted she would accept any explanation I gave.

Dane and I headed along the service corridors to the garrison. His profile was steely, his brow heavy, but that could have been a result of the shadows cast by the torches in the dark recesses.

"I'll escort you back to the cottage," he said. "I can wait while you make up the concoction for the maid then bring it back. There's no need for you to also return."

"I could return to the village now that it's safe."

"I'd prefer you stayed at the cottage until I depart from the palace. I won't leave until I know Mull is completely safe."

"Ah. About that…" I cleared my throat. "Can we talk?"

"That depends," he said.

"On what?"

"On whether you're going to use your femininity on me."

My heart did a little flutter. "Do you want me to?"

His pace slowed. "Yes," he murmured.

I caught his hand and stopped, forcing him to face me. Slowly, slowly, his gaze lifted to meet mine. My heart skipped a beat at the intensity in the deep orbs. He hadn't looked at me like that in some time.

I wanted to reach up and capture his face, to kiss him senseless right there in the light of a flickering torch. I wanted to tell him I loved him, and that I knew he had feelings for me. But I didn't want him to discard his vow either. Not until he was ready.

I warred with myself and in the end, he made the decision.

He sighed then dragged his hand through his hair and looked away. "You wished to say something."

"Right. Yes." I searched for a way to tell him. After that interlude, I suspected everything I had planned to say would come out wrong. So I just gave him the simplest version. "I'm leaving with you."

He cocked his head to the side. "We agreed that you should stay here. I'll come back if…if I am free to do so."

"I didn't agree to that. And if you are not free to come back... at least we can say goodbye."

"You think that will make it easier? Merdu, Josie, it will be hard enough if I learn I have a wife. It will be even harder if you are there."

"I can't simply wait here for your return. It will be torture."

"You can get on with your life."

"Could you, if our positions were reversed?"

He looked down at his boots. "It's safer for you here now that the Deerhorns are gone."

"Safer but lonely without you. There'll be nothing for me here once you've left. If I go, I'll miss Meg but she's the only one. Mull doesn't even feel like my home, anymore."

He tilted his head back and blinked up at the ceiling. "You're making this so hard. I don't want to leave you behind—"

"Then don't."

"But if I have a wife..."

"*If.* It's not a certainty." I touched his chin so that he'd look at me and I offered him a weak smile. "We'll face that obstacle *if* it arises. But I *am* coming with you, Dane. You can't get rid of me that easily."

His lips quirked. "That's the problem. I don't want to."

Andreas, one of the warrior priests, appeared at the end of the corridor. "Thank the goddess, I found someone." He jogged up to us. "I'm looking for the garrison but these tunnels are more confusing than the ones beneath the temple. Can you direct me?"

"We're heading that way," Dane said, setting off.

Andreas looked at me, at Dane's retreating figure, and back at me. "My apologies, Josie. I interrupted something."

"Not at all." We followed Dane to the garrison where some of the guards sat along with several warrior priests, Balthazar and Theodore.

"How is the duchess?" Theodore asked me.

"A little unwell but she'll recover quickly," I said. "She's worried, though. She's certain her husband ordered her maid to add the poison to her food."

"Are you sure she was poisoned?" Balthazar asked.

I nodded.

"What precautions are you employing?" he asked Dane.

"Josie and I will set a plan in motion this afternoon," Dane said. "I'll escort her back to the cottage now."

Balthazar tapped the end of his walking stick into the flagstone floor. "Just a moment, *Dane*. Rhys has a report to give you."

Some of the guards frowned at Balthazar, perhaps wondering if he'd lost his mind. Others repeated Dane's name in curious whispers.

"Dane?" Quentin asked, his head tilted to the side like a quizzical puppy. "Have you remembered his first name, Balthazar? Is your memory returning?"

Balthazar folded his hands over the walking stick head and leaned on it. "It has not. While we know him as Hammer, he has always known his name was Dane."

"He only saw fit to inform us this morning," Theodore added with a pout in his voice.

"Dane," Quentin repeated. "It's a good name. Better than Hammer."

Max grunted. "Why'd you take so long to tell us?"

"I had my reasons. Rhys," Dane said to the master of the warrior priests. "Your report."

"Wait," Quentin said. "I'm confused. Do we call you Dane now?"

"Call me Captain."

Dane and Rhys spoke quietly at the table while the rest either watched on or returned to their conversations. Max pulled out a chair and signaled for me to join him.

"You knew, didn't you?" he asked.

"He told me his real name some time ago," I said. "He didn't want me calling him Hammer."

He grunted, but there was no resentment in it.

Quentin sat on the edge of the table near me, a bowl in hand. "Does the duchess need me, Josie? I have a cloth to wipe her brow and a bowl for purging into." He tossed the cloth into the bowl.

"She needs to rest now," I said.

"I should check that she drank all of the tea you made for her."

"Let her rest."

His shoulders slumped before his face lifted again. "I can keep the maid away."

"The guards on duty are doing that," Max said. "Do as Josie says. The duchess doesn't want to look at your spotty face while she's recovering."

"Can I be put on the next guard duty?"

Max nodded at the board where a roster had been written. "Remove Ray's name and add your own."

Dane and Rhys stood and an expectant hush fell over the room. "Master Rhys reports that the riots have completely stopped," Dane announced. "He and his men will maintain a presence in Mull tomorrow to make sure trouble doesn't flare up again. If all remains calm, they will leave the day after. Balthazar is going with them, as is Theodore." He met Max's gaze. "And me."

Murmurs once again rippled around the room, louder this time, but Quentin's voice rose above the noise. "You're leaving us, Captain? But...you can't!"

"I want to find out more about myself. Learning about Balthazar and Amar's lives in Tilting might help. It's not likely, but it's an opportunity I need to explore."

Quentin plopped down on a chair, the bowl in his lap. He looked like he wanted to be sick into it.

"Anyone who wants to do the same is welcome to travel to Tilting with us," Dane went on. "The rest can remain here. If we learn anything in the capital, word will be sent back."

The guards glanced at one another. Three declared they would travel to Tilting, but the rest looked uncertain. Only Max declared his intention to stay.

"The dukes will want some guards to remain at the palace," he said. "Even if they leave, someone should protect the property."

I smiled at him. I knew he chose to stay to be near Meg.

"There will be a need for other servants here too," Balthazar added. "It's likely the dukes will both remain for a little while, at least. Neither of them are willing to give up the power base."

"Balthazar, meet with the heads of each department," Dane

said. "They can inform their staff and find out who wishes to stay and who will go. We depart at dawn the day after tomorrow." He indicated to me that it was time to leave, and I followed him amid an increasing hum of voices as the guards discussed their options.

"Do you think many will come with us?" I asked as we crossed the forecourt.

"Hard to say. Some see this as their home now and aren't interested in learning about their pasts, but most are. Many lack the courage to venture away, however. I expect many to stay and wait."

"Quentin didn't commit to staying or going, but I expect him to follow you," I said.

"He might, but he has a woman here now."

"He does?" That explained some things.

"I'm disappointed Max chose to stay," he said. "I've grown used to relying on him." It was the first time he'd ever shown something resembling friendship to any of his men. He considered Balthazar and Theodore to be friends, but they were his equals at the palace. Max was different.

We passed a sedan chair being set down on the forecourt tiles by its carriers. The Duke of Gladstow stepped out, and his gaze fell on Dane. I stood very still, hoping he would consider the captain's companion as beneath his notice. I didn't think he'd seen me when I rescued Lady Claypool from his clutches on the night of the revels, but I preferred to avoid him now anyway.

"Captain," he said. "Your men are disturbing my wife. Remove them from her chamber immediately."

"I will not, Your Grace," Dane said.

The duke's spine stiffened. "I order you to remove them!"

"I cannot act without the Duke of Buxton's agreement."

"You put them there without mine," the duke ground out through gritted teeth.

Dane bowed. "Your Grace."

The duke's gaze drifted to me for the first time. He frowned, as if he was trying to recollect where he'd seen me. I held my breath, but he strode off without acknowledging me in any way.

"Our plan had better work," I said, watching him go. "I can't leave without knowing Kitty is safe."

* * *

THE FOLLOWING DAY, Dane accompanied me into the village, but we parted ways outside the Divers' house. Meg received me with a bone-crunching hug.

"Max told me you were safe at the palace, but I've still been worried," she said as we settled at the kitchen table with her mother and a loaf of freshly baked bread. "After Lord Xavier took you away, I was so scared."

"We all were," Mistress Diver said.

"The Deerhorns have fled the village," I told them. "You no longer have to worry about their interference."

"Thank the goddess," Mistress Diver muttered. "With them gone and those two thugs from The Row in jail with Ned Perkin, the village can finally begin to return to normal."

"As normal as it can be with so many newcomers arriving every day plus the displaced residents from The Row on the streets," Meg said. "The council needs to build more houses, and quickly."

"Now that the Deerhorns can't influence the governor, conditions will improve," I said.

"Supplies will start to flow into Mull much faster than they have been," Mistress Diver added. "Some say the Deerhorns were controlling how quickly goods were processed in the customs house. Their departure will unblock the bottleneck."

I finished my slice of bread slowly as I tried to think of a way to tell them about my imminent departure, but I lacked the courage. I'd already informed Meg but she mustn't have told her mother or Mistress Diver would have tried to talk me out of it already.

I waited until she left to call on a friend, but I still avoided the conversation with Meg. Instead, I told her the other palace news. "Kitty was poisoned by her husband. It was only a mild dose, and she's recovering well. She looks better today."

"How awful! Has the sheriff been notified?"

"We can't prove who did it, although we're sure the maid administered the poison at the duke's direction. The sheriff won't dare arrest him without solid proof."

"Surely the duchess will leave him now. She can't possibly stay."

"She won't leave. She refuses to hand her husband and title over to Violette Morgrave." I told her about the tisane I'd given the maid to purge her bowels and our plan to replace her with someone who'd do our bidding and not the duke's.

"The tisane has begun to take effect," I said. "When I visited Kitty in her rooms before coming here, she was alone except for the guard. Her maid was indisposed."

Meg chuckled. "Good. I hope she soils herself."

"Kitty says her husband is irritated by the maid's frequent absences. She thinks he'll want to replace her very soon to resume his poisoning scheme."

Meg's smile began slowly, tentatively, until it grew into a sly grin. "Replace her with me."

"Absolutely not! It's much too dangerous. If the duke discovered your duplicity, he might kill you."

"So it's all right to risk the life of a stranger, but not mine?"

"That's not what I meant."

"Josie, listen to me. I'm smart enough to avoid the duke's plotting. I can also try to convince the duchess to leave him. Besides, I want to do something other than sit here and work in my mother's kitchen." She picked up a wooden spoon she'd been using to stir the pot hanging over the fire and waved it in my face.

"I can't put you in the duke's way," I said, taking the spoon off her. "I'd never forgive myself if something happened to you."

"But—"

"No, Meg." I set the spoon down out of her reach. "There's something else I need to tell you before Dane gets back."

"Dane?"

"His real name." I waved off her questions. "I'm leaving with him tomorrow."

She gawped at me. "So soon?"

"We're traveling to Tilting with the priests and some of the other servants. Ever since the priests recognized Balthazar and Amar, Dane has wanted to find out if there's a link between their lives and his."

"I know you said you wanted to leave with him, but I thought I'd have time to change your mind."

"There's nothing for me in Mull if he leaves." I reached across the table. "Except you."

"And I am not enough to keep you here."

I winced. It sounded unkind. "I want to be with Dane. I want to help him find his home."

She sat back, her arms over her chest, a frown on her face. "You're leaving me here, alone, with stifling parents."

"They love you."

"My mother wants me to be just like her, in the kitchen with children at my feet. But I want more. I want..." She sighed. "I'm not really sure what I want."

I understood. After my mother's death, my father had stifled me too. Perhaps it was why Meg and I were such good friends. We both wanted to live fuller lives, although it was a side of Meg that I'd only recently seen emerge. I suspected there was a reason for that.

"Max is staying behind because of you," I said.

Her cheeks flushed. "This isn't about him. It's about me. Just like your desire to leave isn't entirely about the captain."

"It is a little bit," I conceded. "But you're right. It's time to see what's outside Mull."

She clasped my hand. "So you agree I should become the duchess's new maid."

I hesitated then nodded. "But only if Max keeps a *very* close eye on the situation."

Her blush returned, but she smiled too.

* * *

I spent the afternoon saying goodbye to neighbors, friends and former patients. Many were upset to see me go and asked me to reconsider. Some even told me my father would be horrified, but those who remembered my mother's free spirit conceded that she would have let me go with her blessing. By the time I returned to the Divers' house, my heart was full and I'd shed more tears than I cared to admit.

I was about to go inside when Dane hailed me. He rode quickly up the street, and reined his horse to a stop beside me. I knew from the look on his face that something was wrong. Very wrong.

"What is it?" I asked.

"The gem," he said heavily. "It's gone."

CHAPTER 13

J grabbed the bridle as he jumped down, landing softly on his good foot. "What do you mean?" I asked. "Did you lose it?"

"It was dug up and removed. It's possible whoever took it didn't know the significance of it, they simply thought it a valuable jewel."

"Do you believe that?"

He closed his eyes and shook his head. "I don't understand how anyone could have known where it was. And if they saw me bury it, why wait until now to remove it? But...I'm sure I wasn't seen."

"Have you told anyone where it was? Anyone at all?"

He shook his head.

"Where did you bury it?" I asked.

"The graveyard."

"Then it was probably dug up by accident. Brant said the area was decimated by the rioters. I was about to head there for one last visit."

"Brant told you this?"

I nodded. "He returned from the village via the graveyard when Barborough chased him. He said the rioters pushed over headstones and did all kinds of damage. It's a travesty, and now one of those rioters has the gem. We should visit the silversmith in the village to see if someone tried to sell it to him." My voice dwindled as he shook his head.

"The area where I buried it wasn't touched by the rioters," he said. "The gravestones were upright and the only earth that was dug up was the spot where I buried the gem."

"The riverwart," I said on a breath. "You buried the gem when you planted the riverwart at my father's gravestone." I groaned as a wave of nausea swamped me. "It's my fault. I told him."

I sat on the front porch and buried my head in my hands. Dane sat beside me.

"What are you talking about?" he asked gently.

"After Brant told us about the graveyard, I asked him if my parents' headstones were damaged. In describing the location, I mentioned you planted a riverwart at the time of my father's death. He must have guessed you'd planted it to hide the gem buried there."

"Brant," he bit off. "At least we know who has it."

I felt even sicker. "If Brant has it, he can use his wishes to gain whatever he wants."

He got up and put out his hand to assist me to my feet. "Then we'll make sure he doesn't."

We raced back to the palace and searched the garrison and dormitory for Brant. We eventually found him in the commons enjoying a pie in the dining room.

"Brant, with me," Dane barked.

Brant hunched over his plate. "I'm eating."

Dane grabbed him by his sore arm and pulled him to his feet. Brant gritted his teeth but didn't make a sound. Dane marched him from the commons to the palace corridor then to Balthazar's office. I trailed behind and shut the office door.

Balthazar and Theodore looked up from the lists they'd been writing. "Making trouble again, Brant?" asked Balthazar.

"He took the gem," Dane said.

Theodore gasped and Balthazar dropped his pen. The ink spread over his paper, ruining his list.

Dane told them where he'd hidden the gem. Both men realized before he'd finished what had happened.

"I told him where to find it," I said on a groan. "Why didn't I realize earlier that's where you'd buried it? It's so obvious."

"It's not your fault, Josie," Balthazar said gently. "If Dane had informed you, you would have kept quiet."

"Or if he'd told *us*, we could have stopped you," Theodore added with a glare for Dane.

Dane ignored the jibe. "Hand it over, Brant."

"It wasn't me," Brant snapped.

The knuckles on Dane's fingers turned white as he dug into Brant's arm. Brant growled and tried to wrench free, but Dane relentlessly bore down. "Hand it over," he snarled.

"It wasn't me! Merdu and Hailia, don't you think I would have used it by now to get my memory back?"

"Perhaps you wished only for yours to return and you're pretending now. Or maybe you lied and you don't have the wishes. Maybe you plan to sell the gem to the Deerhorns or Lord Barborough. Or maybe you haven't considered how you want to use the wishes yet."

Brant wiped a bead of sweat from near his ear with his shoulder.

Dane whipped out his sword and dug the point into Brant's throat. A drop of blood beaded.

"Don't!" Theodore cried. "Please, Dane, I'm begging you, don't hurt him. You don't want it on your conscience."

"Where is it?" Dane ground out.

"You won't kill me," Brant said with a smirk. "Not if you think I have it."

Dane lowered the sword to Brant's groin. "But I could castrate you."

Brant swallowed.

Balthazar put up his hands for calm. "Let's think about this a moment. Put away the sword."

Dane lowered it but didn't sheath it.

"What if it wasn't Brant?" Balthazar asked. "There were dozens of people in the garrison when Josie told us about the flower."

"Who?" Dane asked.

"Us, for starters." Balthazar pointed to himself and Theodore.

I counted on my fingers. "Erik, Quentin, Zeke, Ray and Yen.

Amar was there and Deanna from the menagerie."

Theodore rattled off the names of the servants and guards I didn't know. "Two dozen, at least," he said.

Brant's lips stretched, revealing the gap in his teeth. "Any of them could have taken it."

"And done what with it?" Dane asked.

"Sold it."

"We all knew you hid it shortly after Josie's father's death," Balthazar agreed. "It isn't difficult to come to the conclusion that you buried the gem when you planted the plant."

"Except *I* didn't conclude that," Brant said triumphantly. "Nor Josie, obviously."

"Nor I." Balthazar looked to Theodore, his bushy brows raised.

Theodore held up his hands in surrender. "Nor I. But someone did."

"Can I go now?" Brant whined.

Dane opened the door. "Get out before I change my mind and throw you in the palace prison."

Brant looked relieved as he headed out the door, only to stop, frowning. "Wait. What if this is all a trick to get me to believe you no longer have the gem?"

"Why would he do that?" Balthazar asked.

"So I'll chase after the Deerhorns or Barborough instead, thinking they have it."

Dane went to close the door in Brant's face. "If I wanted you to leave, I'd make you."

Brant snorted. Dane lowered his gaze to Brant's sore arm and Brant skulked off along the corridor.

"Is he right?" Theodore asked Dane. "Was that just a trick on him? On us?"

Dane gave him a frosty glare. "The gem is gone."

"So what do we do?"

"I'll ask the silversmith in the village if someone tried to sell it to him, but…" Dane shrugged.

"You don't think it was a random stranger who happened to dig it up during the riots," Theodore finished.

Balthazar picked up his ink stained list and sighed. "We have to leave the palace not knowing who has it."

"Show me your lists of who is coming with us," Dane said.

He read the names and pointed out that most of those who'd been in the garrison when I mentioned the riverwart plant wanted to go to Tilting too. "I'll encourage the rest to join us," he said. "We'll keep the suspects close."

Balthazar accepted the list. "By encourage you mean..."

"Ask nicely."

The master of the palace looked relieved. "As long as Brant doesn't have it, it's not a disaster."

"You believe him?" I asked.

"Don't you?"

I looked to Dane and he shook his head. If the person who knew him best didn't trust him, then I saw no reason to either.

"I'd wager Barborough got it," Theodore said. "He knows what it's for and he's slippery."

"He wasn't in the garrison meeting," I pointed out. "He didn't know where it was hidden."

"Someone could have told him where to look."

"If he does have it," Dane said, "he might approach Brant and buy a wish to use for himself or for Vytill's benefit."

"If Brant can be believed and he did inherit them when the king died," I added.

So many ifs. It would seem we would be departing the palace without the gem, and a cloud of uncertainty would follow us all the way to Tilting. At least we'd have the opportunity on the journey to keep an eye on Brant, and the others, and take back the gem if we could discover who had it.

"How is the duchess?" Dane asked.

"Probably wishing Quentin weren't on duty so much," Theodore said with a smile. "He seems to be doubling as her maid."

"So the tisane is continuing to work on Prudence?" I asked.

"Like magic."

"Has the duke talked about replacing her?"

Balthazar shook his head. "There's a possibility that your plan won't work, Dane. The duke might fetch a woman from his own estate, someone he knows he can manipulate."

Dane folded his arms and frowned in thought. "Pre-empt him. Suggest a palace maid first. Do you have one in mind?"

"I do," I said before Balthazar could answer. "Meg wants the position."

"It could be dangerous," Dane warned.

"She knows that and still wants to do it. I think she'd be rather good."

"Advise the duke," Dane said to Balthazar. "Tell him Meg's a palace maid. He doesn't speak to our servants and won't bother to learn the truth."

* * *

I RETURNED to Mull later in the day to inform Meg that the duke agreed to make her Kitty's new maid, and she was to return to the palace immediately to be briefed by Dane and Balthazar. I took the opportunity to pack all my belongings and say a final farewell to the Divers.

It was dusk by the time we left in the palace carriage, my bag strapped to the roof alongside Meg's. She'd taken all of her clothing with her, even though I told her she'd be given a Gladstow maid outfit to wear.

"Just in case they don't have one in my size," she said, waving at her parents and siblings through the rear window.

I waved too as fresh tears welled. "I can't believe I'm leaving," I murmured.

Meg squeezed my hand. "It's not forever."

"I know."

She faced forward, smiling. Ever since I'd given her the news, she couldn't wipe the grin off her face. "No more cooking," she said. "No more scrubbing the floors until my fingers bleed."

"Your fingers never bled from scrubbing floors."

"I'm going to live in a palace!"

"You never struck me as the sort who cared about palaces," I said with a laugh.

"I don't, really. But I've never lived in one before and I find I want to try new experiences."

"You do realize you'll be at the duchess's beck and call. She might be more demanding than your mother."

"I doubt that. My mother's a tyrant when it comes to cleaning and cooking. The duchess seems like the sweetest thing."

"She is. That's why I'm worried about her. She's not wily enough to avoid her husband's traps."

"That's what I'm for." She put her arm around my shoulders and hugged me. "Don't worry, Josie. I'll take care of her."

"And yourself too." Even so, I would give her a copy of the poison antidote recipes before I left.

* * *

WHEN THE CARRIAGE deposited us at the palace gate, it became clear plans had changed. Several servants carried trunks and boxes across the large forecourt and out of the gate. Theodore stood with an air of authority, overseeing them.

"What's happening?" I asked him. "Who do these belong to?"

"The Duchess of Gladstow," he said, checking a list in the flickering light of a torch. "The duke is sending her home to their estate near Tilting."

"With me?" Meg asked.

"With you." He looked up from his list. "Welcome to domestic service, Meg. I'll show you to the duchess's rooms soon. Don't bother unpacking."

"Why is he sending her home?" I asked.

"He claims it's not safe this close to Mull after the riots." He urged a footman struggling with a heavy box to hurry up. "I don't think anyone believed him."

"So what's his real reason for sending her away?"

"To control her?" he said with a shrug. "To put her among servants he has complete authority over?"

That did seem likely. According to Kitty, her husband ran the household, and the housekeeper was employed by him. Meg would be her only ally in a nest of vipers.

"I don't like this," I said. "Meg, you shouldn't go with her. It's too dangerous now."

She picked up her bag from where the coachman had deposited it. "I'm going, Josie, and that's final."

I appealed to Theodore, but he was no help.

"They'll travel with us to Tilting, and men from the duke's retinue will collect her from the city," he said. "The estate isn't far. Come on, Meg. I'll take you up now. At least you won't have to say goodbye to Josie just yet."

I watched them go, wondering if I was the only one who thought it was too dangerous for her. Dane would probably agree, and Max certainly would. I headed to the garrison, where I found them both enjoying some rare time off duty with other guards and several warrior priests. Dane even had his feet up on the table, although he lowered them upon seeing me.

Andreas pulled out a chair and invited me to sit with a friendly smile. "I hear you'll be riding in style with the duchess in her carriage," he said.

"I'm prepared to walk with the others." I indicated the guards and servants.

"The guards are taking horses, since we're now on official business for the duke," Dane said. "You can ride with me, but you'll be more comfortable in the carriage. Rhys has assured me the road to Tilting is fair at this time of year, barring any storms."

At the mention of his name, Rhys looked up from the cup he'd been staring into. "The journey will take twice as long, since many of the servants are walking," he said, a hint of frustration edging his tone.

"Your men can ride ahead," Dane said. "We don't need guides."

"The roads are dangerous," Rufus said. "Nobles' carriages in particular are a beacon for bandits."

Erik tossed the long ropes of hair off his shoulder with a jerk of his head. "Bandits will not worry us."

Max got Rufus's attention. "Do the bandits only want money and jewels?" he asked.

Rufus nodded. "Fine clothes, too, shoes…anything of value."

"What I mean is…" Max glanced at me. "What about women?"

Rufus followed his gaze. "Sometimes."

Max's grave look settled on Dane. "You're fine with Josie traveling on these roads?"

"The women will be safe," Dane assured him. "Unless you doubt your abilities as a swordsman."

Erik tapped his chest. "I will look after Meg for you, Max. And the duchess and Josie, too. I will have all the women."

"I think you mean *protect* all the women," Vizah said.

Yen snorted. "No, he means have."

"Is it too late to swap Meg for one of the palace maids?" Max asked no one in particular.

"She won't agree to it," I told him. "She wants to leave Mull. She wants to live a more interesting life."

"She'll be in Gladstow's house without anyone to protect her. It won't be interesting, it'll be treacherous."

"I tried telling her that. She's unfazed."

"She's brave," Vizah said with a nod. "I admire her."

Max folded his arms and fell into silence.

"It's not just Meg we should be concerned about," I said. "The duchess is returning to a place where she has no friends. It'll be easier to poison her there." I didn't need to mention the duke by name. Everyone understood, even the priests.

The rest of the group joined Max in morose silence, cutting their evening revels short.

I didn't see Meg again until the morning. She handed a letter to a palace footman on the forecourt and asked him to take it to her parents after she'd left. When we'd departed from Mull the day before, she hadn't known she was leaving the area.

"You should say goodbye in person," I said. "We can wait for you,"

"Absolutely not," she said. "My mother and sisters will cry, my father will forbid me to go, and my brother could very well lock me up until after you've all gone. It's better just to write a nice letter."

I didn't agree but kept my mouth shut. I wished I had a chance to say goodbye to my father before his death. Saying that out loud—even just thinking it—made me fear for her even more.

We followed dozens of other servants through the gate and along Grand Avenue. Some went to the stables but we diverted to the coach house where a carriage and a cart waited, laden with trunks and boxes of varying sizes. Footmen checked to make sure the luggage was secure while grooms looked over the horses one final time. The servants traveling with us assembled nearby, saying farewell to those staying behind. According to Balthazar, almost fifty wanted to leave with us. It made us a large traveling party, and yet the number was small when the total in service was close to a thousand.

Max broke free of the group and strode up to us. "It's not too late," he said to Meg.

She tilted her chin in defiance, a gesture that mere weeks ago she wouldn't have made in front of him. "I'm going."

His lips flattened, but he seemed to know he would be wasting his breath and only angering her if he argued.

"I thought *you* were staying behind," she added.

"I changed my mind." He turned and strode off to join the other guards.

Meg watched him go, a secretive smile on her lips.

I spotted Quentin standing a little apart from the group. He was talking to a small, broad-hipped girl with a sweet face who looked no older than him. She was crying, and he tried to console her, albeit unsuccessfully.

A sedan chair entered the large stable yard, followed by a second. The carriers deposited them and the duchess stepped out of one while Balthazar emerged from the other. Meg joined her new mistress.

Kitty still looked pale but otherwise healthy. She stood erect, a regal figure dressed in a deep blue skirt and matching jacket with a high collar and black braiding stitched down the front. It was a simple, elegant outfit, sensible for traveling. I hoped she'd hidden her jewels.

She beckoned me to join them. "You will travel with me, Josie. I wish for your company." Her ability to switch between friendly Kitty and grand duchess never ceased to amaze me.

"Yes, Your Grace."

She bestowed a smile on me then held out her hand to a hovering footman. He took it and assisted her into the carriage. Meg and I had to make our own way up the step.

Once inside, Kitty relaxed. She spread her skirts out on the seat beside her and folded her gloved hands in her lap as we set off at a slow pace behind several mounted guards, including Dane and half of the warrior priests. Behind us rode the other guards and priests, with the servants on foot bringing up the rear. Hundreds of other servants watched on, waving and wishing us good luck. Some were in tears. I waved at Dora and spotted Remy up ahead, a big grin splitting his face as he kept pace with the leading horses.

"Goodbye, Josie, and good luck," Laylana called out. She wore a gardening uniform, her hat in her hand. A man standing very close to her waved at us as we drove past. He was dressed in gold and crimson livery of the palace footmen yet the fingers of his right hand were stained dark. He must be the one sketching pictures of faces for Laylana so she could recognize people when she awoke without a memory. It was an enormous relief to know that her frequent memory losses no longer frightened her. Her life would always be stranger than most, however, unless her memory returned.

The footman stopped waving and rested his hand on her shoulder. She smiled up at him.

"Everyone has someone seeing them off," Kitty said quietly. "Except me."

It was true. Her husband hadn't escorted her to the coach house. No noblewomen had come to say goodbye. The only friend she'd made among them was Miranda, and she'd already left.

"Why are so many servants coming?" she asked, peering out the window.

"The palace has no need of them now that many of the nobles have left," I said.

"But why are they all going to Tilting? They can't all be originally from the capital."

Meg and I glanced at one another.

"What is it?" Kitty asked. "What haven't you told me?"

I didn't like giving away the servants' secret. It wasn't mine to tell. However, I couldn't think of a lie that would satisfy her. Besides, if she was going to spend the next few days with us, she was going to grow more suspicious.

"You have to promise not to tell a soul," I said. "Swear you won't."

She placed a hand to her heart. "I swear."

"Do you remember the rumors of magic?"

"Of course."

"They're true."

She didn't look at all surprised.

"Leon found a gem that granted him three wishes," I went on. "He wished to be a rich king."

Her eyes widened. "The king should never have been king?"

"In order to fulfill Leon's wish, the sorcerer needed a palace." I indicated the building behind us, a dominant presence in the landscape. "And a palace needs servants."

She gasped. "Are you saying he *created* them? They're not real?"

"They are real. We believe they already existed somewhere. The thing is, they have no memories of their lives before coming here."

She frowned. "None of them?"

I shook my head. "Not the highest servant nor the lowliest."

She sat back and blinked at me. "Miranda was right after all."

"She guessed about the memory loss?" I asked.

"Not that. She simply knew something was amiss with the palace staff." She looked past me through the rear window at the trail of servants following, waving at those who stood watching them go as if they were in a parade. "How very strange it must be for them."

I followed her gaze to see some of the remaining servants trudging back to the palace. Some of them might regret not coming with us. I suspected many of the servants who left would not return.

I, however, intended to. Mull was my home, as was the palace, in a way. It felt like a part of the village now, like an extra limb. But who knew how long I'd be away. When I came back, Mull might not even be recognizable. It would certainly change, but whether I would like those changes remained to be seen.

I faced forward again, towards my future, and clutched Meg's hand tightly.

CHAPTER 14

*P*rogress was slow, but those of us in the carriage didn't mind. Balthazar joined us and, for a while, we were content to talk quietly. Kitty asked us about village life. She seemed genuinely interested in what chores we did, how and where we did the marketing, and my somewhat unusual role as doctor's daughter, apothecary and midwife.

"I cannot believe that your parents simply allowed you to enter into service to me," she said to Meg. "Josie has no family to stop her doing as she pleases, but don't your parents have expectations for you?"

"They wish me to marry and have children, just as my mother did," Meg said.

"Naturally. But you defied them. I do hope I'm not the cause of dissent between you and your family."

"Not at all, Your Grace. I didn't defy them. They've never *insisted* I marry, nor did they forbid me to enter into service."

"Extraordinary," Kitty murmured. "To be free to make choices about when you marry, and whom…I envy you both." She laughed. "I sound like Miranda. At least her parents will never force her to wed an old, gouty beast."

"You could become a priestess," Balthazar said. "That would free you from your husband."

"Not quite," I said. "Because her husband is still living, she won't be accepted as a full priestess. The duke wouldn't be free to remarry either."

"I have to die if he is to get what he wants," Kitty added flatly.

"You would be safe in a temple, at least," Meg said.

"Or I might bring trouble to the temple's door."

We plunged into silence that lasted until Erik rode up. He rested a hand on the window sill and peered into the carriage.

Kitty, still jittery after the attempt on her life, reeled back.

Erik had been about to smile, but it disappeared without properly materializing. "Please, do not fear me, Kitty. I do not hurt women, only men who are my enemies. And maybe women who are my enemies too." He shrugged. "I do not yet know if I have any woman enemies, but I think I would not. I like to bed women, not fight them."

She swallowed and resumed the regal air of earlier. "That's all well and good, but in future, do not thrust your rather large head into a lady's carriage if you are not aiming to frighten her."

Erik grinned, which only seemed to irritate Kitty more.

"And you must refer to me as Your Grace. I will forgive you this once, since you have no memory of how things are."

"He's also from The Margin," I told her. "I don't think they have duchesses there."

"The Margin? But that's the other side of the world!"

"Just the other side of Widowmaker Peaks."

Erik frowned. "My Grace?"

"*Your* Grace," Kitty said, raising her voice.

"Why must I call you this when your name is Kitty?"

"Because I am a duchess."

"Then why not Duchess Kitty? The king was King Leon."

Kitty hesitated then with a toss of her curls said, "It's the way it is."

He drummed his fingers on the window sill. "Your husband wants to kill you."

Kitty wrinkled her nose. "Must everyone know my business?"

"Yes, if they are to keep you safe on this journey," Balthazar said.

She sighed.

Erik tapped his chest. "I will not let him harm you, Duchess. Stay close to me."

"Thank you," she said. "That's very kind."

"Very close. Especially at night. We will share a room at the inn."

Kitty looked appalled. "We're sleeping in an inn? But there are noble houses on the way, some of them quite grand." She folded her hands in her lap. "We shall stay in one of those. Erik, please inform the captain."

"We won't be staying in noble houses," Balthazar said. "Or even farm houses. Your husband will expect it."

"Oh. Yes, of course. It is probably best to stay at an inn."

Erik beamed. "So you agree? I will look forward to it. You will enjoy me."

"No, I didn't—" Kitty leaned out the window but Erik had already ridden off. She pulled her head back in, a hand to her hat to hold it in place. "Did he mean what I think he means?"

"Yes," I said, trying not to smile. "Don't worry. I'll explain later that you didn't agree to his proposal. Unless you don't want me to."

"Josie! Honestly, you are as wicked as Miranda sometimes. Not only am I a married woman, but I certainly wouldn't want to go near that man. Just because he's extraordinarily handsome and intriguing, we cannot overlook his ill manners." She turned back to the window and stared out of it for the rest of the afternoon.

* * *

THE PROBLEM with traveling in such a large group was that a single inn couldn't accommodate all of us. The priests camped outside the village with some of the servants also willing to do so, but the rest of us filled out the inn's rooms and stables. I squeezed into Kitty's modest bedchamber along with Meg.

"I've never shared a room with anyone before," Kitty said as Meg undressed her. "Not even my sister, the mean little frog. Do you know, I haven't seen her in two years, since my marriage."

"I find that so strange," Meg said. "My sisters are a lot younger than me, but we're quite close."

"I'll wear the green dress with the gold braid on the sleeves for dinner, thank you, Meg."

"Are you sure?" Meg asked. "It's a lovely dress and you don't want to attract unwanted attention from the locals."

"You mean thieves. Don't worry. I won't wear my best jewels, just the choker with the pearl pendant and matching earrings. It's very subdued. Perfect for dinner at a rustic countryside inn."

I left them to their chatter and went in search of Dane. The ancient floor of the inn creaked with every step and I had to duck my head to go through doorways. Downstairs, it smelled of ale and, more faintly, of wood smoke.

I expected to see the guards and servants drinking, but there were only the servants, dressed in ordinary clothes, not palace livery. Balthazar and Theodore were not among them.

I found Dane outside, helping the stable hands with the horses, some of his men also assisting. The rest of the guards were nowhere to be seen.

"Settled in?" he asked me as he brushed down Lightning's coat.

I rubbed the horse's nose. "I think so. Kitty is changing for dinner now. She seemed to think it important to have at least one clothing change today. I hope there's enough food for everyone."

"Rhys sent men ahead to warn all the villages along the way. Speaking of the priests, they might leave us tomorrow. The master is anxious to return to Tilting and we don't need their guidance."

"He doesn't like leaving the city for long."

"I think he's worried about friends or family getting caught in the troubles. Vizah told me that Rhys feels responsible for a street urchin he took under his wing."

"He's a good man." I continued to rub Lightning's nose since the horse seemed to enjoy it and I couldn't touch Dane. "Where are the rest of your men?"

"Scouting, looking out for signs that the duke has paid someone to attack the duchess."

The thought sent a chill through me and I shivered. My hand

stilled and Lightning nuzzled it. "Sorry," I told him. "Your master distracted me."

"You don't have to worry." Dane's voice was molten gold, and suddenly very close. "I'm staying in the room next to yours and Max is on the other side."

I gave him a reassuring smile. "The floorboards creak like an old man's joints. We'll hear someone approaching."

He rubbed Lightning's nose too, his hand inches above mine. And then it covered mine. It was warm but not soft thanks to the calloused palms. "Josie..." he began, not looking at me.

"Yes?" I whispered.

"I'm glad you came with us."

I smiled. "So am I."

He removed his hand just as suddenly as he'd placed it there and turned. It wasn't until I turned too that I realized he'd heard someone approach.

"Sergeant," he said to Max. He waited until Max joined us before continuing. "What did you find?"

Max gave his head a slight shake. "Nothing."

Dane nodded and Max walked off.

"What was that about?" I asked.

"He searched Brant's pack in the stables but didn't find the gem."

"That was a risk."

"Brant is with the others, scouting the village. I was keeping look out." He glanced down at my hand. "Badly."

I almost apologized for being a distraction, but it seemed a little absurd. "If I were him, I'd keep the gem on my person. If I had it."

"Captain!" called Erik, striding up to us.

Dane took a small step away from me. "Is there a problem?"

"Aye." Erik's earnest look worried me.

"Did you find something?"

"Nothing. The others are on their way back, but I walk quick to speak to you. Captain, I wish for a room inside tonight, not a straw mat in the stables."

"No," Dane said without a blink of an eye.

"You don't like sleeping in stables?" I asked Erik. "I didn't think you sensitive about such things."

"I do not care where I sleep. In stables, pig pen...I will sleep anywhere." He shrugged. "But the duchess will not like to come to me out there."

I pressed my lips together to suppress my smile.

"That's why you're in the stables," Dane said.

Erik didn't seem to understand. "I will go to her—"

"You will go nowhere near the duchess."

Erik sighed then walked off, only to stop and turn back. "Unless she wishes me to be near her, yes?"

"Fine. Unless she wishes it. Otherwise, stay away."

Erik grinned.

"This will be interesting," I said, watching him go.

Dane flashed me a rare smile. "We need something to entertain us on the journey."

* * *

WE SET OFF EARLY, meeting the priests just outside the village. After exchanging words with Dane, Balthazar and Amar, they rode off at a swift pace. We continued, slowly.

I spent much of the day walking with the servants. My legs needed the exercise after spending most of the previous day in the carriage, and I wanted to keep an eye on Brant. He looked comfortable on his horse, his injured arm resting on his thigh rather than held close to his body. Not once did he touch his doublet at his chest or anywhere the gem could have been hidden. What he did do with regular frequency was glare at Dane's back.

Except for when he had to relieve himself by the side of the road, that is. He didn't even go into the bushes, but simply stood there, whistling as if he didn't have a care in the world.

Meg made a sound of disgust in the back of her throat. "Don't look," she told the duchess. "He's revolting."

We rounded a bend and Dane's head suddenly jerked to the left. He dismounted and drew his sword before plunging into the thick bushes that edged the road. "Surround the carriage! Josie, get inside. Yen, Ray, with me!"

The two guards followed but they were well behind Dane by the time they crashed through the forest underbrush. The carriage came to an abrupt stop and I jumped in.

"Keep away from the windows," Balthazar ordered as the guards formed a wall around the carriage.

"Hailia, protect us," Kitty murmured, reaching for Meg's hand.

I desperately wanted to search for Dane, but didn't dare glance through the window. Several pounding heartbeats later I heard the bushes rustle.

"Captain?" Max said. "Did you see anyone?"

"They're gone," came Dane's voice.

Those of us in the carriage released a collective sigh of relief.

"Was it bandits?" Quentin asked.

"We found their camp," Yen said. "It was hastily abandoned, the fire still warm, but there was no sign of them."

I opened the carriage door and went to step out, but Dane ordered me back inside. "I feel better if you're somewhere I can see you," he said, gentler. "Somewhere I can keep an eye on you."

"I suppose I can protect the duchess better from in here," I said, closing the door again.

He frowned, and I suspected he was regretting ordering me to be nearer the duke's intended target.

He rode up ahead, only to be replaced by Erik. "Is My Grace all right?" he asked.

"I am quite well, thank you," Kitty said, dismissing him with a turn of her head.

"I do not know why the duke wants to kill you. You are very beautiful."

She regarded him coolly. "It is none of your affair, Guard."

"Erik." He gave her a shallow bow. "If you were my wife, I would cherish you. Every day, I would say you are beautiful and kind, and every night I would lie with you and worship your body."

Kitty gave a little cry then covered her mouth.

"Don't you have something better to do?" Balthazar asked Erik.

Erik gave him a blank look. "There is nothing better than being with the duchess."

Balthazar groaned. "I think I'll get out and walk."'

"You can't," I told him. "You'll slow us down."

"Then Erik, you have to go before I'm sick."

"Yes, do go away," Kitty said with a haughty lift of her chin. "You are too arrogant."

Erik reached through the window and grasped her hand. He drew it to his lips and kissed it. "And you are too lovely for me." He let her hand go and rejoined the other guards.

Kitty's gaze followed him, her entire body tilting to the side to see him better the further away he drew. He cut a fine figure on the horse, sitting comfortably in the saddle and moving as one with the horse. I didn't blame her for desiring him, and I was quite sure from her lingering blush that she did.

"He's very handsome," I said, teasing.

She shut the curtain. "He's got too much nerve."

* * *

"I DON'T LIKE IT," Dane said that night as we gathered in the small sitting room off the inn's larger taproom. "To disappear so quickly in thick forest is no easy task. I don't think it was a ragtag group of opportunistic bandits."

Kitty gasped. "You think it was someone hired by my husband?"

"Or the Deerhorns. They have as much of a reason to want you dead as he does."

"Perhaps more," Theodore added.

Meg and I had accompanied Kitty into the room when Dane requested a word with her. Balthazar and Theodore had insisted on coming too and Max invited himself.

"I have another reason for thinking it wasn't simply bandits." Dane held up a strip of black cloth. "This was caught on a branch. It's fine quality and clean. Too fine and clean for bandits living in the forest. The assassin is well paid."

Kitty let out another small cry.

"Assassin," Meg repeated dully.

Max shifted his weight to his other foot and I willed him to go to her, comfort her, but he continued to stare at the back of her head from the door where he stood guard.

"You're an easy target out here, Your Grace," Dane said. "Even with all of us guarding you, an arrow can slip through. There are too many opportunities, too many bends and stops along the way."

"What do you propose we do?" Theodore asked.

"Move faster," Balthazar said. "We split into two groups. Everyone on foot continues at the same pace, while the carriage, cart and guards ride on at speed to Tilting."

"And then what?" Max asked, moving into the room. "Hand the duchess and Meg over to the duke's men? We can't do that. I *won't* do that."

"Agreed," Dane said.

There was only one thing to do. We couldn't outrun the duke and Deerhorns, and Kitty couldn't escape them. Even in a priestess's temple, she would not be safe. Miranda had known what needed to be done and now I agreed with her.

"Kitty," I said, taking the duchess's hand. She was close to tears, her face as pale as it had been after she was poisoned. "Miranda was right. You have to pretend to be dead or your life will always be in danger. You have to leave this life behind, forget you are the duchess, or you'll never be safe. There's no other way."

"But...what will I do? Where will I go?"

"We'll stay with the palace servants," Meg said. "Travel with them." She took the duchess's other hand and crouched beside her. "It'll be an adventure. We can go with Josie and the others to search for the servants' memories."

Kitty sniffed and dabbed at the corners of her eyes with a handkerchief. "I suppose."

Max looked pleased. "It's an excellent idea. Everyone in agreement?"

We all nodded, except Kitty.

"But...my jewels and clothes, and..." She lifted a shoulder. "I'll just be an ordinary person."

"You can never be ordinary," I assured her.

"When your husband dies," Meg said, "you can announce your miraculous survival and resume your old life, but as his widow. With him gone, there'll be no need for you to remain dead. Even if he marries Lady Morgrave, her marriage would be nullified when you reappear in public, and it'll be too late for her to do anything about it."

"It *would* be rather satisfying to see her face when I walk into the house." A smile touched Kitty's lips. "And my husband is much older than me. He'll probably die while I am still quite young. In the meantime, I can be...well, I can be just like you, Josie. Free as any woman can be without a family." She blew out a measured breath. "Very well. I'll do it."

Max looked to Dane. "How will we do it? Bandits? Burn the carriage?"

Dane looked out the window to the dense evening sky. "I have a better idea. One where we don't need a body."

* * *

WE TRAVELED the following morning with only the people we could trust. Those of us who'd been at the meeting were joined by Quentin and Erik. Theodore rode on horseback for the first time on the journey, having taken Brant's horse at Dane's order. Brant had been furious and vocal about it until Dane spoke quietly to him.

He wouldn't tell me what he'd said when I asked. It was then that I'd voiced my concern about leaving Brant behind.

"If he has the gem, we're leaving it behind too."

"I know," he said. "But keeping the duchess safe is our priority, and if we don't act today, we won't get another chance before we reach Tilting, and we can't afford to have him come. He can't know what we're doing or he'll go straight to the duke and Deerhorns."

"He has no reason to."

"He doesn't like me. That's reason enough."

Balthazar rode in the carriage with Meg, Kitty and me, but we did not stay dry, with only a curtain covering the window aperture. Those outside were barely visible through the veil of rain. They must be soaked. The servants we left behind decided to stay in the village another day to wait for the rains to ease, but we'd told them we wanted to push on and get the duchess home. No one had questioned it, not even Brant.

Meg said something but I had to ask her to repeat herself. "I can't hear you over the rain on the roof!"

She leaned forward. "I said that this is the perfect weather. The captain was right."

"Perhaps he was a weather predictor in his past life," Balthazar shouted.

"There's no such thing," I told him. "And I happen to know he simply asked the innkeeper. Apparently when the clouds over the hills are that dark by nightfall, there'll almost certainly be a torrential storm."

We settled back into silence, partly because it was too difficult to talk, and partly because we were so anxious. Kitty in particular hadn't said a word all morning. I wondered if she was considering her future and all the possibilities ahead of her, spreading out like the branches of a giant oak, or if she was simply mourning the loss of her luxuries and status. We had decided not to take any of her jewels with us except those she'd worn every day since leaving. Anything more would look suspicious.

We arrived at the river around midday and ate the food packed for us by the inn's kitchen staff. The rain had eased a little but still fell consistently. The road was slick with mud, and rivulets connected the large puddles. The rivulets almost became streams themselves as the road sloped down to the bridge.

"It's time," Dane said, opening the carriage door. "Your Grace."

She refused his offered hand. "If I am to be a commoner from now on, I must act like one."

"A woman can still accept assistance from a man to alight from a carriage," I said. To show her, I took Dane's hand and stepped down.

I drew my hood tighter around my face and waited as the duchess emerged, followed by Meg and Balthazar. We were very soon wetter than ever.

"Go carefully," Dane said.

I took Balthazar's arm while Meg held Kitty's hand. With our heads bent against the rain, we continued, our steps cautious on the road then just as cautious as we crossed the bridge. It was narrow, the stones slippery. The side of one section had been washed away in a previous storm, and the swollen river was threatening to take another toll today. Heaving, churning, muddy water smashed into the stones with a thunderous applause that we could not even shout over. The bridge builders hadn't made it high enough to clear the river in flood. It was a mistake that had given Dane an idea, thanks to Rhys's warning about the damaged crossing.

We four picked our way over the bridge, carefully setting one foot in front of the other. Balthazar clung to my arm, his walking stick searching for purchase within the grooves between stones.

At the halfway point, Meg and Kitty stopped. Kitty removed her cloak, revealing one of my plain gowns underneath. She briefly hugged the velvet cloak to her chest before tossing it into the river.

Meg went to remove her cloak to hand it to the duchess, but Kitty refused with a shake of her head. They continued on and safely met the river bank on the other side.

I dared a glance over my shoulder. Theodore was not far behind us, holding his horse's reins, his other hand on the mount's neck. The animal's ears twitched and his head was raised high, but he didn't look as though he would bolt. Behind Theodore came Quentin with the mount he'd ridden. With my heart in my throat, I watched the slender youth try to encourage the anxious horse onto the bridge. It made one tentative step then another and another before accepting its path.

Dane had selected the calmer, older horses for Theodore and Quentin today, while Max acted as coachman. Dane always rode Lightning and Erik usually rode a particular horse too, so they continued on them today. If they'd ridden out on different horses this morning, someone might have become suspicious.

Balthazar and I made it safely to the other side. Theodore joined us just as Erik started his crossing. Or tried to. Lightning tossed his head and refused to set a hoof on the slick stones. Lightning's fear infected the second horse and Erik battled against both, using his shoulders to keep them from crushing him between them. I could see his lips working as he tried to soothe the animals but Lightning was having none of it. He flatly refused to move.

Erik glanced over his shoulder at something Dane said then he mounted onto Lightning's saddle. After a comforting rub on his neck, the horse seemed to calm which, in turn, calmed the second beast, and Erik was able to move them forward onto the bridge.

When Quentin joined us, and Erik was halfway across, Max and Dane set off with the four carriage horses pulling the vehicle itself. The bridge was barely wide enough at the point where some of the stones had been washed away. The horses seemed to sense the danger and stopped altogether. Like Lightning, they wouldn't budge.

"They'll have to unhitch the carriage and leave it," Balthazar said. "The horses won't move any further with it."

Just as he finished speaking, the torrent swallowed a section of the bridge wall and gnawed away at the remaining stones. The horse nearest Dane reared and Dane was forced to let the reins go. When it settled again, he jumped onto the horse's back. Without a saddle, he was not secure.

The move seemed to quiet the horse a little, enough that Max and Dane were able to encourage the two in front to move forward. All four horses slowly but successfully passed the damaged portion of the bridge. And then it was the carriage's turn. Both Max and Dane looked back at the wheels. They eased the pace right back and kept the horses straight, steady. From where we stood, it looked like they had a mere inch either side. If the horses stepped off course, the carriage would tumble over, taking the horses with it into the river, and Dane too.

I squeezed my eyes shut.

"They should let it go over," Meg said. "We don't need the carriage."

I opened my eyes to see Kitty let go of Meg's hand. She cupped her mouth. "Unhitch it!" she shouted.

But they couldn't hear her. With every part of me tense, I watched as they inched the horses and carriage past the narrow, damaged part of the bridge where the hungry river tried to bite off another morsel. The front set of wheels cleared the gap and the second set looked as though it would too until suddenly the stones beneath the rear left wheel disappeared into the river.

The carriage tilted. Dane's horse reared and all four bolted. Max pressed himself to the bridge wall to get out of the way. Dane somehow managed to hang on.

I hustled Balthazar to the side of the road where Erik stood with his two horses, just as the contraption passed us at speed. It didn't stop. The carriage wheels slid on the muddy road, unable to get purchase. It was in danger of overturning.

It rounded the corner on two wheels, the other two spinning in the air, then disappeared from sight.

"Come on," Theodore said. "Your Grace, can you walk?"

Kitty wasn't listening. She was staring downriver at some debris that had been tangled up with a web of thick tree roots growing out of the bank. Among the branches was a sodden blue strip of fabric. Her cloak.

She turned away, her face wet from the rain, her eyes bright and clear. "I can walk. And please, call me Kitty. I am no longer a duchess."

I picked up my skirts, a rather pointless exercise with the hem already caked in mud. "Meg, help Balthazar."

I ran ahead, splashing through the puddles too large to leap over. Erik rode past on his own horse, leading Lightning. Max and Quentin followed on horseback while Theodore kept pace alongside me in silence, his own horse trotting behind.

"He'll be fine," he said with a confidence that I needed to hear.

Theodore was right. The carriage had stopped some distance away beneath a thick overhang of trees. It was upright and the horses calmly waited in the middle of the road while Dane inspected them. Erik dismounted and helped.

C.J. ARCHER

"Don't do that again," I snapped when I reached them. "Next time, unhitch the carriage and bring across just the horses."

Dane straightened. "That would be a sign that we knew the carriage wouldn't make it. We'd have to explain why we attempted the crossing at all in these conditions if that were the case."

He was right but I wouldn't admit it. Leaving behind the duke's carriage would have people questioning why we crossed with the duchess on foot. What did we plan to do with her on the other side? If the carriage couldn't cross, we would be expected to return to the village and attempt the crossing when the waters receded.

We *had* to take the carriage with us. We couldn't leave it behind, nor could we send it over the bridge with Kitty's cloak. If we wanted to make it look like a vehicular accident, we'd not only have to push the carriage off the bridge, but the horses too, and we'd also have to pretend that Meg and I died in the accident, not just Kitty. We couldn't do that to Meg's family.

The only way to fake the death of the Duchess of Gladstow, and only her, was to tell everyone we all got out of the carriage and walked across the bridge while the men brought the horses and empty carriage across. Alas, the duchess had slipped and fallen in. We'd searched for her body for the rest of the afternoon, but unable to find it, we'd assumed the floodwaters had taken it.

In Tilting, we would hand over the carriage and her luggage to the duke's men. If they searched downriver, they would find Kitty's cloak among the flood debris, but nothing else.

With everyone accounted for, Meg, Kitty, Balthazar and I climbed back into the carriage. Kitty rearranged her hair into a simpler style and removed her earrings and the choker necklace. She tucked them into her pockets and settled back in the seat.

She closed her eyes and sighed. In the clothing she'd borrowed from me and her bedraggled state, she looked like a village girl. But if someone looked past the clothes and hair, and saw the soft hands, the noble bearing, they would know she was not one of us. Meg and I had a big task on our hands turning the regal duchess into plain Kitty.

CHAPTER 15

*K*itty didn't say a word until we reached the village later that afternoon, and even then, she remained silent until we closed the door to our shared bedchamber.

"Do you think they believed me?" she asked, removing her soaked jerkin and dropping it on the floor.

Meg picked it up and wrung it out over the basin. "Why wouldn't they? You look like a maid."

"I tried very hard to walk like you two and look down at my feet. It wasn't easy. I couldn't see where I was going."

"Maids can look up," I said.

"Meg, help me with these fastenings on my skirt. They're complicated." They were simply hooks and eyes, and any woman could undo them, even though they were located at the back. It would take some time before Kitty grew used to being a commoner.

"Perhaps you should keep your face averted in public," Meg said. "We don't want anyone describing you to your husband if he comes here and asks questions."

Kitty made a miffed sound through her nose. "He won't ask questions. He'll accept the captain's explanation without hesitation because he wants to believe me dead."

She was probably right. Indeed, we were counting on it.

Even so, we dined in our room. Afterwards, the men joined

us and reported that they'd given their account of the accident to the innkeeper who'd directed them to the village governor and sheriff.

"We wrote a letter to the duke, informing him that we'll continue to Tilting as planned and hand over the carriage and horses to his men," Balthazar said.

"Did the inn staff or patrons say anything about me?" Kitty asked. "I mean, the me that is a maid?" She plucked at her skirt. "Did they believe I was just an ordinary woman?"

"Yes," Dane said at the same time Erik said, "No."

"No one will believe you are ordinary," the Marginer explained. "The men see how very beautiful you are, how desirable." He took her hand and kissed it, his gaze lifted to hers through his lashes.

She plucked her hand away. "As long as they didn't mistake me for a duchess."

"No one suspected a thing," Max said. "You're safe." His gaze flicked to Meg. "Thank the god and goddess."

We discussed further aspects of our ruse, the lies we would have to form, and made sure we all had the same story memorized.

The following morning, we set off early and maintained a swift pace to the next village then finally, the day after, we arrived in Tilting.

I hadn't known what to expect, but it wasn't the sea of buildings that hugged the Upway River at Glancia's south western corner. The buildings within the walled city were taller than the cruder structures outside, some reaching as high as three stories. Some even had panes of glass in the windows, like the palace.

In the distance, rising above the city on a hill, was a turreted castle built of dark stone. Glancian kings had made it their base for generations, until the sorcerer had built Leon something different and spectacular outside Mull. The castle reminded me of a beast, squatting on the hilltop, keeping watch over its dominion.

One other structure also rose above the others, but it was more elegant than its fortified neighbor. The high temple was topped with domes and spires, and a single tower shot into the sky from its center. The bell housed in the tower was silent.

"It stinks," Meg said, wrinkling her nose.

"It's worse downriver," Kitty said. "That's where the tanneries and slaughter houses are. But that's not near here. You can probably smell Merdu's Pit."

"Merdu's Pit?"

"The worst of the slums."

I followed her gaze but it looked the same as the rest of the city. The streets were narrow and crowded, the sun blocked by tall buildings. Washing hung from tenement windows and children played in the side streets. The cobbles were slick with mud, dung and slops. Our carriage fought for space on the main thoroughfare, jostling with carts and barrows, and a drove of pigs being urged on by a lad younger than Quentin. The stench became worse downwind.

No one paid us any attention. In Mull, such a fine carriage would have been a spectacle, but ours was not the only fine carriage in Tilting. We passed several, all going at a pace too fast along streets too small for so much traffic.

"It'll improve soon," Kitty said, peeking through the curtain on her side of the carriage. We'd agreed that she should remain hidden in Tilting in case she was recognized. The duke had too many eyes spying for him in the capital.

Before the city "improved," we had to skirt the large market, teeming with people carrying their goods; not just women but footmen, maids and errand boys. It must be open all day. There seemed no sign of any of the carts closing up, despite the lateness of the hour.

"Oi! Watch it!" a boy called out as he ran past.

The carriage suddenly stopped to allow a man to follow, shouting for the thief to stop. The boy ducked behind a cart, wove through the crowd then disappeared from sight, a breadstick tucked under his arm.

Up ahead came another shout then a shriek. I poked my head out the window to see two uniformed constables drawing swords on a youth while a third pummeled his fist into another man on the ground. He was bleeding from the nose. Papers were scattered nearby, the breeze curling the edges and flipping some over.

I placed my hand to the door handle to push it open, but Meg held me back.

"We have to keep our heads down," she warned.

She was right, but I hated doing nothing. The constables didn't need to use such force. The man couldn't fight back.

"Help is on its way," Balthazar said, looking through the other window. "Rhys's men."

Four warrior priests led by Brother Rufus rode up and ordered the constables to ease back. The constables hesitated before one sheathed his sword and began collecting the pamphlets.

"I wonder what's going on," Kitty said as we passed Rufus. "I've never known the brothers to interfere in a constabulary matter."

Balthazar pointed at one of the pamphlets that we almost ran over. "Josie, I can't see that far. What does it say?"

"It's a drawing of a large man wearing the governor's chain of office and badge over his fur coat. He has the head of Okoa. That's a horned monster the ancients used to believe in," I explained. "It was said to roam through forests and enter villages at night to steal children and rape women."

"This is why Rhys was worried about leaving the city," Balthazar said. "His men are needed here."

"If the king had built his palace here, we wouldn't have such lawlessness," Kitty said. "The nobles would have stayed."

"If the governor wasn't a monster, Tilting wouldn't have this problem at all, with or without the nobles," Meg said. "No doubt he's taking advantage of them being away at Mull. At least some are coming back now the king is dead."

"Others are staying away because of this lawlessness," Balthazar told her.

We drove on and the city began to improve, as Kitty said it would. The buildings looked newer and more substantial, with many protected by high walls.

"That's our townhouse," Kitty said, pointing at a high wall. Above the wall, I could just make out an expansive gabled roof and multiple chimneys. "We stay here when my husband has business in Tilting. The houses on this side are the best in the city. Behind these walls are beautiful gardens and fountains—and the biggest houses. The governor lives in that one, and Lord and Lady Esses in the one with the green door. She has rather dubious taste and likes to keep peacocks in the garden. She used to keep swans in their pond too, but they got into the bath house and frightened the guests."

"Where's the river?" Balthazar asked.

"On the other side of these houses. They all have their own private pier, some with waterside pavilions, and others have gardens down to the water's edge. We have both, of course."

A beggar emerged from the shadows, bowl balanced between two stumps where his hands should be. "Please, sir, for my children," he said to Dane.

Dane reached into his pocket but before he could give the coins to the beggar, two mounted constables rode up. "Get away!" one shouted as he drew his sword. "Get going!"

The beggar dropped his bowl and cowered as the constable raised his sword.

"Stand down!" Dane ordered. "This man is doing no harm."

"Begging ain't allowed in this quarter," the constable said.

Quentin dismounted and gathered the beggar's bowl. "Let me help you."

"It's best not to encourage 'em," the constable said. "If you do, they'll only be back, and more too."

Quentin ignored him and assisted the beggar to his feet.

The constable pressed his sword to Quentin's shoulder. "I said, let him be."

Dane and Erik both drew their swords. "Let the man go on his way peacefully," Dane said.

The constables eyed them up and down, while Quentin quickly tucked the money from the bowl into the beggar's clothes, as well as the coins Dane handed him. One of the constables moved his horse forward to follow the beggar as he hurried off, but Erik maneuvered his horse to block the way.

"Now you go," Erik said. "That way." He pointed his sword in the opposite direction to where the beggar had gone.

The constables gave him a fierce look but must have decided not to test the big Marginer. They steered their horses away. We waited until they were out of sight and continued on, warier than ever.

The walls of the grand residences gave way to the municipal buildings situated around a vast paved square. Made of dark stone with turreted roofs, they were as solid, imposing and grim as the castle. The heavy presence of constables at the front of the grandest structure identified it as the council building.

We headed towards the temple of Merdu's Guards, occupying the entire north side of the square. Instead of stopping out the front, we passed it, turned a corner and stopped at a second entrance. Two arched doors positioned between white columns could be opened to allow carriages through. On the stone lintel the words *For The Glory Of Merdu* were carved between two long horizontal swords. According to Rhys's directions, this must be the garrison where the warrior priests lived and trained.

Dane opened the carriage door and assisted Balthazar down the step. "Stay hidden," he said to Kitty. "The priests know you, and I'm not yet ready to inform them of our duplicity."

I got out to stretch my legs, and I nodded at the priest who'd opened the door to receive us. He smiled back and invited Balthazar inside.

Balthazar hesitated.

"I've got your pack," Quentin told him. "Go on in, Bal. This is your home."

Balthazar looked to me. "Are you coming, Josie?"

"I can't," I said. "Women aren't allowed."

"I forgot." He rubbed his forehead. "My memory isn't what it used to be." He smiled, and I laughed.

I hugged him and received a brisk pat on the back in response. "Goodbye," I said. "And take care."

"This isn't goodbye." He flapped his hand at me. "Stop making a fuss. I'll see you tomorrow."

He walked off, his walking stick tapping on the cobblestones. Quentin followed with Balthazar's belongings, and Dane went inside too. The priest shut the door.

Some moments later, a piercing whistle sounded and both the

doors opened. A rider approached and rode straight through without stopping. The doors were shut behind him.

"Wasn't that Rhys?" Meg asked.

"Aye," Max said. "He's in a hurry."

When Dane and Quentin returned, we set off again. Kitty peeked through the curtain and pointed out the best goldsmith shop, and the finest cloth and wine merchants. I was hardly listening. I couldn't help thinking how strange it must be for Balthazar, being in a place that was his home yet unfamiliar, with people who were his friends yet he didn't know them. Hopefully something in the temple or garrison would jog his memory.

* * *

DANE, Theodore, Max, Quentin and Erik left the inn early the following morning. They planned to show their faces and ask questions about missing people at the river docks. Tonight, they'd frequent the inns and taverns in the area. If they had no luck, they'd try the markets tomorrow, and then move outward from there. The city was so large that it would take weeks to cover every street. Hopefully someone would recognize them soon.

Kitty had the opposite problem. She didn't want to be recognized and had to remain indoors. Meg and I kept her company, but I was regretting my decision by midday. I itched to explore the city and help the men. Kitty and Meg seemed just as bored. Our idle chatter grew stale, and there were only so many card games we could play.

"I don't know how the noblewomen can play so many rounds," I said, throwing down my hand after losing to Kitty yet again.

"Wine helps," Kitty said, gathering the cards. "Lots of it. And gossip. Do either of you know any gossip?"

"Not about people you know," Meg said.

"Tell me something scandalous. I don't care who it's about. The ruder the better."

Meg and I exchanged a glance. "We could tell her about

Teddy having an affair with another man's wife. Oh, I know! Olleander's baby."

"What about Olleander's baby?" Kitty asked.

"He had Zemayan coloring."

"And neither she nor her husband are Zemayan?" Kitty clapped her hands. "This is excellent gossip. How did her husband react?"

We were saved from giving her the details by Erik's return.

"The others are still at the river," he said, removing his sword belt. "It is a very large dock, with many people."

"Any luck yet?" Meg asked.

He shook his head. "No one knows us, and no one is missing."

"Why did you come back?" I asked.

He indicated his forehead tattoos. "The people stare at me. Some spit."

"That's awful," Meg said. "I thought Tilting was a diverse city."

"It is," Kitty said. "But I have never seen a Marginer here. Freedlanders, Dreens and Vytillians abound, and there are a handful of Zemayans, but not a single Marginer. I thought they might be found at the docks. I am sorry for the behavior of my fellow countrymen, Erik."

"Do not apologize. I like it better in here with the ladies. So what are we doing?" He rubbed his hands together. "Cards? I like cards. I win many times."

"You won't today," Kitty said. "I'm very good."

"A challenge! I accept. Josie, deal."

We played a few rounds before another arrival put an end to card games.

"Balthazar!" I embraced him before he'd even stepped through the doorway. "It's so good to see you."

His thick brows drew together. "You must be bored." He pointed his walking stick at Erik. "Shouldn't you be out searching for your identity?"

"I do not like Tilting," Erik said. "The people are not nice. Not like Mull."

"It is certainly a different place," Balthazar muttered. "It took an age for the carriage to get here through the traffic. I would have been quicker on foot."

"The priests gave you a carriage?" I asked. "That's generous."

"They have several carriages, and I have my pick of them. The position of archivist is a senior one, and the use of vehicles is one of the privileges. A larger room to myself is another, although it's very bare."

Erik nodded sagely. "You are old, it is true."

"Is it the same room as the one you occupied before you left?" I asked.

Balthazar nodded. "The new archivist, Elliot—my assistant back then—insisted on vacating it. He thought staying in my old room might help my memory loss."

"And did it?"

"Not a bit." He sighed as he eased himself onto a chair.

"Any clues in the room as to why you left all those months ago?" I asked.

"No. Nothing in my office either. Brother Elliot showed me the text he believes I was reading at the time. It might be a clue but I don't know what answer it points to. I don't even know the question."

"What was it about?"

"It was a collection of accounts about the Freedlandian civil war of forty years ago. They were all written by various priests, including the Master of Merdu's Guards at the time. The warrior priests fought there."

"On whose side?"

"The royalists."

"So they failed," Meg said.

"One of the few times throughout their history, according to Elliot. He says the order doesn't like to talk about it, which is a shame. The lack of discussion means the younger generation knows very little about the order's involvement in Freedland's civil war."

"You'll have to seek out the older generation," I said. "There must be people your age who remember it."

"Warriors don't have long lives. Even the retired priests who still live on the premises weren't in the order forty years ago.

That's why I'm going to visit another priest now. Apparently he's as ancient as me." He smiled. "We were good friends, so the brothers tell me. Very good friends. There was a letter from him waiting for me at the garrison, urging me to visit him at my earliest convenience."

"Then what are you waiting for?" I said. "Go and see him."

He folded both hands over the head of his walking stick. "I hoped to find Theodore here, but you'll have to do, Josie."

"For what?"

He cleared his throat. "To accompany me."

I tried very hard not to smile. "I'll be happy to."

* * *

BALTHAZAR'S very good friend turned out to be none other than the high priest himself. The most senior priest in all of Glancia oversaw every order in the kingdom and answered only to the Supreme Holiness in the city of Fahl, located in Vytill. He lived in the temple I'd seen on our way into Tilting with the enormous bell tower looking down on the streets below. Positioned next to the old king's castle at the heart of the city, it would be where the monarch worshipped. The temple of Merdu's Guards, while impressive in both size and location, was for the private use of the warrior priests. It wasn't as daunting as the high temple.

I tilted my head back to take in the view of the bell tower. The spire seemed to pierce the scudding clouds and the bell itself seemed small, yet I'd heard it ringing for morning prayers from our inn, some distance away.

"I wish you'd told me your friend was the high priest," I said.

"Would it have made a difference?" Balthazar asked.

"I might have worn a nicer dress."

"He's a priest. He doesn't have worldly possessions. He won't care if you're wearing a potato sack."

Balthazar had sent the high priest a message to say he was on his way, so we were expected and shown immediately to his office. The temple reminded me of the palace with rooms dedicated to both public and private use. Like the palace, ceilings were high and rooms could be vast. But the similarity ended there. While we didn't enter the room where the public worshipped, the audience chamber and other rooms were simply furnished. There was no gold or silver, no glass in the windows, no plaster on the walls. The temple's stonework was left exposed, covered in places with enormous tapestries. Even in these early autumnal days the rooms were chilly. They must be freezing in winter.

The sound of our footsteps on the flagstone floor announced our progress before the priest escorting us opened the final door to the high priest's office. It must be used as a meeting place, because it was very similar to the main audience chamber, only smaller. In the center of the floor was the same mosaic tiled image of the bright yellow sun, each ray touching a different scene. In one, Merdu was shown creating the world by throwing thunder bolts down from his perch on a cloud. In another scene, the god raised a sword above the head of a cowering Zemayan, and in a third scene, he watched over a field of wheat. Hailia was depicted in only two scenes, one with a baby in her arms and, in the other, she healed a sick man with a hand to his heart.

The mosaic was clearly meant to be the room's best feature. All chairs had been pushed to the edges except for the one behind the large desk on which a man with white hair and neat white beard sat.

"Bal!" He rushed out from behind the desk, arms extended, a warm smile on his face. "How I've missed you, friend." He embraced Balthazar, only to quickly pull away, his smile turning awkward. Balthazar hadn't returned the embrace. "Come in, sit. Tell me about your adventures at the palace." He signaled for the priest to leave, then his gaze fell on me.

"This is Miss Joselyn Cully," Balthazar said. "A friend from Mull."

I curtsied and said, "Your Eminence." The title was correct, but I wasn't sure about the curtsy.

The high priest smiled. "Welcome, Miss Cully. Any friend of Bal's is a friend of mine."

He walked back to the desk at a steadier pace compared to Balthazar. He wore a black robe, not brown like the regular priests and priestesses, his belt clasped with a gold buckle in the shape of the sun; an ordinary priest's belt was made of rope and was simply tied in a knot without a clasp. Balthazar's belt hung loosely from his thin frame, but the high priest's was tight over a portly belly.

The buckle was the only adornment on the high priest's person. Indeed, it was the only piece of gold in the room. It would seem the abandonment of worldly goods extended to the second highest office in The Fist's priesthood.

The high priest offered us wine, served in plain wooden cups, and pushed a bowl of nuts toward Balthazar. "You look as though you haven't eaten properly since leaving here. Didn't they feed you at the palace?"

"I wasn't this thin the last time you saw me?" Balthazar asked.

The high priest shook his head sadly. "The food at the guards' temple is awful. I've tried it myself." He pulled a face. "But you were never like this. You seem...older."

"I am older, by a year, apparently."

The high priest's wrinkled features settled into grim lines. "Master Rhys's letter told me you'd lost your memory. He says that's why you never wrote to inform us of your whereabouts. It seems so remarkable, so fantastical."

"Yet it's true."

The high priest smiled. "Thank the goddess for your safe return. She watched over you. Although she has not fed you sufficiently." He nudged the bowl of nuts closer to Balthazar. "Eat, eat."

Balthazar took a nut and nibbled. He didn't look comfortable sitting across from the high priest, and that worried me. In the palace, he'd been authoritative, even toward the king. Leon had looked up to Balthazar when I first met them. Leon might have been the ruler of all Glancia, but Balthazar had been the ruler of the palace.

"Master Rhys said you have no recollection of how you ended up at the palace or why you were employed there." The high priest separated his clasped hands and drew them together again, resting them on his stomach. "Didn't you ask?"

Rhys had agreed not to tell anyone about the rest of the

servants' memory loss, but he'd said it was necessary to inform the high priest of Balthazar's, since he'd immediately know something was amiss upon seeing him again. He'd also agreed not to mention magic in his letter, leaving the decision up to Balthazar. In the carriage, Balthazar told me he hadn't yet decided whether he would say anything about the sorcerer and Leon's use of magic to gain the throne. From his guarded look now, I couldn't determine whether he'd come to a decision or not.

"The king employed me," Balthazar said. "Only he knew his reason for employing me and it's not something you simply ask a king."

"And of course he's dead now." The high priest rubbed his forehead. "Messy business."

I wasn't sure if he was referring to the death, its aftermath, or Balthazar's employment.

"You're back where you belong now," he went on. "Have you settled in to your old room?"

"Yes, Your Eminence."

The high priest smiled wistfully. "You used to refuse to call me that for a long time after I gained the office. You said it was too formal for old friends. I insisted just to annoy you. It worked, eventually, but there was always an edge of sarcasm to your tone. Is he still sarcastic, Miss Cully?"

Surprised at being directly addressed, I stumbled my way through an answer. "Er, y—yes, Your Eminence."

"I'm glad to hear it. You might look older, Bal, but it would be grave indeed if that sharp tongue had been blunted. Tell me about life in the palace. What was King Leon like?"

"Childish, impetuous, selfish," Balthazar said. "He looked up to me at first, and listened to my advice, but later…he changed."

"I suppose that led to his downfall. Was the guard who assassinated him ever caught?"

"No."

"Any suspicions about who paid him?"

"Several. The Vytill representative—"

"Lord Barborough? Possible, I suppose, considering King Phillip is the next in line, theoretically. Glancians won't accept him, though, and I'm quite sure he knows that." The high priest clasped his hands over his stomach again. "Who else?"

"Both of the dukes."

The high priest sat forward. "You've spent some time with them in the palace. Do you believe they would assassinate the king in order to take his place? After all, it means plunging the kingdom into war, first. It's a drastic measure with an unpredictable outcome."

Balthazar agreed. "The Duke of Buxton is a reasonable man. Gladstow is the ambitious one. It's possible Buxton is only considering vying for the crown because he thinks Gladstow would make a poor king."

"That's a good observation. I see your mind hasn't dulled. We used to enjoy our political discussions, right here in this room. We had them regularly."

"Did we agree?"

The high priest chuckled. "Sometimes."

Balthazar grunted, but it was one of his friendly grunts. Talk of the dukes and king had relaxed him, and he seemed more like his usual confident self again. The high priest clearly respected his friend's opinion, and Balthazar was in his element.

The high priest's smile faded. "Terrible business about the Duchess of Gladstow. It must have been awful, Miss Cully."

"It was," I said, trying to sound saddened. "She was kind to me and those around her. She'll be missed."

"Not by her husband, I hear."

"What have you heard specifically?" Balthazar asked.

"That Gladstow will choose another wife as soon as a suitable period of mourning has passed."

"And what is a suitable period of mourning?"

"For Gladstow, as short as possible, I expect. Do you know whom he favors for his new bride?"

"Lady Violette Morgrave," Balthazar said.

"Merdu," the high priest muttered. "That's not good news. I hate to think of Gladstow's power coupled with the Deerhorns' ambition."

"And their ruthlessness." Balthazar told him about the village riots, the political situation in Mull both before the fire and after, and my brushes with the Deerhorn family.

The high priest knew about most of it from Rhys, but the specifics shocked him. "No wonder you left the village to come here," he said to me. "Although I'm not sure how safe it is for you in Tilting. The Deerhorns are here. You must be very careful."

"It's a big city, and we're unlikely to come across one another," I reassured him.

He didn't look reassured, however. "The tales of your encounters with them in Mull confirm some of the stories I've heard. They're a nasty family with no morals and no one to rein them in."

"They've been weakened after the village killed many of their men and took their grain," Balthazar said. "And the Tilting governor isn't in their pocket, unlike Mull's governor."

"He's in no one's pocket," The high priest said wryly. "Sometimes I wish he was controlled by someone. He's a law unto himself. The sheriff gladly does his bidding and in the most brutal manner. In many ways, the two of them remind me of the Deerhorns. Their reasoning is twisted, they wield torture and cruelty like weapons, and their power grows stronger every day. The governor has all dissenters in his sights lately yet their numbers increase."

"Are the dissenters responsible for the pamphlets littering the city?" Balthazar asked.

"Not litter. Important political statements."

"I saw one with the governor's bare arse hanging out of his pants."

"Balthazar!" The high priest's gaze flicked to me.

I held up my hands. "I've heard worse."

"Much," Balthazar said with a smirk.

The high priest shifted his weight, clearly uncomfortable to have me exposed to crude talk. "The residents are tired of living in filthy, stinking conditions. They want industry moved out of the city to clean up the river. Fresh water, free for everyone, will go some way to appeasing them, yet the governor won't order it. He owns many of those businesses, as well as the land they rent. He'd lose money if they were forced out. The people will continue to press for change, however. There's talk of marching through the streets, demanding something be done."

"This is beginning to sound terribly familiar," Balthazar muttered.

"Thankfully Merdu's Guards are back in the city to protect us. Master Rhys will see that order is maintained and the governor's bullying curtailed."

"He's distracted by his missing friend at the moment," Balthazar said.

The high priest cocked his head to the side. "What friend? Who's missing now?"

Balthazar waved his hand in dismissal. "A friend from outside the priesthood disappeared while Rhys was in Mull."

The high priest blew out a measured breath. "That's unfortunate, but I'm glad it's not another priest. I couldn't cope if another friend went missing. When they told me you'd vanished, Bal, I'd never felt such panic." He tapped his chest. "It was like I was stabbed, right here."

Balthazar rubbed his hand over the head of his walking stick. "Do you have any idea why I might have left? No one knows."

"Unfortunately not. You never confided in me, which makes me wonder if you left of your own accord at all."

"What do you mean?"

"You always told me everything, Bal. We were—are—great friends. If you were leaving Tilting, you would have told me where you were going and when to expect your return. But you gave me no clue. You simply vanished. It's very unlike you. And the fact that no one knows where you went…it leads me to think you were kidnapped."

I gasped. "But who would do such a thing? I assume there was no ransom note demanding payment for his return."

"No one would kidnap a priest if they wanted money," Balthazar told me.

"No note of any kind was found," the high priest said. "Perhaps your kidnappers weren't aware you were a priest until the morning. Knowing they wouldn't get much for you, they set you free, but perhaps the shock affected your mind. That would account for the memory loss."

"There are no known cases of memory loss from shock," I said. At the high priest's narrowed gaze, I added, "My father was a doctor. He looked into the medical aspects of memory loss before his death."

"What are the medical reasons for memory loss?"

"A blow to the head."

The high priest turned to Balthazar. "Perhaps they beat you before they released you."

"Possibly," was all Balthazar said. "Your Eminence, do you know why I would have been researching Freedland's civil war before my disappearance?

"Why do you ask?"

"Brother Elliot said I was looking through accounts of the war. I thought the research might be linked to my disappearance."

"Sorry, I can't help you." He twiddled his thumbs in thought. "You always discussed your research with me, but Freedland wasn't one of your interests. Not in the days before your disappearance or even the years before." He shrugged. "Perhaps you finally grew bored and simply picked a topic you knew little about for something to do."

Balthazar sighed. "Elliot said the same thing. I never discussed Freedland with him, either. Tell me, Your Eminence, what do you know about magic?"

I held my breath, not quite believing he'd finally broached the subject. I'd begun to suspect he wouldn't.

"Magic?" The high priest looked taken aback. "Don't tell me you believe that nonsense about the palace's creation."

"Lord Barborough believed."

"Barborough is a crackpot. I don't know why King Phillip allowed him to be his representative in Glancia."

I knew why but I kept my mouth shut. Barborough had forced King Phillip's hand, killing the man the king had originally chosen. King Phillip only agreed to let him come to Glancia because Barborough had promised to discover whether the rumors of magic were true or not.

The high priest regarded Balthazar down his nose. "Tell me, Bal. Did the palace seem real to you? Was it solid?"

"Yes."

The high priest spread out his hands. "There you are. No magic, just efficiency and superior craftsmanship. Everything can be explained."

Balthazar's hand rubbed the head of the walking stick faster. "What if I tell you I do believe in magic, that the palace was created by magic, the staff put there by magic. And Leon gained the throne through magic."

The high priest stared at him as if he'd never seen him before then barked out a humorless laugh. "What evidence is there for any of it?"

"None," Balthazar said.

"Well, there you have it. Come, Bal, it's not like you to believe in something you cannot prove. You're a man who requires evidence."

Balthazar's brows arched. "Then how do you explain my being a priest? Isn't the very definition of faith a belief in something despite a lack of evidence?"

The high priest's lips flattened. "There are books about the god and goddess. Ancient books written by those with direct experience of the deities. You have some in your temple, and there are many more in the library here. The evidence is in those, and I urge you to re-read them." He suddenly sat forward, his palms flat to the table surface. "I know your memory loss has affected your mind, but *trust* yourself, Bal. Trust in the person you are—a man of reason and logic. You've never questioned your faith before, never believed in the Zemayan stories of magic. Doesn't that tell you something?"

"It tells me that I am not the same man as I was when I left here."

The high priest sat back and crossed his arms. "The very notion of magic is ridiculous."

Balthazar's direct gaze would make most people look away, but the high priest held it. As affable as he'd seemed up to now, it was a timely reminder that he was used to dealing with powerful lords and fierce warriors, but he was also used to Balthazar.

"You must have a reason for believing in it," the high priest said. "What is it? Tell me why you would set aside your very nature and believe in something most Zemayans no longer do."

Balthazar plucked a nut out of the bowl and held it between his thumb and forefinger. "King Leon was like this nut. He wasn't special, just one of many."

"I know he wasn't aware of his heritage. Not long after you disappeared, a document written by Prince Hugo Lockhart, many years ago, was discovered right here in this very temple. The document stated that he, Prince Hugo, heir to the Glancian throne, had married a woman in secret in Freedland and she'd given birth to a boy named Leon. Prince Hugo had entrusted the document to this temple, but the high priest at the time kept it such a secret that no one knew of its existence. Prince Hugo died shortly after the boy's birth, and the high priest died shortly after Prince Hugo. The document was forgotten until one of my archivist's assistants discovered it. Despite my reservations about its authenticity, it was shown to King Alain who, I am told, found the young man named Leon and declared him the legitimate heir."

"How did he find him?" Balthazar asked. "*Where* did he find him?"

The high priest frowned. "I'm not sure of the details. It was a very confusing time. The point is, Leon knew nothing of his lineage." He indicated the bowl of nuts. "You're right. He was an ordinary man. None of this is in dispute, however. King Alain declared him the rightful heir and that is the end of that."

"It *is* in dispute," Balthazar said. "Leon admitted to me, and others, that he found the sorcerer's magical device and freed the sorcerer from it. As a reward, he was granted three wishes. He wished to be a rich king. The sorcerer chose Glancia, creating a falsified document for your archivist to find, and made Mull a vital port where riches would flow in on the tide with new trade and increased taxes. Then the sorcerer built a palace nearby, where few could witness its rapid construction. It populated the palace with a thousand servants, but wiped their memories first so they wouldn't bear witness to the magic. I know this because I am one of the thousand, and I know every single other servant. None have a memory from before their time at the palace."

He put the nut in his mouth and rose.

I quickly got to my feet and followed him out, very aware of the man sitting behind the desk, staring at us. At the door, I glanced back to see the high priest looking as though the ground had fallen away beneath him and he was frozen in the moment before he fell through.

It was only when I went to shut the door behind us that he rallied. "What happened to you, Bal? What did those kidnappers do to you?"

Balthazar sighed. "Come on, Josie. There's work to be done."

CHAPTER 16

*W*e dined in a private dining room at the inn that night. It had been a long and frustrating day at the docks for Dane and the others, with not a single person recognizing them. No one matching their descriptions had been reported missing either.

"There is still much of the city to explore yet," Theodore said, trying to sound cheerful but failing. "We haven't exhausted all of our options here."

Quentin hunched over his tankard of ale. "Maybe we should just go back to the palace."

"You can go back," Dane said. "No one will think any less of you if you want to return."

Quentin sighed. "You're not going back, are you?"

"Not until I have answers."

The lad straightened. "Me too." He downed his ale then called for another.

Max pointed a chicken leg at Balthazar. "How did your meeting with the high priest go?"

Balthazar shredded a piece of chicken off the bone and placed it with the others on the side of his plate. "He believes I was kidnapped and beaten up, resulting in my memory loss."

"And the loss of your common sense too," I added with a wry smile.

Quentin laughed, but when no one laughed with him, he shoved a piece of chicken into his mouth.

"Was he able to tell you what you were researching before you disappeared?" Dane asked.

"Unfortunately not," Balthazar said, pushing his plate away.

I pushed it back again. "The high priest was right about one thing. You're too thin. Eat everything on that plate."

"I'm not hungry."

"I don't care."

"I'm not a child, Josie."

"Then stop acting like one and eat."

Erik waved his half-eaten chicken leg in Balthazar's face. "Do not pick at your food. Eat like this, like a man." He bit into the chicken and tore the meat from the bone with his teeth. He chewed with his mouth open.

"That's disgusting," Kitty said. "Just because you're a barbarian doesn't mean you have to act like one."

"I am a Marginer, not a barbarian." He traced the line of tattoos across his forehead, leaving behind a streak of chicken grease.

"Ugh," Kitty said, rising. "I'm retiring. Goodnight, everyone."

Erik wiped his mouth with the back of his hand. "Do not go, Kitty. I will eat with manners."

"My reason for going to my room has nothing to do with you and everything to do with being tired."

"It's probably just as well," Dane said. "Rhys and his men are coming. We can't tell them about you. They're too loyal."

"And honest," Balthazar added.

Erik rose. "I will come. We play more cards."

"I'm tired of cards," Kitty said.

"Then we talk." He winked.

"About what? We have nothing in common."

Erik rolled his eyes. "When I say talk and wink too, I do not mean talk. I mean we should lie together."

Kitty's eyes bulged.

"It is a good time now," he went on. "Meg and Josie will stay here with their men, and we will be alone."

"Erik," Dane snapped. "Kitty doesn't want your company."

"She does." Erik sat again. "But she does not yet know it."

Kitty made a miffed sound through her nose, turned, and strode out. Erik chuckled as he watched her go. There was a definite sway to her hips that had not been there before.

Rhys and his closest advisers arrived just as our plates were being cleared away by the innkeeper's daughters. Balthazar's assistant, Elliot, accompanied them.

One of the serving girls brought in a tray laden with cups. She set one down in front of each of us then flashed a smile at Andreas. He lifted his cup in salute.

"We didn't order these," Theodore told her.

Rhys studied the contents of his cup with a morose intensity, as if he could see his future in the clear liquid. "The innkeeper knows us. The first round is always on him."

"That's generous."

"You protect him," Dane said, nodding. "You keep troublemakers from his door. The free drinks are his way of thanking you. Now I know why you recommended this place."

Rhys didn't look up from the cup.

"He's a good man and runs a clean, honest inn," Rufus said. "Both are hard to find in this city. They need to be protected or we're left with bad men running dishonest businesses."

Quentin sniffed the contents of his cup and wrinkled his nose. "It's strong."

Vizah chuckled. "It'll put hairs on your chest, boy." He downed the entire contents of his cup.

Quentin followed suit, only to immediately suffer a coughing fit.

Erik clapped him on the back then downed his own drink in its entirety. Vizah looked impressed.

I sipped and my eyes began to water from the strong, bitter taste. I looked to Meg, to see what she thought of it, but it was hard to tell. She cradled the cup in both hands, hunching over it in an attempt to hide the birthmark on her face from the priests. Just when I thought she was growing more comfortable with it, I was reminded that she was only comfortable in the presence of familiar friends.

Rufus turned to Balthazar. "You didn't return to the garrison after your meeting with the high priest."

"I wanted to spend time with my friends," Balthazar said. "Josie and I explored a little of Tilting before coming back here."

"The high priest summoned Rhys this afternoon," Andreas said. "He wanted to hear Rhys's account of the palace."

We all looked at Rhys. "And what did you say?" Balthazar asked.

Rhys set down his cup without taking a sip. "With regards to magic, I told him that all the servants claimed to have lost their memories, and that you told us what the king had said with his dying breath. I told him the nobles never mentioned magic. Not once."

"What was the high priest's reaction?"

"He wanted to know whether I believed you. I said I was convinced that *you* all believed in magic."

"And then?" Dane prompted.

Rhys lifted his broad shoulders in a shrug. "And then we moved on to politics." He sat forward, his full attention on the conversation for the first time since his arrival. "The Deerhorns have been telling the masters of the city's religious orders that the Duke of Gladstow would make an excellent king. The only order they haven't spoken to is ours."

"They know we won't support them," Rufus said. "Not after what we saw in Mull."

"And the priestesses?" I asked. "Have the Deerhorns approached them for support?"

"There are only three orders dedicated to the goddess in the city," Rhys said. "They've spoken to two. The mistress of the third order, Hailia's Handmaids, despises Lady Deerhorn."

"She must be wise," Theodore said.

"Will the other orders support Gladstow and the Deerhorns?" Balthazar asked.

"It's not yet clear. They never outwardly like to show who they support."

"Some will have made up their minds already," Andreas said. "But some will wait for the high priest to guide them."

"Who will he support?" Dane asked.

"Buxton," Rhys said.

Balthazar nodded. "Josie and I had the same opinion after our meeting with him. King Phillip is certainly not his favorite choice for ruler and he dislikes Gladstow and the Deerhorns. He sees them as too powerful and corrupt."

"How much does it matter who the orders support?" Max asked. "Aside from Merdu's Guards, they are not fighters."

"It matters because many people will be guided by the priests," Rufus said. "They trust us to support the right side, the side of good."

Rhys picked up his cup again and swirled the contents. "It's not just the religious orders the Deerhorns are petitioning. They're trying to build support among the nobles and merchants too. The lords have private retinues they can use in battle if necessary, and the merchants have money to pay mercenaries."

"Is Buxton petitioning anyone?" Balthazar asked.

"Not to the same extent. He hasn't approached any of the orders, for instance."

"Is that because the high priest has already told him he supports his claim?"

Rhys met his gaze. "The high priest doesn't confide in me."

"He should," Dane said. "You're the master of the most powerful order in Glancia."

"On the entire Fist," Vizah pointed out.

"If the high priest commits Merdu's Guards to fight for the Duke of Buxton, will you do so?" Balthazar asked.

"You mean will *we* fight?" Rufus said. "You're one of us, Bal, even if you don't wield a sword."

"Don't you have to do as the high priest commands?" Theodore asked.

"Our charter states that we can choose our battles as we see fit," Rhys said. "But if we go against him, it will cause a rift between Merdu's Guards and the other orders. We don't want that."

"Luckily, the high priest agrees that Buxton is the right candidate," Andreas said, raising his cup to his lips. "If we're called on to fight for his cause, we will."

Vizah gave a deep, contented sigh. "It's been an age since we've fought a battle against a properly trained enemy."

"Vizah," Elliot hissed. "You sound bloodthirsty."

Vizah rested a hand on his thigh and lowered his gaze to the small, wiry man with crooked teeth and prematurely thinning hair. "I'm tired of minor skirmishes. I want to put my training to good use."

Elliot pushed his spectacles up his nose. "War isn't a good use of anything. It's destructive, both socially and economically. There are no real winners in a war, particularly a succession war."

"Except the winner." Vizah looked at Elliot as if he were stupid. "In this war, the winner will be the Duke of Buxton because he'll have Merdu's Guards on his side."

Elliot rolled his eyes.

The archivist had an ally in his master, however. "That's the sort of talk that will get you killed," Rhys told Vizah. "Arrogance makes you lazy. Lazy soldiers die." After a weighty silence, he said to Dane, "We'll stay out of the battle between the dukes for as long as possible. Neither is a threat to the faith, but if it goes on too long, and there are too many casualties, we'll step in to end it. Elliot's right, no one wins in a succession war."

Elliot shot a triumphant look at Vizah.

Rhys was just as arrogant if he assumed his order could end the war. After all, they hadn't been successful in Freedland's civil war. Balthazar was right; the order ignored that failure at their peril. Without knowing their own history, they were doomed to repeat their mistakes.

After the priests and Balthazar left, Meg retired too. One by one, the others followed. Max had to assist Quentin. The strong liquor had sent him to sleep, and he was too drowsy to walk steadily. Theodore left with them, leaving Erik behind. Dane had to glare at him and clear his throat before Erik got the message and departed.

I held my breath and waited for Dane to say something. Or perhaps say nothing and just kiss me.

He got up and filled two cups with water from the jug and handed one to me. "You didn't finish the...whatever that stuff is."

"If I had, I would have been snoring by now."

"You don't snore."

"You don't know that."

He set the cup down in front of me, avoiding my gaze, and sat on the chair beside me.

"You seem dejected," I said.

"I hoped to have some answers after today, even if it was to learn that several people had gone missing."

"Tilting is a big city. When the rest of the servants arrive, you can spread out and cover more ground." I rested my hand on his arm. "Give it time."

He covered my hand with his and rubbed his thumb along mine. "I'm not a patient man."

"I disagree. You didn't rush to interrogate Leon about magic when others pressured you to. Nor did you leave the palace and go in search of your past until the time was right."

"It wasn't timing that kept me in Mull." His dark murmur washed over me like a vibration, warming my skin, putting a blush in my cheeks.

I wanted to cup his face, his jaw, make him look at me so he could see that I knew what he really meant. But I didn't know how the intimate gesture would be received, so I did nothing.

He sat back in the chair and crossed his arms with a huff of breath. "We need to talk about something less…just something else. Anything. How is Balthazar?"

I also sat back. I hated avoiding intimate discussions, hated the distance he wanted to put between us. Yet forcing a discussion or throwing myself at him could push him away altogether. It would also make me look desperate. I might *feel* desperate, but I refused to show it.

"I'm not sure," I said. "Unsettled, I think."

"He's been that way ever since discovering he's a priest. I don't think he likes the idea of belonging to the priesthood."

"He would have preferred to be a scholar, or the bookkeeper for a merchant."

"You once thought he might be a smuggler." He smiled. "Your guess was a little off."

"So was yours. Spy, wasn't it?"

His smiled widened. "He might still be a spy. The position in Merdu's Guards could be his cover."

"You don't like to be proved wrong, do you?"

"I haven't been proved wrong."

I groaned and he laughed softly.

"Come on," he said, rising. "I'll walk you upstairs. You've got another long day tomorrow, keeping Kitty entertained."

"No thank you. I'm coming with you."

He arched his brows. "Is that so?"

"It is. Erik can stay with her. He's far better at entertaining Kitty than me or Meg."

"I want to ask what he did to entertain her today, but I'm afraid of the answer."

* * *

WE SPENT all day at the market, stopping at every street seller's cart, every stall and shop. We spoke to farmers, grocers, and craftsmen, to maids and their mistresses, errand boys and grooms, but no one knew of any missing people and none greeted Dane or the others as long lost acquaintances.

The closest we came to success was when the cobbler suggested we ask around the slums because people went missing in there all the time, so he'd heard. We decided to visit the biggest slum area the following day. I didn't have much hope of finding the answer to Dane's past there, however. He'd never been a slum dweller, I was certain of it.

We returned to the inn at the end of the day and found Meg lying on her back on the bed, staring up at the canopy. Erik and Kitty were arguing over a card game at the table.

"You cheated," Kitty cried.

"Aye," Erik said. "That is how you win this game. By cheating. It is allowed."

She sniffed. "It shouldn't be."

"It is a game without rules. That is why it is fun."

"Rules are necessary."

He gathered up the cards. "No."

"What do you mean, no? Of course they're necessary. We can't all live like you, Erik, free to roam the peninsula, to have dalliances with whomever we please. If most of us didn't follow the rules, there'd be anarchy."

"There'd be freedom," he shot back. "I will show you how to live without rules when we leave Tilting. It is too hard for you here. You are known. Here, you cannot be free." He looked to Dane. "When can we leave?"

"In a few days," he said. "Unless we find something of interest."

"It's looking more and more doubtful," Max said.

Meg sat up. "We need to get out of this room before we all go mad."

"I am not going mad," Erik said with a smile. "You should go out with Josie in the day, Meg. Ask questions. Or shop. You were always in the market in Mull."

"I'd rather stay inside," she muttered, dipping her head.

"But you just say you want to get out."

She lifted a shoulder in a shrug.

"Tell me, Meg. Why do you not want to leave the inn?"

"Leave her alone," Max growled.

Erik sat next to Meg on the bed. "It is the mark on your face, yes?"

Meg shook her head, but no one was convinced.

Erik touched her chin, forcing her to look at him and expose the birthmark to everyone in the room. "Do not be ashamed of it."

She jerked her head away. "That's easy for you to say. You're handsome."

"And you are pretty. But we both have marks on our faces that get us noticed." He tapped his forehead tattoos. "You do not like people to stare at your mark, and I do not like them to point at mine. But they do and they always will."

She blinked at him. "I suppose. I never thought of you being in the same predicament as me."

"You hid away in here today too, Erik," Quentin pointed out.

"I *tell* you I stay in here because of the staring. It is really because of Kitty." He winked at Meg.

She smiled, and Kitty blushed.

"Tomorrow we will show Tilting we are not ashamed of our marks," he said to Meg. "They are part of us, they make our faces unique." He nudged her with his elbow. "No one will forget us." He looked to Dane, Max and the others. "I should have come with you today. My face is not only the most handsome, it is the most recognized."

"Recognizable," Theodore corrected. He clapped Erik on the shoulder. "I think you're right. If any face is remembered a year later, it will be yours."

"Mostly because I am so handsome. A little because of the tattoos."

Meg laughed. "Very well. I'll come too." She threw her arms around Erik. "Thank you."

I glanced at Max, expecting to see jealousy, but he simply looked satisfied.

Kitty sniffed and dabbed the corner of her eyes. "All of you go out tomorrow. I can amuse myself here."

"Are you sure?" Meg asked.

"Quite sure. I insist that you go with the others. I'd come myself, but someone might recognize me."

"In the slum?" Quentin asked.

"I'm very well known."

* * *

THE PARTY of servants we'd left behind a few days ago arrived at dusk, tired and grateful to have their accommodation organized. Not everyone could fit into the inn where we stayed, but Rhys had rented rooms at other inns nearby when he'd returned. Among those accommodated at our inn was Brant.

He sat with us at dinner, which surprised me. It surprised everyone at our table, going by the curious way they eyed him. "Someone's been watching me," he said without as much as a "Good evening."

"Who?" Theodore asked.

"If I knew that, I wouldn't be sitting here."

"What makes you think you were being watched?" Dane asked.

Brant picked up a fatty slice of pork. "Just a feeling."

Quentin snorted. "You aint' got feelings."

"I got instincts. Good ones." Brant shoved the pork into his mouth and chewed loudly. A piece spilled from the corner of his lips onto his chest. He flicked it off onto the table.

"Why didn't you confront them?" Max asked.

"He was too quick."

"Let me know if it continues here in Tilting," Dane said, accepting a note from the maid.

"I reckon its Barborough," Brant said. "He wants my wishes."

"They ain't yours," Quentin said. "They're the king's. You just stole them from him when you killed him."

"Shut your hole," Brant hissed, watching the maid leave. "She could've heard you. Ain't no one but us knows what I did, and that's the way it's going to be. Got that, you sniveling little shit?"

"I'll make inquiries about Barborough," Dane said, folding up the paper again. "If he's newly arrived in the city, it may well have been him." He held up the note between his fingers. "Gladstow has made arrangements for the duchess's belongings to be collected the day after tomorrow. The royal horses will also be collected and returned to the palace."

"Anyone here recognize you?" Brant asked.

"Not yet. Tomorrow we're trying the slums."

Erik pointed his knife at Brant. "You should come. You are probably from the slum."

"And you should go back to where you came from, Marginer. You don't belong in Glancia."

"We don't know that," I said. "Perhaps he's half Glancian. Perhaps you're the one with no Glancian blood."

With a grunt, Brant snatched up his plate and joined another table.

* * *

THE LARGE GROUP of servants split up the following morning. Some went to the market and docks to try their luck there, while many came to the largest slum with us. We divided ourselves into smaller groups of three or four and spanned outward, promising to meet back at the inn later.

The slum reminded me of The Row with its derelict tenements, dark courtyards and narrow alleys. The quality of accommodation decreased dramatically the further in we went. The lean-tos and crates offered little shelter from the elements but some folk didn't even have that. It was what it would be like in Mull now, with many slum dwellers forced onto the streets after their homes were destroyed.

"Is this place called Merdu's Pit because it's like an armpit?" Quentin asked as we passed a drunkard lounging against a wall, scratching his groin with one hand and his head with the other. "Dirty, smelly and full of fleas?"

"I think the god would find that offensive," I said. "Also, I'm quite sure it's named Merdu's Pit because it resembles the hole the god throws the souls of evil folk into after death. You're right about the dirty and smelly part. Merdu's Pit—the hole, not the slum—is supposed to be a horrible place."

"I'll try to remain on the god's good side then."

A prostitute offered herself to Dane before turning her attention to Quentin when he refused. Quentin blushed and pulled free of her clutches, only to find himself careening into the arms of another.

She spun him around, laughing, and pushed him back to her friend, but not before pinching his bottom. "What a handsome boy you are," said the first. "Want me to show you something you ain't never seen before, love?"

"No, thank you," Quentin muttered.

She laughed, revealing rotting teeth, and went to grab his crotch. Dane pulled Quentin out of the way. "How long have you lived here?" he asked the women.

"A while," said one. "Why?"

"Do you recognize us?"

"Nope."

"You answered very quickly."

"I'd remember *you*, love." The prostitute draped an arm over Dane's shoulder and squashed her breasts against his chest. "You sure you don't want to come inside with me? It'll be worth it."

"Inside" was a room in a house made of wooden boards as rotten as the woman's teeth. I counted seven other prostitutes leaning out of windows across the two levels, watching us with a mixture of boredom and mild curiosity.

"Do you know of anyone who went missing from here several months ago?" Dane asked. "It could be a year or more."

One of the prostitutes shrugged. "Girls go missing all the time. Some get themselves a man and leave, others just never come back after walking out at night. Those that ain't got shelter ain't safe." She jerked her thumb at the brothel behind her. "We're lucky. We don't have to go into the streets to get trade."

"We run a clean house," said the second prostitute.

An older woman with streaks of gray through her hair leaned further out of the whorehouse window and whistled. She beckoned us with the crook of her finger. "I know someone who went missing about then," she said. "Two people, in fact."

"And they never returned?" Dane asked.

"Nope."

"Men? Women? How old? What did they look like?"

"Slow down, handsome." She rubbed her fingers together. "You want answers, you got to give Mama some bread."

"We haven't got bread," Quentin said.

Dane pulled out an ell but didn't place it on her outstretched palm. "If the information's good."

She folded her arms beneath her large bosom, pushing them up so that the tops of her nipples were visible above her bodice. Quentin fixed his gaze on her face without blinking.

"Two men, early twenties," she said. "About her height, they were," she said, pointing at me. "Light brown hair, good teeth, lean." It described half the male servants.

"If I bring some people back with me, do you think you could pick these men out?" Dane asked. The odds of the two men missing being among the ones who'd left the palace with us were slim, but we had to try.

"Aye," she said with a shrug. "But there's one more thing. They were brothers and looked alike. Not twins, mind, just real similar."

Dane and Quentin exchanged a glance. "Paddy and Percy," Quentin said on a breath.

"Aye, that's them."

"You knew their names?" Quentin asked the woman. "Why didn't you say?"

"You never asked for their names, just what they looked like." She pointed at a lane opposite. "They lived through there with their ma. She used to run her own whorehouse, but after they left…she didn't want to work no more. She ain't in a good way these days."

Dane handed her the ell. "I know where her boys are. I'll write to them and tell them to come—"

"Merdu, no! Don't do that. Tell them to stay away."

"But this is their home," Quentin said. "Won't it make their mother happy to know they're safe?"

"Aye, and you can tell her that yourself. But don't let them come back here. They'll be arrested if the constables get wind of their return. They were wanted by the law for theft, see." She waved a hand in dismissal. "Maybe they stole something, maybe they didn't. Those boys were always up to no good, but so are a lot of folk around here. The sheriff thought they were guilty, and that's all that matters. The sheriff sent his constables here looking for them one day. Paddy and Percy got away that time, and the next and the next. Then one night, they went out and never came back."

"The constables finally got them?" I asked.

She spat on the ground near my feet. "Merdu, no. They left the city."

"Where did they go?"

"That's what I been telling you! Ain't no one knows. That's why they're missing. That's why their ma's dying from wondering what happened to her boys. They told her they would find a new home and send for her. They never did."

"If you were on the run from the constables," Dane said, "where would you go?"

She shrugged. "Out of Tilting."

"Out of Glancia," said one of the women who'd accosted us

on the street. "Vytill's just over the river and Glancian constables can't touch you there."

The woman told us where to find Paddy and Percy's mother and we headed into the narrow lane. This part of the slum was darker and smelled of urine. Drunkards slept in gutters and women lounged in doorways, watching us pass with a mixture of hunger and suspicion. Even the children watched us warily. None played, they merely sat on stoops like soulless puppets.

Quentin pinched his nose. "Paddy and Percy won't like finding out they were from this place."

"What role do they have at the palace?" I asked.

"Footmen. They pride themselves on having their gloves the whitest, their hair always neatest. Ain't nothing of this filthy place in them."

We found their mother lying on a stained mattress, the straw poking through rips in the fabric. An empty wine jug had fallen over next to her. She stank worse than the gutters. We managed to wake her and inform her we knew where her boys had gone. It was impossible to tell if she understood us through her drunken stupor, however.

Dane paid two neighbors to clean her and buy new clothes, but whether they would do it or run off with the money, we couldn't be sure.

"I don't think we should tell Paddy and Percy they came from here," Quentin said as he eyed the man following us as we left.

"We have to tell them," Dane said. He seemed oblivious to the man on our tail, even when he was joined by two thuggish friends. They slunk in the shadows, keeping their distance. They weren't a direct threat.

"Josie, you better stay close," Quentin said. "The captain and I'll protect you."

"They won't harm us," Dane said.

"How do you know?" I asked.

Up ahead, three more men emerged from the shadows like wraiths. They blocked our exit from the lane. Behind us, the other three blocked our rear escape. One of them cracked his knuckles.

"We're leaving," Dane told them, his stance still relaxed. "But I know forty men new to this city who might come here to conduct business." He nodded at the brothel where the women hung out of the windows, watching us. The one who'd given us the information about Paddy and Percy perked up at Dane's news. "They won't come if they feel threatened," he finished.

The men up ahead didn't move. They looked unsure what to do next.

"Let 'em be!" called the older whore from her window. "They know Paddy and Percy."

The man in the middle, the largest and ugliest, said, "You speak to their ma?"

"Yes," Dane said. "I'm not sure she understood, but we told her we'll have Paddy and Percy send for her soon."

The thug closed his hands into fists. Then he stepped aside. "I'll see she understands."

Dane signaled for us to follow him. "Hands at your sides," he said to Quentin. "Not near your sword."

I stayed close to Dane as we passed the three thugs in front.

"Tell the lads not to come back here," the thug called out. "It ain't safe for 'em."

"The constables might have forgotten about them," Dane said.

"They won't forget. Rumor is, the magistrate's going to punish thieves with death."

"He's the governor's man?" Dane asked.

The thug nodded.

"Can he change the law like that?" I asked.

The thug lifted a shoulder. "Ain't no one to stop him. Ain't no king, and the nobles don't care. One less thief is all right by them."

We left them and Merdu's Pit behind. Instead of going to the inn, we went to see Balthazar at the garrison. Dane would ask him to send a letter to Paddy and Percy, informing them of all we'd learned here, including a warning to stay away. Balthazar knew them better, and they would listen to his advice.

I waited outside the garrison with Quentin. We chatted to the priest on guard duty at the gate until Dane rejoined us with Balthazar in tow.

"I'd rather be out with you three," Balthazar told us. "There's nothing to do here."

"But you're the archivist," Quentin said. "You can read books and papers."

"Elliot is the archivist. I won't take that position away from him now. Besides, I've read everything I wanted to read."

"You mean the accounts of the Freedlandian civil war?" I asked.

Balthazar nodded and watched a cart drawn by a single horse drive up to us. It would seem he was giving us a ride through the city. The driver, one of the warrior priests, jumped down and handed the reins to Dane before helping Balthazar up to the seat. I climbed into the back with Quentin since there wasn't enough room up front, and dangled my legs over the edge.

"Did you discover anything in those accounts that would set you off on a path out of the city without telling anyone?" I asked.

"No," Balthazar said over his shoulder. "But the accounts are loose, not bound. It would be easy to remove one without anyone knowing."

"Where are we going?" Quentin asked.

"There's a street of booksellers and stationers not far from the market," Balthazar said. "Apparently I went there a lot. I might have friends there."

"Do the priests think you confided in someone who sold you books when you didn't confide in your fellow priests?" I asked. It sounded dubious to me, but I supposed it was possible.

"The priests don't think that. I do. I kept information from them for a reason. Perhaps I didn't trust them. Perhaps I did have a friend outside of the priesthood whom I confided in. It's not likely, but it's worth checking."

We spent a large part of the day going into every bookshop and stationer's shop on the street. Many did indeed know Balthazar and wanted to ask him where he'd been.

"Didn't I tell you?" Balthazar asked each of them casually.

They all claimed he'd simply stopped coming to their shops. More than one assumed he'd died of old age, and I suspected the rest had thought it but didn't want to admit it.

The journey had been a waste of time. We headed back to Quentin, who'd remained with the cart at the end of the street, out of ideas for where to try next. I was about to suggest we return to the inn to see if the other servants had any success, when a man stepped out of a map shop in a hurry and almost barreled me over.

"I am sorry, miss," he said. "I didn't see you there. Are you all right?"

"Fine, thank you," I said.

He smiled at me. Then his gaze fell on Dane at my side and the smile slipped.

"My apologies again, Miss. Excuse me." He went to lock the door, his gaze once again falling on Dane before shifting to Balthazar.

"Oh! Good afternoon." He squinted through his spectacles at Balthazar and smiled. "I'm sorry, I've forgotten your name, Brother...."

"Balthazar," Balthazar said. "Have we met?"

"Just once. I never forget a customer's face." He adjusted his spectacles and smiled.

"You're the proprietor of this shop?" Dane asked.

"Yes. Are you in need of a map? I was just stepping out a moment to deliver this one to a customer, but I can do it later." He indicated the rolled map under his arm. "The errand boy is supposed to do it, but he hasn't returned from his last job." He pushed open the door and pocketed the key. "Come in, come in. How was your journey, Brother?"

"Journey?" Balthazar asked.

"To Freedland. You bought a map. Two, in fact. One of Vytill and one of Freedland."

Balthazar looked to Dane then back at the mapmaker. "Can we ask you some questions?"

CHAPTER 17

"I never forget a face or a map," the mapmaker said.

"Can we see copies of the maps he bought?" Dane asked.

The mapmaker frowned. "Of course. Did you lose them?"

"Yes," Balthazar said.

"Such a pity." The mapmaker rounded the counter and scanned the labels on a series of narrow, wide drawers until he found the one he wanted. The room wasn't very large. Indeed, it seemed to be used as both shop and workshop. A desk near the window held ink bottles and quills, mortar and pestle, a closed box, and several unlit candles in various stages of use. A half-finished map was laid out on the desk, a smaller, completed version beside it.

"Here we are," the mapmaker said, laying a cloth map on the counter then placing another over the top of it. Neither were as large as the unfinished map covering much of the desk.

Balthazar picked up one and studied it while Dane picked up the other.

"Were the roads accurate, Brother?" the mapmaker asked. "Did you successfully reach Freedland using these?"

Balthazar nodded and smiled.

"That is good news. I've sold only a handful of maps of Freedland and none of those customers have ever returned.

You're the first one I've been able to ask." He admired his work in Balthazar's hands and gave a satisfied sigh.

"Did I tell you why I was going there?" Balthazar asked.

"No." The mapmaker smiled again. "But I wouldn't expect a brother to tell a humble mapmaker his affairs. The affairs of Merdu, I suppose." He chuckled.

"How much for these?" Dane asked.

"Twenty-four ells."

Dane set the money on the counter while the mapmaker rolled up the maps. He handed one to Dane and the other to Balthazar.

"You wish to go back?" he asked.

"I'm not yet sure," Balthazar said. "But I like these maps. They're works of art."

The mapmaker looked pleased but his smile quickly turned to a frown. "You're allowed to decorate the temple walls with maps?"

Balthazar hesitated then said, "Only in the library."

We thanked the mapmaker and left. "You have to remember you're a priest," I told Balthazar. "Not the master of the palace with maps and plans on your walls."

"Nothing on the walls," he muttered. "Four walls of gray stone. It's a bland existence in the temple."

"Only if you exist solely within your room and never go out. But you do go out, Balthazar. You're not a prisoner."

He grunted. "It's little better than a prison. There are prayer times and meal times and an entire hour for reflection during which I'm not allowed to speak, read or do anything except sit and think."

"You like to think."

"At a time of *my* choosing."

"The position of master of the palace is still open," Dane said. "Even without a king, the palace needs someone to oversee operations."

Balthazar grunted again but gave no answer.

* * *

ON ARRIVING BACK at the inn, I parted ways with the men in the taproom and headed straight to the room I shared with Kitty and Meg. Poor Kitty must be terribly bored by now.

I thought we were the first group back, but I spotted two palace servants and a guard in the taproom. They raised their tankards in greeting. I smiled back and headed up the stairs.

A woman's cry stopped me on the first floor landing. I followed the sound to the open door of the third room. Inside, Brant had a knife to the throat of one of the inn's maids.

"Let her go!" I said. "Don't do this, Brant. You won't get away with it."

His lips peeled away from his teeth in a snarl. "Get lost. This ain't none of your business."

The woman looked terrified. Her huge, tear-filled eyes begged me to help as she backed away from the knife.

Brant lunged at her, pushing her into the wall. She cried out again as the knife bit into the skin above her collar.

"Stop!" I shouted.

"Who paid you?" Brant snarled at the maid. "Tell me who paid you and I might not carve up your face."

The maid started shaking and crying, her tears spilling down her cheeks, her nose running. She could barely say a word let alone speak an entire sentence.

"Who paid her to do what?" I asked, venturing across the threshold.

"Stay out of this!" Brant shouted at me over his shoulder.

I inched further into the room, stopping at the chair, far enough that I could run out before he caught me.

"Tell me who paid you to come in here?" Brant ordered.

"It's her job to come in here and clean," I said.

"I gave instructions that no one be allowed in."

"Perhaps the innkeeper didn't pass on those instructions."

The woman started to sob. "P—please don't kill me."

"Someone paid you," Brant snapped. "Tell me who and I'll spare that ugly face."

"He told me he'd kill me if I said a word."

Brant raised the knife to strike.

The maid screamed.

I picked up the chair and smashed it over Brant's head. It wasn't enough to render him unconscious but he staggered backwards, allowing the maid to slip away. She ran out.

Brant straightened and flexed his grip around the knife handle. "You stupid bitch!"

I backed up to the doorway, keeping my gaze locked on Brant. When he suddenly lunged at me, I was ready for him and darted to the side at the last moment. He careened past me, straight into Dane.

Dane grabbed Brant's wrist, punched the inside of his elbow, and took the knife off him when his hand opened involuntarily. Brant grunted as Dane twisted his arm behind his back. He didn't struggle but the look on his face was one of pure frustration and hatred.

"I was trying to find out who paid that maid to look through my things," Brant snapped.

"Slashing her across the face isn't going to get you answers," I snapped back.

"You want answers, you got to force them out of people. Ain't no one going to talk if you give 'em flowers."

Dane let him go, shoving him in the back as he did so. Brant stumbled but caught himself before falling. He picked up his pack and put the things back in that the maid must have removed in her search.

"I reckon it was Barborough," he said. "But we won't know now because *you* let her go." He shook the pack at me. "Get out of my room. Both of you."

"Leave the staff alone," Dane said. "Or there will be consequences."

"I don't answer to you no more. You ain't my captain."

Dane tucked Brant's knife into his sword belt. "The consequences aren't dependent on me being your captain."

He followed me out, Brant's glare burning into our backs.

"I'm going to speak to the maid," I said.

Dane caught my hand, halting me. "Are you all right?"

I blew out a breath in an attempt to steady my racing pulse. "I'm angry at that oaf. I'm surprised we didn't find out he was from the slums. The men in Merdu's Pit seem like his kind."

To my surprise, Dane's lips twitched. "You seem fine."

"I can take care of myself sometimes. I don't always need you to rescue me."

"Sometimes," he repeated to drive the point home. "And you have to allow me to rescue you once in a while or why have me around at all?"

I stood on my toes and kissed him lightly. "You have other uses."

I walked off, leaving him looking a little dazed.

He caught up to me on the stairs and together we went in search of the maid. We found her in the large kitchen, crying into a cup of tea. The innkeeper's wife was trying to talk to her but the maid wouldn't, or couldn't, speak.

"May I talk to her?" I asked.

The innkeeper's wife nodded and stepped back.

I sat beside the girl and pulled my chair close. "My name's Josie," I said. "What's yours?"

"Yana." She sniffed and wiped her cheeks with the back of her hand. "Thank you for saving me, miss."

"Brant is not a man anyone should cross," I warned her. "Stay out of his way."

"How?" she whined. "He'll keep coming for me until I tell him who paid me."

"Then you must tell. It's the only way."

"He'll kill me, he says."

"Not if we threaten to kill him if any harm comes to you."

Her gaze settled on Dane. "Will you protect me, sir?"

Dane nodded. "As will my men. It's your choice, Yana, but I can assure you, Brant won't give in until he knows who paid you."

She sniffed. "I don't know…"

The innkeeper's wife clicked her tongue. "She don't know his name," she told us. "But he was dressed real nice and spoke like a gentleman. He seemed to have a sore arm. All limp it was."

"What are you going to do?" I asked Dane after we left the kitchen. "Tell Brant it was Barborough?"

He nodded. "If he wants retribution, he can get it himself."

We didn't reach the stairs, however. Several more groups of

palace servants had returned from their day of searching and congregated in the taproom to discuss their efforts. Among them were Max, Meg, Theodore and Erik. And Lord Barborough.

"Look who we found lurking outside," Max said with a nod at the Vytill spy.

Barborough tugged on his doublet hem. "Captain, Miss Cully. How do you do?"

"This inn has just become a dangerous place for you," Dane told him. "You paid the maid to search Brant's room for the gem."

Barborough's nostrils flared. A muscle in his jaw pulsed as his gaze focused on the kitchen area behind the counter.

"If you so much as harm a hair on that girl's head, I'll see that you lose the use of your other arm." Dane said it as casually as if he were ordering a tankard of ale.

"Does Brant know?" Barborough asked.

"He will soon."

As if summoned, Brant came down the stairs. He paused on the bottom step then hunched his shoulders and lowered his head like a bull preparing to charge. He pushed through the crowd and strode up to Barborough. He towered over the small lord, but Barborough didn't back down. Like many nobles, he seemed to think the lower orders wouldn't dare harm him. It had led to their downfall on more than one occasion in history, in more than one kingdom, most notably in the country now known as Freedland.

"My men are just outside," Barborough said with a tilt of his chin. "I only have to shout the order and they'll come."

"Who says you'll have time to shout?" Brant snarled.

Barborough's chin lowered a little. He swallowed.

"We outnumber you, Barborough" Dane said.

"It's 'my lord' to you."

"You're not my anything." Dane pulled out a chair. "Sit. Tell us why you paid that girl to look through Brant's things."

"So it *was* you." Brant pushed Barborough in the chest, forcing him to sit.

Barborough immediately stood again. "I'll buy the gem off you."

"I don't have it," Brant said.

"You're lying."

Brant grabbed the front of Barborough's doublet. "I don't have it. They do." He jerked his head at Dane.

"I don't have it either." Dane crossed his arms. "Nor do any of my friends."

Brant let Barborough go, his narrowed gaze on Dane. It was impossible to tell whether he believed Dane or not.

"I want to help you," Lord Barborough said. "I want to help you find out about your pasts. We could use the magic in the gem to do that."

"If we had it, I wouldn't give it to you," Dane said. "We don't want or need your help." He went to walk off, but Barborough grabbed his sleeve.

Dane glared at his hand and Barborough let go. "This isn't about King Phillip or Vytill," Barborough said. "I'm not offering to help you so I can gain advantage with him. Nothing like that. My interest isn't political, it's purely personal. I want to help because I want to find out all I can about magic."

Dane walked off leaving Barborough glaring at his back. Dane went only so far as the counter where he ordered ales.

"I'm going to our room," Meg said in my ear. "Coming?"

I watched Lord Barborough leave and nodded. Dane and Quentin could inform the others what we learned today. I needed some peace and quiet.

I was ready to tell Kitty and Meg about the mapmaker, but Kitty didn't give us a chance to speak when we entered.

"Thank Hailia you're back," she said, sitting up on the bed. "I'm utterly, totally, completely bored."

"Then we are at your disposal," Meg said. "What would you like to do? Play cards? Shall I do your hair? It looks like you've been lying on it all day."

"Arrange it while I talk. I sorely need to say something. I haven't spoken a word all day, except when someone tried to open the door."

Meg and I stared at her. "What do you mean?" I asked.

Kitty sat on the chair and ruffled her hair. "Don't worry. They didn't get in. Someone tried the door but it was locked. They didn't give up, though, and I worried they were going to get a key and let themselves in. So I put on a Zemayan accent and pretended to be a maid cleaning the room. Whoever it was left and never came back."

"Any clues as to their identity?" I asked. "Were their footsteps loud, like a man's?"

"Yes," she said as Meg brushed out her hair. "It was either a man or a heavy woman."

"It could have been Lord Barborough," Meg said. "He sent a maid to look through Brant's things," she told Kitty.

"The poor girl was accosted by Brant," I said, "and was terrified of Barborough."

Kitty wrinkled her nose. "He is a strange one, Lord Barborough."

"In what way? Was he nasty to you at the palace?"

"Not at all. He ignored me. It was as if I wasn't even there. Very odd behavior, considering I was a duchess."

"You couldn't get him what he wanted," I said. "He only sees those he can use or manipulate."

"And I was useless." Kitty sighed. "My husband made sure I had no real power. Anyway." She picked up the handheld mirror from the table and smiled at her reflection. "The duke is Violette's problem now, not mine."

Meg set down the brush. "And what a perfect match they are."

Kitty suddenly turned to us. "I've been thinking about something all day and haven't come to a conclusion. Perhaps you two can help. Tell me: am I still a married woman?"

"Of course," Meg said. "Your husband isn't dead. That's the only legal way you can be free of him."

Kitty's entire body slumped. She turned back to allow Meg access to her hair.

"I think your situation is unique," I told her. "While you are legally still married, morally I'm not so sure."

"Morally?"

I raised a finger. "Your husband is trying to kill you." I put up a second finger. "You left behind your old life as his wife at the bridge." I raised a third. "He is going to remarry."

Kitty's face lifted. "So can I remarry too?"

"No!" Meg said. "Josie, stop making up the rules. She's already married. That's the end of it."

"I agree," I said. Kitty's face fell again. "I don't think you can remarry," I went on. "But you are also an independent woman now. Your husband can't tell you what to do, nor can your parents. You're guided by your conscience alone. You're free to make your own choices, Kitty. That's what I meant. Of course you can't remarry until the duke dies. But you can be the woman you've always wanted to be *without* a man at your side."

"Free," she murmured to her reflection. "I am, aren't I? Free to do as I please. And as long as I don't remarry, I am not breaking any law."

"Precisely." I looked to Meg and even she nodded, agreeing with my assessment of the situation.

"We are all three of us free to do what we like now," Meg said as she braided Kitty's hair. "None of us have family or husbands to make our decisions for us. Well, no family near enough to try. I'd wager there isn't a trio of female friends in the whole of Glancia who can say that."

* * *

I REGRETTED GOING with Dane to meet with the Duke of Gladstow's men the following morning at the city's public stables the moment I saw Lord and Lady Deerhorn with them. Even Dane's step slowed with his uncertainty.

"Keep walking," I told him. "I won't let them know I fear them. They can't harm me here."

"They can," he said. "But I won't let them."

His words bolstered my confidence, and I met the Deerhorns with my head high.

Lady Deerhorn eyed me coolly while her husband took in my presence with a quick glance. Then he ignored me and addressed Dane. "Inform the grooms that we are His Grace the Duke of Gladstow's representatives in Tilting," he demanded. "Let's get this over with. I'm busy."

"I'm surprised you bothered with such a trivial matter at all,"

Dane said, leading the way to the coach house. "This is a menial task for the duke's servants." The duke's men now followed in our wake. I counted nine of them in addition to Lord and Lady Deerhorn.

"We wanted to inform you of some good news, Captain," Lady Deerhorn said. "Our daughter Violette will marry the duke."

"After a suitable period of mourning," Lord Deerhorn added.

Lady Deerhorn's lips tightened, perhaps displeased that the protocol had to be followed at all.

The confirmation of their marriage chilled me. Kitty's life was most certainly in danger now. If the duke or Deerhorns learned she were still alive, they'd stop at nothing to remove her. With Kitty supposed to already be dead, they could get away with her murder.

"You should congratulate us," Lady Deerhorn went on. "As the duchess, our Violette will wield enormous power. She'll have the power to destroy her enemies."

"I wouldn't be so sure," Dane said. "The last Duchess of Gladstow had no power. She couldn't even sneeze on her enemies."

"That girl was stupid," Lord Deerhorn said. "Violette is not."

"Are you returning to your home near Mull?" Dane asked. "Or the palace?"

"That is none of your affair," Lady Deerhorn said.

Dane met with the head groom and instructed him to bring out the horses and carriage we'd stabled there on our arrival in Tilting. "These men will take them," he added, indicating the duke's liveried servants. "And Lord Deerhorn will pay."

Lord Deerhorn's nostrils flared.

"Can't pay?" Dane asked idly. "Did you leave all your money behind at the castle? Perhaps you should have stayed longer to collect it all. And answer for your crimes."

Lord Deerhorn rounded on him, his hand raised to strike. Dane caught it.

Anger flashed in his lordship's eyes. "I'll thrash you one of these days."

Dane waggled Lord Deerhorn's hand. "Not with this limp thing."

One of the duke's men snickered.

Lord Deerhorn snatched his hand back. "Get out of my sight before I have you arrested."

Dane stood with his hands loosely at his sides and didn't move. He had one more thing to do, something important to him, and he wouldn't let the Deerhorns bully him out of doing it.

The resulting silence stretched until Lady Deerhorn broke it. "It was useless, wasn't it?"

Neither Dane nor I responded.

"The gem," she went on in a triumphant voice. "It didn't perform how you expected it to."

Again, we remained silent.

She moved to stand in front of us, giving us no choice but to look at her. "The world has not changed. No one else has become king or suddenly become rich. You are staying at a mediocre inn, wearing ordinary clothes, with no horses of your own. I've made inquiries about you all," she went on. "I know what purchases you make, what meals you eat, and how generous you've been to the inn staff. I know you're living modestly."

"If you say so," Dane said.

"Your lackadaisical air belies what you're truly feeling. And what you feel is devastation that your gem doesn't work. It contains no magic or you would be rich and powerful by now."

"Perhaps we wished to be free," I said. "Free to do as we please."

She stepped up to me, toe to toe, her deep blue eyes drilling into mine. Beside me, Dane tensed. "You might be free to do as you please, but you are not safe." She grabbed my chin, pinching it. "I will grind you under my boot."

I slapped her hand away. She smiled cruelly and walked off. Her husband watched, then, when he realized she wasn't going to stop, he followed, tossing a coin purse at the head groom.

I turned away and watched a groom bring out Lightning.

"Don't let her get to you," Dane said quietly.

"I won't. Now go and say goodbye to your horse. Try not to cry in front of the duke's men."

I waited as Dane rubbed Lightning's neck and exchanged a

few words with the head groom. We walked off together, leaving the horses, carriage, and Kitty's luggage to the duke's men.

"Are you all right?" I asked him.

"I will be as long no one mentions horses, lightning or storms in general."

I laughed softly. "You're much softer than you seem."

He took my hand. "Don't tell anyone."

We rejoined the others at the inn where some of the palace servants were about to set off again to roam the city and show their faces. It unnerved me to think that Lady Deerhorn had spies here, but I suspected those spies were among the inn staff, not the palace servants.

Dane, however, wasn't ready to leave yet. He suggested we meet with the others in our room so Kitty could take part in the conversation.

"I propose we leave Tilting tomorrow," he said when we were all settled. "The city is restless, and I don't want to become entangled in any trouble."

"Thank the goddess," Kitty said on a breath.

"It will be just us. We can't risk anyone else knowing about Kitty."

"What about Balthazar?" I asked. "He'll want to come."

"We'll inform him now."

"He won't need much notice," Quentin piped up. "He ain't got no belongings to pack."

Max smacked his arm. "You can come with me today. I reckon we start in the dyers and weavers districts. Meg, you joining us?"

"I'll stay with Kitty. Not because of this," she assured Erik, indicating her birth mark. "She'll go mad if she spends another day alone in here."

"Then I will stay too," he said.

Max grabbed his arm. "You're coming with us."

Erik allowed himself to be led out, blowing a kiss to Meg and Kitty from the doorway. Quentin followed. He also blew a kiss back at them, but stumbled over his feet because he wasn't looking where he was going.

Theodore, Dane and I were about to head out of the inn when

a note arrived, delivered by a priest. He waited for an answer as Dane read it.

"Tell the high priest I accept his offer." Dane handed the note to me. "You two have also been invited, along with Balthazar and Rhys."

"I accept," Theodore told the priest.

"As do I." After the priest left, I said, "What do you suppose dinner at the high temple will be like?"

"Flavorless," Theodore said. "Certainly nothing like palace food."

We traveled to the garrison of Merdu's Guards, but Balthazar informed Theodore and Dane he would remain there. He would see us that evening, at the high temple.

"What about tomorrow?" I asked. "Is he leaving Tilting with us?"

"That's why he's remaining behind today," Theodore said as we set off on foot. "He wants to spend time with Elliot and the other brothers so he won't feel guilty about leaving them."

I was relieved that Balthazar had decided to travel with us. It wouldn't be the same without him. Indeed, I would miss him. I smiled to myself. A few months ago, I wouldn't have expected to miss the grumpy master of the palace. How things had changed. I was far from Mull and my home, with people I'd met only at the beginning of the summer. My father would never have allowed me to go on this journey. Everything would have been different if he were still alive, yet I missed him terribly.

Dane's hand slipped into mine, and we walked side by side until we reached the dyer's district. Curtained behind cloth newly dyed and hanging out to dry, the air smelled like my kitchen after I made up tisanes and ointments, with an underlying stink of ox blood used to dye fabric and leather a dark reddish brown.

We returned to the inn at the end of the day without success, but were met by a group of enthusiastic palace servants sharing a round of celebratory drinks.

Yen had been recognized.

CHAPTER 18

"*A* woman came up to me in the street, claiming she was my cousin," the guard named Yen said. "She took me to a house to meet my family. A nice house in a good area." He seemed more pleased about this than about meeting his cousin. "I have a mother and two older brothers, both married, and nieces and nephews too."

"Were they overjoyed to see you?" Theodore asked.

Yen grinned. "They couldn't stop feeding me." He glanced at Dane. "I told them I lost my memory and somehow ended up working at the palace. I didn't tell them everyone was the same."

"When did they say you went missing?" Dane asked.

"That's the thing. I wasn't missing, as far as they were concerned. I simply left Tilting to go traveling. They said I had itchy feet and always wanted to go on adventures, even as a boy. I set off in the spring before last with my pack, a good horse, and plenty of money to see me all the way to Freedland."

"Freedland?" Dane echoed.

Yen nodded. "That was my ultimate destination."

"Why?"

He shrugged. "Because it was the furthest place from Glancia? No real reason, so they said."

Freedland again. The number of times it had been mentioned lately was adding up.

"When I didn't return and my letters stopped, they were a little concerned," Yen went on, "but they assumed I would write to them eventually, or just show up. Apparently I wasn't a good letter writer."

"What did they say about your memory loss?" asked Deanne. "Did they think it strange?"

"They just took it in their stride."

"What are you going to do now?" asked one of the footmen.

"Move back here, I suppose. This is my home. They're my family." His smile widened. "My mother cried when I walked in the door and hugged me so hard I couldn't breathe."

Yen received congratulatory slaps on the back and Max bought him a drink.

Dane joined in with the celebrations at first, but after the initial raising of the tankards, he went quiet.

I pulled my chair closer to his. "Something wrong?"

"I'm happy for him," he said.

"I know you are. But you're sad to lose him, aren't you? He's the first of your men to leave."

"That's not it." He cradled his tankard in both hands and stared into the liquid. "I'm jealous. I wish it was me." He shook his head and looked away. "I'm being selfish."

"You're being human." I rested a hand on his arm then withdrew it when Theodore and Max joined us.

"That makes five from Tilting," Max said. "Balthazar, Amar, Paddy, Percy and Yen. I expected more."

"So did I," Theodore said. "But the Fist Peninsula is a big place. There are many cities and villages."

"Too many to visit in a lifetime," Max said heavily.

I eyed Brant, sitting alone in the corner, the only one not joining in with Yen's celebrations. He hunched over his tankard, watching us with a bitter curl of his top lip. He still thought we had the gem. I no longer thought he did. He would have used one of the wishes by now.

But the Deerhorns and Lord Barborough might have it, despite claiming they didn't. I didn't trust either of them. Whoever had the gem must realize it didn't work alone. It remained to be seen if they knew Brant had inherited the unused wishes.

"It's time to tell them we're leaving." Dane finished his ale and stood. The guards instantly fell silent and the rest of the servants soon followed until a hush fell over the taproom. "I have an announcement to make."

* * *

"How did they take it?" Balthazar asked us when we met for dinner in the high temple that night.

"Well enough," Dane said.

Theodore arched his brow. "Most of the guards wanted to come with us," he said. "Some were put out that we were heading off alone."

"They were fine once I explained we can cover more ground by splitting up and traveling independently," Dane said. "Most agreed."

"Most?" Balthazar asked.

"Brant wanted to join us."

Balthazar leaned heavily on his walking stick. "Because he thinks you still have the gem. Can we expect him to cause trouble in the morning?"

"He wouldn't dare."

The high priest entered the reception room where we'd been waiting and welcomed us. "You must be the captain," he said to Dane.

Dane bowed his head. "Your Eminence."

"And this is Theodore," Balthazar said. "My very good friend and valet to the late king."

"So you are calling him the king again now, are you?" the high priest said as he watched Theodore bow.

"I thought you might prefer it, Your Eminence, however I stand by what I told you. Leon used magic to gain the throne. The sorcerer removed our memories so we couldn't divulge Leon's secret."

The high priest slapped his hands together at his back and regarded Balthazar with sympathy. "I have been thinking about what you said. I do not doubt that you all lost your memories, and I can concede that King Leon gained the throne under unusual circumstances. But it was not through magic or any efforts of a sorcerer. It is the will of Merdu."

"Not Hailia?" Balthazar asked.

"The goddess has no interest in the whims of kings and the jostling for their crowns. It's the God of Change you have to thank for your predicament." He directed us towards the far door. "Come, dinner will be served in a moment."

Balthazar led the way, the sound of his walking stick dulled by the rug covering the flagstones. "So we should not bother to search for our pasts? Since it's Merdu's will, we should merely accept what happened to us?"

"Not at all. Search for your pasts, by all means. But you will only regain your memories when the god wishes it. Not before."

Balthazar made a scoffing sound. "You make it sound as though our fates are not in our hands."

"Fate is not what you think it is, Bal. It is a combination of the god and goddess's wills, but it must be combined with the will of men and women. For instance, Merdu might decide to return your memories to you, but if you do not go searching for your pasts, he cannot present the opportunity to you." He held out both hands, palms up, as if weighing two objects. "Merdu's will and your own must be in alignment."

Balthazar grunted. "As a man of reason, I don't like your theory."

"But as a man of Merdu, you do. I know you better than yourself, Bal. At this point in time, at least."

Balthazar's pace quickened. I suspected he didn't like what the high priest said. I also suspected he knew he was right, to a certain point. Trust Balthazar to not want to admit it, however.

The dining room was much like the high temple's main audience chamber with a mosaic floor. The tiles on this floor were arranged with images of the sun and moon. A long table that could seat at least twenty filled the room. It was set for only six tonight. Several brothers stood around the edges of the room, holding jugs. As soon as we sat, they filled our cups with wine. The cups were ordinary pewter, the tableware simple. A trail of white and pink flowers decorated the center of the table, but they were the only adornment in the room aside from two large tapestries depicting the god and goddess hanging on the walls. Even the candlesticks were made of iron rather than silver or gold.

The brothers melted back to the edges of the room once our cups were full. Another door opened and six more priests entered, each carrying a covered bowl. The bowls were set before us and the lids lifted to reveal a thick soup. It smelled of beef and a blend of herbs and spices.

"Start," the high priest said with an irritated glance at the vacant sixth place. Rhys had not arrived.

"This is delicious," Theodore said, digging his spoon into the bowl for another taste.

The high priest smiled. "You sound surprised."

"I thought it would be blander."

"I entertain kings and queens here, lords, ladies and the Supreme Holiness himself. They are willing to overlook the simple room and table setting, but not bland food. My cook is one of the best in Glancia, although I hear the cook at the palace could rival him."

"I'll judge after I've tasted the rest of the meal."

The door leading to the reception room burst open and Rhys strode in. He bowed to the high priest and nodded a greeting to the rest of us. He looked exhausted. Dark smudges underscored eyes red from lack of sleep, and he hadn't shaved. Indeed, he looked like he'd just walked in from patrol in dusty boots and gloves.

"You're late," the high priest said.

"My apologies, Your Eminence." Rhys didn't offer an explanation and the high priest didn't ask for one.

"Your men will be busy this evening," Dane said as Rhys sat. "The people are restless, and from what I've witnessed these last few days, the constables are more than happy to use violence to keep them at bay. How many men are you sending out each night?"

Rhys stared into his soup. "Rufus is in charge of the duty roster at the moment."

Dane frowned.

"Your friend is still missing," I said gently.

Rhys paused then gave a slight nod before plunging his spoon into the soup.

"Did the men tell you I'm leaving tomorrow?" Balthazar asked.

Rhys nodded, whereas the high priest set down his spoon. "Leaving?" he asked. "Bal...why? This is your home. We are your people, your family. You belong here, not at the palace. There isn't even a king to serve."

"I'm not returning to the palace. Dane, Theo and the others will continue searching for their memories, and I want to go with them."

The high priest's brow plunged with his frown. "Dane?"

Balthazar indicated Dane, sitting opposite. "The captain."

The high priest blinked owlishly. "Your first name is Dane?"

"Have you heard of me?" Dane asked. "Of someone named Dane who disappeared?"

The high priest shook his head and picked up his spoon again. "I'm afraid not. It's not a common name, but it's not all that unusual either. My apologies, I feel a fool for not asking your name when we arrived. I assumed you preferred to simply be called Captain."

"Not anymore," Dane said. "I've given up the position."

"To go in search of your memory. Where will you look?"

"We'll cross the border into Vytill tomorrow."

The high priest set his spoon down without finishing his soup. "You should continue your search in Glancia first. You're tall."

"But too dark to be full Glancian," Dane said.

The high priest indicated Theodore. "Why not travel to Dreen? Theodore is most certainly from there."

"We're going to Freedland first," Theodore said. "Via Vytill."

The high priest's frown deepened. "Freedland? May I ask why? It's so far away."

"We have reason to believe some of us might come from there." Balthazar indicated Dane. "Dane, for one, considering his olive complexion and dark hair."

"Are you sure it's wise to go all the way to Freedland? It's quite a journey, particularly for a man of your years, Bal."

"I'll manage."

"They say it's a wild place, being so isolated from civilization. I hear there are pockets where savages roam and marauders take advantage of travelers. You'll have to be very careful, particularly with a woman to protect. If they capture her…" He shook his head. "I don't think it's wise for Josie to go."

I narrowed my gaze at Dane, daring him to order me to stay behind. He did not, but I suspected I might have to fight that battle back at the inn.

"What's it like politically?" Balthazar asked. "Is it stable?"

"It is now and has been for almost a decade," the high priest said. "Before that there were some clashes between the republicans and royalist supporters."

"The royalists weren't all killed during the civil war?" Dane asked.

"Some survived. They would come out of hiding from time to time in an attempt to overthrow the republic, but they were always suppressed. They must have all since died or given up their quest because there's been no trouble for several years. Thank Hailia."

"You're a supporter of the republic?" Balthazar asked.

"I'm a supporter of peace. The last king was a tyrant, his rule filled with bloodshed and fear. I'm not sorry about his end. He deserved to be overthrown and Merdu must have agreed. Rulers of the other kingdoms on the Fist should take the last king of Freedland's life and death as a lesson to try and be better, kinder."

We fell into silence as the brothers collected our empty bowls and the next course was brought in.

"What did the surviving royalists want to replace Freedland's high minister and his advisers with?" I asked, watching a priest lift the lid off a platter to reveal an entire roasted turkey. "Did any descendants of the last king survive?"

"None," the high priest said. "His two sons and daughter were killed in the uprising. They were children at the time so had not yet married."

"Children! How awful."

I lost my appetite, despite the parade of delicious food being brought in from the kitchen. The brothers placed platters of fish, oysters, pheasant, eel, salads and vegetables before us. The priests who'd been standing at the edges of the room with wine jugs refilled our cups.

The high priest signaled to one of the servers and whispered something in his ear. The priest left through the service door only to return a short time later and hand the high priest a small bottle stopped with a cork. It looked like the ones I filled with tonics. The high priest pocketed it.

"Have you heard any more from the palace?" Balthazar asked him.

The high priest stared at him for a long moment without answering. He seemed distracted, as if he hadn't heard a word, and he'd gone pale. The food must not be agreeing with him. If he dined as sumptuously as this only rarely, it wasn't surprising.

"Your Eminence," Balthazar prompted. "The dukes. Have you heard any more?"

The high priest picked up his knife. "I have, in fact, and it's a little concerning. Several Glancian lords have written to me, stating which duke they will support."

"Why is that disturbing? It's good that they keep you informed."

"It's disturbing because the information they're basing their decision on seems false to me. For instance, Lord Laxland threw his weight behind Buxton because he'd been informed that Grenlee was supporting Gladstow. But I received a letter this morning from Grenlee saying he was, in fact, supporting Buxton."

"Laxland and Grenlee despise one another," Rhys told us. "What one does, the other is sure to do the opposite out of spite."

"Like squabbling children," the high priest spat.

"Why does it matter?" Theodore asked. "Setting aside their petty disputes, why should the nobles care what the others are doing?"

"If the lords are told lies, then the dukes might hear them too.

If they believe they have more support than they have, they'll strike early."

"Glancia could be plunged into war soon," I murmured.

The high priest nodded gravely.

"Is the false information coming from Vytill?" Dane asked.

"Most likely," the high priest said. "It would suit King Phillip to set the dukes against one another before the nobles have truly made up their minds."

Balthazar looked grim. "He wants to cause chaos to weaken Glancia."

"So he can come in with his army and take over," Theodore finished. "This is terrible."

"This is how kings operate," the high priest said. "King Phillip's ambition has been known for years. Ever since Prince Hugo's death, he has been waiting for King Alain to die so he could claim the Glancian throne. If Leon hadn't been found and declared legitimate, he would have started these rumors months ago. Leon's rise to the throne put a halt to his plans."

"And his death revived them," Rhys said.

"It's a good time to get out of Glancia," Balthazar said.

"And into Vytill?" The high priest shook his head. "Hardly."

"We're just passing through Vytill," Dane said.

"I still think Dreen is the better choice right now. Give your friend Theo a chance to find his family while Glancia and Vytill fight their battles."

Theodore smiled. "That's kind of you, Your Eminence, but my curiosity about Freedland has been piqued. It seems like an interesting place."

"I haven't been there myself."

Dane and Rhys fell into conversation about which routes to take, what sort of supplies were needed, and which inns had the best reputations. It seemed Merdu's Guards often traveled into Vytill on peaceful pilgrimages to the religious capital of Fahl.

Balthazar and the high priest grew quiet as they ate. I suspected they were both considering the political landscape and the potential for war in Glancia. Politics seemed to be a matter that interested them both. In the high priest's case, it would be an important part of his position. He needed to keep abreast of the machinations of kings. For Balthazar, it seemed to be an interest deeply ingrained in his character.

Neither man ate much and both abandoned their plates without finishing. The high priest looked pale again, his brow furrowed.

"You should take that tonic," I said.

He blinked at me. "Pardon?"

"The tonic your priest gave you earlier. Does it soothe your stomach after rich meals such as this?"

"Yes. My apologies, Josie, my mind was elsewhere." He patted the pocket of his robe where he'd slipped the bottle. "I don't like to use it unless absolutely necessary. It causes other… unpleasant problems."

Then it must be for indigestion. The most common tonic to treat it caused wind in some patients. "You can get a different tonic. Tell your apothecary to use a formula that contains less borrodi spice and more inkspur. It's milder on the stomach."

"I will, and thank you, Josie. You're very observant."

"Only when presented with medical conditions and medicine."

He nodded, thoughtful.

"My father taught me everything he knew. He and my mother often used to experiment with new medicinal recipes. I've kept their book and have expanded on several of their formulas. It's something I enjoy." I was rambling yet I couldn't stop myself. The high priest made me anxious in a similar way to the king when I first met him. I was used to dining with villagers, not powerful leaders.

He smiled gently. "Don't be nervous with me," he said. "I'm just an old man who can't feast on rich food anymore. You, however, are quite the interesting young woman. It's no wonder the captain likes you."

My face heated. "It's not like that between us."

"No? But the way you two look at one another… Forgive me if I've misspoken."

"You haven't. It's just that he could be married. We don't know."

He pressed a hand to his heart. "I'm sorry. I didn't think.

You're right. It's very commendable of you to...abstain." He looked to Dane, still having an earnest conversation with Rhys. "Commendable of you both."

"He's a good man," I said. "Very honest and kind to his friends. The thought of betraying a wife goes against his very nature, even though he can't remember if he has one or not."

"Good men are hard to find. But have you considered that he might not be a good man? That when he rediscovers his memory, he might change back to what he was before, and that it might not be good?"

His suggestion took me by surprise and made my tone harsher than I intended. "As I said, it's in his nature. I'm not worried at all."

"Then I wish you luck, Josie. And I pray that he is not married. You seem like you deserve happiness."

A well of emotion suddenly filled my chest. I knew Dane might be married or otherwise committed, but I rarely allowed myself to think about it. There was no point in speculating. It only led to these emotions surfacing at awkward moments, like now.

"I've upset you," the high priest said. "I'm sorry, that wasn't my intention." He passed me the cup of wine and watched as I sipped. "Forgive me for what I'm about to suggest, Josie, but I think it should be said. Perhaps you should not pursue this course of action."

"Finding their memories? Thank you for your concern, but we must find out who they are. If they don't know their pasts, they can't move forward. That includes Dane. Especially Dane. His honor won't allow him to be with me unless he knows he's free."

He shifted his weight in the chair and leaned closer. "Their memory loss is the will of the god. If Merdu decides to reinstate their memories, it will be done. Leave it to the higher power to act as he sees fit."

"That goes against what you said earlier. You claimed an alignment of the god's will and the actions of man are necessary to force change. While the god might want to restore their memories, he can't do so if they are not searching for them."

He stared at me and I felt a little sick for throwing his words back at him. Who was I to tell the high priest he was wrong about a theological matter?

But his low chuckle dissolved my concern. "I can see why Balthazar likes you. You're right. Put it down to an old man worried about a young couple's future." His gaze turned serious. "Consider what I've said, Josie. Consider that it might be best to let sleeping dogs lie."

Rhys suddenly stood and bade us goodnight. "I have work to do tonight," he said.

"But you haven't eaten dessert yet," the high priest protested.

"I'm not hungry."

The high priest eyed Rhys's empty plate. He'd eaten more than one helping of the main course.

"I don't like desserts," Rhys added. He bowed. "Your Eminence."

He left without as much as a goodbye for Balthazar. He must be troubled indeed to ignore his friend on the eve of his departure. It would be some time before they saw one another again.

We ate our dessert and left too. The remainder of the discussion for the evening centered on more trivial matters rather than politics. The high priest told us stories about Balthazar's past, most of which had us laughing, even Balthazar.

"I like him," I said as we rode in the high priest's personal carriage back to the inn. "I can see why you two were friends, Balthazar."

"I can't," Balthazar said. "But then I can't see how I liked being a priest either, so perhaps I'm not the best judge."

Theodore grinned. "Are you admitting to a weakness, Bal?"

"I blame the good food and wine. I haven't dined like that since I ate food intended for the king's table."

"You stole the king's food?" Theodore cried.

"I was tasting it." Balthazar straightened. "I had to see if it was worthy of his palate."

"Leon probably couldn't tell a good wine from a bad one," Dane said.

"And you can?" I teased.

"The good wines come from southern Vytill." The moonlight

streaming through the window caught the impish gleam in his eyes.

Balthazar grunted. "You read that in one of the palace library's books. I know because I read it too."

Dane crossed his arms. "I haven't much occasion to sample wines. Unlike some, I never stole from the king's table."

"Tasted, not stole." Balthazar clicked his tongue. "How long will it take us to get to Freedland again? I'm having second thoughts about spending it with a pack of boors."

I laughed. "You can sit in the cart with me and we can discuss more civilized matters."

"Like wine?"

"I don't know much about wine. I know a lot about childbirth though."

He groaned.

* * *

I'D BEEN wrong about Rhys. He came to say goodbye to Balthazar on the morning of our departure. He stood alongside his men lining the street outside the inn.

"It's not too late to reconsider," Andreas said to Balthazar.

"I want to do this," Balthazar said.

"We just found you and now you're leaving us again." Andreas threw his arms around Balthazar with such vigor that Balthazar would have fallen if Andreas hadn't held him so tightly. "I'm going to miss you."

"You're soft," Vizah muttered before also embracing Balthazar.

Balthazar shook hands with each of the priests, and endured more hugs from Elliot and Rufus. When he came to Rhys at the end, Rhys remained in the line, unmoving.

"There were a lot of things I wished I'd told you last time you left but never got the chance," the Master of Merdu's Guards said. "I repeated them in my head dozens of times, and promised myself that if I did have the chance to say goodbye to you, I would speak them aloud." He rested his hand on the hilt of his sword. "But now I find I can't remember the words."

"There's no need for this," Balthazar said. "I know I'm old but I have no intention of dying on this journey."

"But do you have any intention of coming back?"

Balthazar looked away.

"I wish you were content here," Rhys went on. "I wish you wanted to stay with us, your friends. Your brothers. But I understand your need to learn more. I wouldn't say I'm happy for you to leave, but I'm satisfied that this is your new calling."

Balthazar lifted his gaze to Rhys's, and Rhys suddenly drew him into a fierce hug. When he let him go, Balthazar rested both hands on the head of his walking stick, shoulders hunched. "I'll write."

Dane assisted Balthazar onto the wagon seat beside Max. I had already said my goodbyes to the palace servants and now I shook each of the priests' hands in turn. When I came to Rhys, he didn't let my hand go.

"Take care of him, Josie," he murmured. "He's like a father to me."

"I'll try," I assured him. "If he'll let me."

He smiled sadly and released my hand.

I joined Max and Balthazar on the driver's seat, and we set off. Kitty had been smuggled into the back of the covered wagon with our luggage, early that morning, and Meg now sat with her. Dane, Erik, Quentin and Theodore rode ahead on their hired mounts. Quentin and Theodore waved to the gathered servants and priests, and Erik blew kisses to the women.

I searched the crowd for Brant and found him standing with the other guards. I released a pent-up breath, glad that he wasn't following us. Our pace would be slow, however, and it would be easy enough for him to catch up.

"Either he is truly happy for me to go or he's a good actor," Balthazar said.

I thought he meant Brant at first, but then I followed his gaze to the powerful figure of the Master of Merdu's Guards. "You still don't trust them?" I asked.

"I don't know, Josie. I really don't."

It took some time to make our way through the busy city to the bridge over the Upway River. Once on the other side, we waited at the checkpoint while Vytill border guards looked through our luggage for taxable goods.

I stood on the riverbank while they worked, and gazed back across the river to Tilting. The king's castle rose above the sea of slate roofs but it was the bell tower of the high temple that drew my eye.

The document conjured by the sorcerer and found in the temple archives had set in motion events that led me here. I was far from my village and I was about to travel far from my country. Trepidation and excitement both gnawed at my gut, but a feeling of hope rose above everything.

Dane drew up beside me. He stood close, our arms touching, and gazed at Tilting too. "You'll be back, Josie," he said quietly.

"I know." But whether I'd be back with or without him remained to be seen.

Available from 5th May 2020:
THE PRISON OF BURIED HOPES
the 5th book in the After The Rift series

A MESSAGE FROM THE AUTHOR

I hope you enjoyed reading THE TEMPLE OF FORGOTTEN SECRETS as much as I enjoyed writing it. As an independent author, getting the word out about my book is vital to its success, so if you liked this book please consider telling your friends and writing a review at the store where you purchased it. If you would like to be contacted when I release a new book, subscribe to my newsletter at http://cjarcher.com/contact-cj/newsletter/.

ALSO BY C.J. ARCHER

SERIES WITH 2 OR MORE BOOKS

After The Rift

Glass and Steele

The Ministry of Curiosities Series

The Emily Chambers Spirit Medium Trilogy

The 1st Freak House Trilogy

The 2nd Freak House Trilogy

The 3rd Freak House Trilogy

The Assassins Guild Series

Lord Hawkesbury's Players Series

Witch Born

SINGLE TITLES NOT IN A SERIES

Courting His Countess

Surrender

Redemption

The Mercenary's Price

ABOUT THE AUTHOR

C.J. Archer has loved history and books for as long as she can remember and feels fortunate that she found a way to combine the two. She spent her early childhood in the dramatic beauty of outback Queensland, Australia, but now lives in suburban Melbourne with her husband, two children and a mischievous black & white cat named Coco.

Subscribe to C.J.'s newsletter through her website to be notified when she releases a new book, as well as get access to exclusive content and subscriber-only giveaways. Her website also contains up to date details on all her books: http:// cjarcher.com She loves to hear from readers. You can contact her through email cj@cjarcher.com or follow her on social media to get the latest updates on her books:

facebook.com/CJArcherAuthorPage

twitter.com/cj_archer

instagram.com/authorcjarcher

pinterest.com/cjarcher

bookbub.com/authors/c-j-archer

Made in the USA
Monee, IL
19 April 2023

32109117R00156